Mark of the Green Dragon

SPARX Incarnation Trilogy

Book I: Mark of the Green Dragon
Book II: Order of the Undying
Book III: Dark Waters

Mark of the Green Dragon

SPARX Incarnation Book 1

2ND Edition

K.B. SPRAGUE

GaleWind BOOKS — AN IMPRINT OF WHISPERWOOD PUBLISHING | CANADA

SECOND EDITION, 2020

MARK OF THE GREEN DRAGON, SPARX Incarnation
Book I by K.B. Sprague

ISBN: 978-1-988363-17-2 (paperback)
ISBN: 978-1-988363-18-9 (epub)
ISBN: 978-1-988363-19-6 (mobi)

Cover designed by Damonza
Maps by Josephe Vandel of MapForge

Published in Canada by GaleWind Books,
an imprint of Whisperwood Publishing, Ottawa.

www.galewindbooks.com

To second chances

As a tree with the passage of time...

TO GLACE VALLEY
Western Tor
Dim Lake
HARROW
Dim River
Upper Malcumin River
Harrow's Gate
WHISPERWOOD
DEEP WEALD
BEARDED HILLS
Webfoot
TO SCARSANDS
Turnsby
The Mire
The Crossing
Doncaster
Blackmuk Creek
THE FLATS
Lower Malcumin River
Akeda Ruins
ABANDON BAY
FORT ABANDON
Abindohn Ruins

BLACKTIP Mnt.
JAKKA HILLS
Rapier Isle
HIDDEN CITY
OF
GAN
DEEPWEALD
Bitterhelm
Trading Post
IRONEAGLE PEAK
Wellspring Creek
Mining
Camp
OUTLANDS
MAP OF
THEIA
TO THE GREAT
EMBERS

With the vows of my former life fulfilled or pardoned by my untimely departure, I am now released of them, and make one and only one vow anew. By sun, wind, rain and earth I take this final oath, to protect the woodlands and the valleys, the lowlands and the marshes, the stands of tall pines and the fields of grass. I hereby declare my acceptance of the earthen form granted to me – Hurlorn of Deepweald – and accept all duties and responsibilities commensurate with that great honor.

—The Spirit Hurlorn Oath

CHAPTER I

Such an awkward thing

The grove is as perfect a place to write as a lumbering beast might find, as bright as the day and sheltered from the wind. Though by the creak in my limbs, I daresay rain is coming, so I must make haste. And Hadamard is waiting.

It is an awkward thing, to tell a tale in such a state, so huge and halting and overgrown. And a burl over one eye has it sealed shut since early spring. The other is sure to follow. But I have my quill, at least, specially fixed to a long, deft claw by the ranger in these parts, whose grandfather I knew very well, and I have my paper from my friend the birch. The monument central to this grove is wide and flat, and serves just fine as a tabletop. The inkbottle is small and awkward though, and its contents may very well dry up before I ever get the lid back on. That cannot be helped.

This part of the story, this first record of events, I will tell as I saw unfold. It is the beginning of my story, the middle of others and, most importantly, the beginning of the end for some great thing. It is that which set things in motion.

Beware in the telling, as I have little patience to spare once stirred into action. I may skip a few years, or tens of years or maybe even a hundred years. Watch for shifts in the time-line. I am not always careful. And I may, at times, draw upon others within this grand consciousness. In many ways, we are one now, even moreso than I am one with my former self – I haven't gone by the name of "Nud Lenokin" for a long, long time. Please bear in mind that I also may have to break off, at times, to accommodate the weather and such, and possibly lose my train of thought in the process. Oh, what I would do for a writing desk, a lamp, and a roof over my head! Such simple luxuries are now lost to me.

How did I become such a gnarled old thing anyway? Any who see me must wonder. The entire notion is ridiculous, I admit, but knowing that won't change bark to skin. Is there such a thing as magic? What else could it be? That will all become clear, soon enough, in the telling.

This tale begins before thick, heavy scales burdened my body. My legs were nothing like tree trunks and my shoul-ders did not bear the weight of a leafy crown. Don't get me wrong... I am not complaining. I can still get around. Slow? Well... mostly yes, but also quiet and well camouflaged if I stick to the tree lines, the copses, and the gardens – but not the bog. That which once sustained my former being is now poison to the heart root through which I drink. That quaggy water would be the end of me, much like the unfortunate soul I once stumbled upon...

Mind you, I wasn't the only person to have discovered a corpse or two in the bog. My experience was one of the most bizarre ever recorded in Webfoot though. Besides me, there was this man and his son that had found a bog body while digging for peat to burn as fuel. Then there was that lady's head with red hair that popped up the same way – digging for peat. She wore a braided leather noose around her neck. Even "Pops" – the father of a good childhood friend of mine – once stumbled upon a soup of pickled body parts while setting footings for a building in town. One might think bog people are lurking everywhere. Well, as far as I know, they are not. But the stories accumulated over the years and decades into one long list of celebrity bog-body appearances. They became the sources of many a legend and the stuff of tall tales.

I, however, was the only one to have at the same time discovered a very ancient seed in the bog from the long-forgotten past; a kernel of admittance into a world I didn't even know existed, a world not so far from any of us. I was the only one to have discovered *fire amber*.

Yes, the bog is doom, and I know of many who would agree, if only they could speak from their muddy graves…

And if I could speak as I once did, none of this would be necessary. This task would be trivial if I did not have to write it all down. But I am without choice in the matter – my spoken words are the baritone notes of a deep wind instrument, my sentences are melodies, this tale a song… all I have are these inked words and the Hurlorns' *whisper*. But who will hear if I do not get this out, in writing, to those who need to know? Who will think to listen for the rustling of leaves in the summer breeze for a message across, as the vow states, *the woodlands and the valleys, the lowlands and the marshes, the stands of tall pines and the fields of grass*? Who will hear the Hurlorns whisper my song? Or yours for that matter, perhaps, someday?

Let us now begin, before the rain hits and spoils the pages…

CHAPTER ii

Suspicious contents

A bulging moon peered in through the reed-screened window. A single, flickering candle burned low and threatened darkness. On the verge of sputtering out, the flame renewed itself, steadied, and blazed on, unbroken. Nud Lenokin, "Leno" to his friends, sat cross-legged on his night sack, eyeing the deepwood box on his bedside table. A hard knot had formed in his belly over it. *Is this what I think it is?* he wondered. *The last time I opened one of these, it didn't end so well.*

Old Paplov muttered to himself in the next room, while sitting in his chair and flipping through important papers for the lord mayor.

"You should be paying more attention," Nud heard him say, amidst other rumblings. The teen huffed. The criticism was in reference to Nud's first pass through the same documents earlier that day. Paplov had been busier than ever lately, hopping from town to town on official business and leaving Nud with all the paperwork. For months now, the teen had begun to act in some formal capacity as his grandfather's aide in diplomatic affairs. But no matter how much effort he put in, the work he did never seemed to be quite good enough. Paplov pushed him to do everything better, and to accept more and more duties and responsibilities. It was getting in the way of everything to do with having fun.

Paplov's other rumblings seemed to follow part of an ongoing negotiation that played out in his mind, complete with all its semantic thrusts, feigns and parries. He sounded like a madman arguing with himself.

That evening, Nud had declined the usual invitation to help his grandfather with "a special task of great importance." Since becoming a full apprentice, every other task seemed to be "a special task of great importance." Nud had decided long ago that Paplov just said that to spice up the boring work he wanted to offload. Most times, Nud let him get away with it. But not that night. That night, he'd simply gone to his room, but with little intention of sleeping any time soon. In his own mind, thoughts were churning.

The casket lay quiet, motionless, as did he.

Paplov had just finished hanging up his weathered traveling cloak on a peg near the front door of their hut, when he'd produced the wooden box from his sidebag. His face was kind and his smile warm, the way he usually came off after a good visit.

"Take it," he'd insisted, hand shaking as he held the box out for Nud to grab. Its contents knocked and rattled as he did so. Paplov had been looking older lately – seventy if he was a day, with little more than wisps of white fluff to show on the top of his head. Somehow, his hair still managed to look messy though, especially on a windy day, which was just about every day. Even his eyebrows were messy – bushy and white with an inquisitive flick to them. But his beard was always in order, soft as down and stroked smooth to a point.

"Straight from the gnarly old woodsman himself," he'd gone on, "Uncle Fyorn sends his regrets that you missed visiting the cabin again." Fyorn wasn't Nud's real uncle, but Paplov always referred to him that way.

Nud had taken the box – a gift from the woodsman. *Why would he do this now, after so long?* he thought. *Is he sending me a message?* And as the teen lay deliberating whether or not to open it, he reminded himself that he could hear no shuffling from within and could see no drips of black ooze spewing from its seams. Nothing stirred whatsoever. In fact, the box, in-and-of-itself, was not intimidating or frightful to look upon in the least. It was elegant. Only the haunting memory it elicited gave Nud cause for concern. Thinking back to that afternoon long ago in Deepweald Forest, it all seemed so unreal…

Over the years, Nud had heard many tales of terrible abominations lurking deep in the woods, and in the dark reaches of rivers, and in out-of-the-way corners of the bog: wolf men that waited among pines for stray travelers to mount on a spit and roast alive; giants in the hills that stripped the flesh off their victims and ate it raw; and then, of course, creatures in caves more dead than alive who hated all life. These stories, Nud believed, held grains of truth, but really were dreamt up to keep children in line, to make them eat their suppers and keep them from roaming wild through the mires, forests and hills. *Where,* Nud wondered, *are the grains of truth in what I saw in the forest that day, perched on a mossy boulder at the edge of a rocky grove?* Even campfire tales never alluded to such a thing.

The flame continued to waver as it pumped short, fluid bursts of liquid orange into the cool night air, darkness merely half a shadow away. And as the fire gasped for breath, the half-shadows grew fuller, longer. And when the light finally snuffed out, the subtlest of shades came out of hiding. The box became swathed in a faint net of threaded shadows, crisscrossing over diamonds of pale moonlight. The woodsman's offering held Nud's every thought within its confines, his every suspicion under its lid.

Nud closed his eyes and thought back to a time out of memory. He thought back to when he could fly.

Like a bird, he'd soared over water, swaying reeds, mounds of grass and even treetops; cool winds numbing his cheeks, whipping his hair and drying out his eyes. And when a strong gust arose, he'd skipped along the turbulence with unparalleled elation. The air had pushed at Nud so hard and blew past him so fast that it sucked the breath right out of his windpipe. He'd struggled against the forceful hand that drove him ever downwards to the mudflats, and fought against crosswinds aiming to rifle him into a rogue tree skeleton.

Here it comes… Here it comes. His chest tingled as he braced himself. He drew in a shallow breath. *I'm gonna hit… I'm gonna hit…*

Nud opened his eyes.

He was only dreaming then, but even long after, in those early moments of morning slumber when the sensation of freefall returned, and when he could feel his body rise and fall on a cushion of air, Nud still believed he could fly. Even when fully wakeful with his thoughts set adrift, he sometimes had to pause to remind himself that he never really flew in the world he knew to be real. It simply never happened, and could never really happen at all.

But what about that black orb with the central eye and legs like a spider? And that crooked forest creature that attacked me?

And that swarm of biting insects so early in spring? Nud was not dreaming then. It all happened. He knew it'd happened. The permanent mark on his arm kept the memory grounded in reality – a reality he'd kept secret all the years since.

Yes, it had been nearly four years since the incident in the woods. And over those four years, Nud had successfully avoided the journey back to his uncle's cabin. Paplov still went to see the woodsman regularly though. Fyorn shared important information with him that helped with his duties as town councilor, plus the woodsman was the only one who knew where to find the rare deepwood Paplov needed for his wood-carving and special arrows.

Looking back, Nud believed he'd just felt awkward about returning, uncertain about how his uncle would react and what he might say. The notion left a sinking feeling in the young Pip's gut, a sinking feeling that'd rolled itself into a hard knot. After all, Uncle Fyorn had spent long hours telling Nud stories about the wide world, teaching him survival skills like how to snare rabbits and how to use a bow. That kind of connection embodies a certain level of trust.

It didn't take long for Nud to realize that the box was not *the box*. A latch of dull black metal kept the lid firmly in place – shaped like a raven's head with a hooked beak for a clasp.

I should've told him what I'd done straightaway, thought Nud. *Why... after all these years?*

Nud gave the lid a sniff. *Smells sort of 'mapley.'* He had to remind himself that he was not that scrawny, naïve little Pip that'd fled the woods that day. Nud was much taller now, springier and well-balanced. He was stronger and much more experienced. On Paplov's insistence, for nights on end he'd studied the old gods and the new ones, the elemental forces, the laws and customs of Webfoot and neighboring districts, on top of accounting, languages, navigation, and maps of lands and oceans both near and far. Still, despite all his training – a future diplomat's required curriculum – Nud had no real explanation for what had happened to him so long ago, that spring day near the cabin. *Really, who would believe me? I can hardly believe me. Branches don't just lash out on their own like that. They just can't.*

Nud sighed, then stood up. He paced in circles about his small room and drew in a few deep breaths. He stretched his fingers apart as wide as they'd go. Even in moonlight, he could see that the scars from the axe blade were still there. He clenched his hand into a fist. The tissue felt tight. Standing over the table, Nud pulled the box to the very edge. It was more ornate than the one in Fyorn's attic had been, and professionally made. The lid bore a depiction of Gan, the Hidden City, inlaid with red-dyed horn. *The time is now,* he convinced himself, and felt a tingle on his wrist where the tree had left its mark.

Finally, hand quivering and body tense, ready to jump back in an instant, Nud lifted the raven latch. Holding his breath, he slowly creaked open the lid, just a crack…

The sweet scent of maple flowed out, nothing more. Nud peeked inside. There were no giant spiders within ready to leap out at him, only maple candy.

Nud let out a deep sigh. Then he shrugged his shoulders, scooped up one of the candies and popped it in his mouth. As his molars crunched down on the morsel, maple flavor melted out of the bits that broke off, dabbing his tongue with sweetness and soaking into his palate. *Not as good as taffy,* he decided, crunching away, *but not bad either… oversweet.* The aspiring diplomat took his uncle's offering as a sign of goodwill. *The next time Paplov visits, I'm going with him.*

That day came sooner than expected. Before long, Nud needed his uncle's advice. The woodsman knew the woods and the lowlands better than anyone did – like the back of his weather-beaten hands. And he seemed to know a great deal about abnormal things. In particular, he was the only one Nud could think of who might know something about a certain artifact that originated in the bog. Above all else though, he was the only Elderkin Nud knew personally.

The bog is a peaceful place. The blood shed there has long soaked into the black earth, and although a battle rages, it is unseen to the untrained eye, and unheard to the untrained ear. Ever it looms though, dark and ominous and terrible and free, but silent and invisible to the simple folk that live among the rushes. They are the Pips, and they are happy.

—*The Diviner*

CHAPTER iii

Bog stone

Early next morning at the onset of a clear day, Nud's good friend Gariff dropped by the hut on his way to the Akedan ruins – the best place for scoring ancient artifacts this side of Jakka. The pair bee-lined to the quickest route by foot: a trail edging the grassy banks of Blackmuk Creek, starting just outside of town.

"Hold up, Leno," Gariff huffed, struggling over the uneven ground. Spring flooding had made for unexpected detours, choked with undergrowth. Nud, being much more agile in bare feet than his Stout friend in his big, mud-sucking boots, found himself way out in front.

"C'mon," Nud called back over his shoulder. "You're too slow. Daylight's wasting."

As Nud rounded a wide pool that brought him away from the creek, the sounds of water trickling around rocks turned to the rustling of small animals rooting around in the underbrush. And as he skirted a mud patch that brought him farther afield still, the animal sounds turned to winds whispering through the high branches of poplar and birch trees.

Well out of sight, the Pip slowed his pace. Then out of nowhere, he caught a shadow and a shimmer over the land. Nud halted. A strange feeling gripped him. A lone crow cawed and took flight. A rabbit darted out in front of him and zig-zagged.

Something's wrong. Nud tensed.

In a flash, the ground gave way beneath his feet. Nud toppled into a wet slide. Slick earth collapsed around him. The forest blurred as he shunted into a deep pit that wasn't there before. Wet mud engulfed Nud's entire body.

His head dipped under. He struggled to resurface.

Can't breathe…

Heart pounding, he forced his way up and gasped for air. He spat the grime out, thrashing his arms and kicking his feet. He sank again.

Like quicksand… Kicking his feet was like digging a hole beneath him – his grave.

Nud barely pushed himself above the soupy mess a second time, with his head tilted back just enough to breathe. His heartbeat raced as he struggled to find the right balance between subtle movement and buoyancy.

"Gariff, help…," Nud sputtered, calling back to the trail. His throat felt raw with the effort and he almost sank under again. A rotten and moldy stench like week-old refuse washed over him. His voice trembled. "Gariff," he gurgled. This time the mud poured into his mouth, grainy and sick-tasting. He coughed up bile.

No one answered his cries, and no wonder – the Pip had left his friend well behind and he knew it. *This can't be happening.*

Seconds felt like minutes. His eyes darted about.

There's no way out.

Nud could almost see the gross mix rising. A steady stream of stagnant water from an adjacent pond flowed over the rim of the sinkhole and poured down its side. But he was already up to his neck in the messy slop. *If this gets any higher, I'm done for.*

He studied the mud wall and spotted tree roots dangling over the edge.

If only I could get to them. The Pip needed a boost.

Gently – trying not to disturb the wet earth beneath him too much – Nud flapped his feet to propel him sideways. His foot banged a sturdy perch, jutting out of the mud wall. He clenched his toes around it and pulled himself to the edge, then reached for a blackened branch sticking out of the mud. It was wet and grainy in his grasp, with a burl that reminded him of a fist. Nud pulled himself towards the dangling roots. The branch snapped. *Rotten… Ugh!* The broken piece in his hand looked like curled fingers… a lot like curled fingers. *It is a fist!*

Wrapped along the stick's greater length were the twisted remnants of tendons and muscles. Nud whipped the severed forearm away, then grasped for another branch, thicker – a leg with only half a foot attached! Nud lost his balance on the root. He slipped back and plunged into the slop, mouth open, eyes stinging. He slipped under.

Nud's arms felt heavy… stuck. Fully submerged, he kicked with his legs and pushed with his arms. For a moment, he could've sworn he was sinking faster for the effort. Somehow, by a twisting motion and frantic flapping of his wide feet, Nud propelled himself upwards and broke surface. He gasped for air, and held there for a long moment, brushing muck away from his mouth and eyes. He spat again, to expunge the earthy grit from his mouth. This time, he got a big glob out. Nud called for his friend again.

"DAMN IT GARIFF! WHERE ARE YOU?"

Crashing noises sounded from the bushes.

"Hold on, Leno," Gariff roared. "I'm coming."

His friend's colossal headgear eclipsed the sun as he peered into the hole. Nud breathed a giant's sigh of relief.

"Quick," Nud said. "There are dead people down here!"

Gariff immediately unshouldered his pack and began rummaging through it.

As Nud waited, water continued to pour into the sinkhole from above. Earth gave way at the rim… down rolled a blackened head to top off Nud's experience. It settled on a sideways lean, floating on the slop.

The eyes were narrow slits, the lips twisted and curled, and its mouth open and oozing red sand. The choking smell, the imagery, and the awful taste in Nud's mouth overloaded his senses. He covered his mouth and began to retch, all the while unable to stop himself from staring at the thing.

The expression on the bog person's face was not one Nud would've expected. It was not an expression of horror or surprise or betrayal. It was not even one of struggle or fight. Rather, the visage was one of normalcy, peace… acceptance, as though laying to rest in a bog were the natural thing to do.

Bile painted Nud's tongue, and the grainy texture of the bog water lined his cheeks from the inside.

"Gariff!" he sputtered.

"Hold on." Gariff had a rope in his hands.

To Nud's horror the gnarled face began to roll towards him, carried by the inflow current. The Pip leaned back as far as he could, to get away. But it kept coming, rolling along towards him as though out for a stroll. Risking everything,

Nud lifted his leg to the surface, stretched it out, and pushed the thing away with his toes. The severed head lingered on the surface awhile longer, bobbing. It spun twice, rolled over, and then slowly sank into the depths of the bog. When it was gone, Nud glanced back to the rim, to the circle of trees that surrounded the hole, and then to the sky.

"Heads up!" Gariff shouted. He tossed Nud the rope.

"Not funny," Nud replied, as he snatched it out of the air.

Gariff's eyebrows squished together. "What?" Then his eyes went wide. "Oh, sorry."

Nud adjusted his grip on the rope, braced his feet against the side of the pit, and signaled to Gariff. Grunting with effort, the Stout began to haul him out.

As his friend pulled him up the slope, a series of bright flashes caught Nud's eye. A brilliant stone jutted out, right where the earth had chunked away. It lay there, cupped by outstretched roots like an egg in a crow's nest. Curious, the Pip swung his body over to the roots.

The Stout let out a heavy grunt. "Stop swingin' around, or I'll let you go."

Nud stretched out a hand, yanked the stone free, and continued up until he crested the rim of the sinkhole. He scrambled onto solid ground, and then waved his prize at Gariff. "Look what I found!"

The Stout wiped his brow with his shirtsleeve, leaving behind a dirty streak on one side of his face. He let out a heavy sigh and brushed off his pants with his hands, but that only made them dirtier. Sticky cobwebs coated his brown bush shirt from top to bottom, splattered with mud and peppered with bits of dry leaves, burrs and small sticks.

Gariff leaned over the pit and looked inside. "Yuk! Bog body soup, if you ask me."

Nud spit out some more grit, then shook mud off his arms. "And I'm covered in it."

Water continued to pour over the rim of the sinkhole and run down its side. A pickled torso, black and shrunken, broke free. It slid down the wet wall and plopped onto the sloppy surface. Across from where the two friends stood, a fist jutted out of the mud—the one Nud had sent flying.

Nud turned his attention to his new find. With his thumb, he wiped some of the mud off the bog stone. He held it to the sunlight. The stone—a crystal of sorts—dazzled red and white. But there was more to its radiance than mere reflection. Trapped within, milky white bands twisted and curled, and every so often they flared a deep red. The stone flashed on and off like a firefly.

The Stout took Nud's hard-earned prize and held it up to the sun, one eye squinting. The first thing he did was shrug, as though it were no big deal. Perhaps the sunlight had made the stone's internal flicker barely noticeable, or perhaps he'd seen better quality stones similar in basic appearance. After having eyed the piece for a long minute, with a quick toss he sent it spinning into the air, then caught the stone in his thick-fingered grip. He nodded his head in satisfaction, then plunked the bog stone back into Nud's hands.

"Not a bad find," he said. "I wonder what it's good fer."

"Lots of things," Nud said, not having thought of even one, but knowing there must be many. "Something this rare has to be valuable."

Spearheads and rusty suits of armor were more Gariff's kind of treasure. "Useful things have value, like this here hat." He went on to adjust his favorite "adventuring" headgear – faded red, floppy and wide-brimmed. The thing was a way-worn monstrosity, and he was the only one that didn't know how ridiculous it looked.

"Well, a rare stone like this can buy lots of useful things," Nud responded.

"Aye," Gariff said. There was no arguing that point. His broad head appeared to sit directly upon his solid shoulders as he nodded.

Gariff Ram and Nud had known one another since before Gariff could remember. The Stout's severe lack of free-spiritedness and imagination didn't stop them from being good friends; it just got in the way at times. As part of what had become an annual tradition, Gariff's father and kinsmen did seasonal work in Webfoot while lodging at the Flipside Inn. His extended family labored long, hard days from early spring through to the better part of the dry season. Gariff's apprenticeship afforded him just enough time for a day trip now and again, usually when work was slow or materials late in arrival.

The pair decided to abandon their trip to the Akedan ruins, on account of their misadventure, and opted to return to the creek, wash up, and follow it back to the Mire Trail. Despite the fact the morning hadn't gone as planned, Gariff seemed content enough to have had an adventure. It wasn't so easy to tell though; he looked on the grumpy side normally, the way his heavy brow seemed to scrunch his eyes into narrow slits.

*

Nud's head cleared noticeably after putting some distance between him and that sinkhole, and by the time they neared the Crossing he realized that, as unnerving as the ordeal had been, they'd stumbled upon an opportunity. And one worth protecting. Nud halted on the high ground, just before traversing over Blackmuk Creek from the forest side to the mire side of the trail.

"Gariff," Nud said, "we both have to promise not to tell anyone about the bog stone, especially your cousin, Kabor."

"What about the sinkhole?" Gariff said.

Nud grimaced. "The sinkhole's fair game, but not until after we know more about staking claims."

"And the bog bodies?"

That one, Nud had to ponder. "We should keep the bodies under wraps too," he decided. "There might be more stones and we don't want to risk giving away the location. People will start digging around while the paperwork is going through, and who knows what they might turn up." As the last words were spoken, they struck a chord inside of him. Nud smothered it with a solid dose of denial.

"Okay, I won't tell a soul," Gariff said.

A voice cut in from across the creek. "Too late."

Nud flushed at the sound of those words. It was the mischief-maker himself. Impeccable timing, as usual. Gariff spun around to look, jaw gaping in surprise. Then he swung his gaze back to Nud, with a chuckle.

"Kabor doesn't count," he jibed. "He has no soul."

Caught with the flashing stone still in hand, Nud deftly closed his fingers around it and slipped the piece into his pocket. *It's bright outside*, he consoled himself, *and Kabor probably didn't notice anything unusual from that far away, not with his poor eyesight.*

"Whatever," Nud told Gariff, nonchalantly. The Pip closed his eyes and let out a heavy sigh, then turned to acknowledge the Stout's sly cousin. Kabor stood casually on the other side of the creek, dressed in dark clothes better suited for a wake than a treasure hunt; always form fitting with him and never a hat. And he wore soft, black boots, unlike Gariff's which were painfully rigid. The cloak he held flapped violently in the wind, which had been gusting up since mid-morning.

The two cousins were both about Nud's age and height, but the similarities ended there. Slight of build and a bit of a runt in comparison to his kin, looks-wise Kabor was not your typical Stout – thin and wiry while most were wide and squat like Gariff. Also, Gariff was drawn to simplicity. Everything was black and white to him. He was stocky, strong and completely inflexible. Kabor, on the other hand, was slippery as oil, and to him everything was a shade of grey. Nud could never get a straight answer out of that one.

Kabor removed his spectacles and shoved them into his pocket. Then he moved to the edge of the stepping-stone-sized boulders that conveniently spanned the creek. From across the gurgling watercourse, he turned his head sideways until Nud was well within his peripheral vision, which was his way of looking straight at a person.

"So, what all did you find?" Kabor asked. The uninvited cousin wore a mischievous, conniving grin that he alone owned. It bothered Nud to no end. Practiced or genuine, he could barely stand to look at it.

"Should we tell him?" Gariff said, anticipation in his voice.

Nud replied in a hushed tone. "Fine, tell him about the sinkhole. Leave the rest to me." Gariff erupted with excitement. The words nearly burst out of him. He called out to his cousin.

"We found bog bodies!"

"I heard," Kabor said, flat-toned. "You're not the first in these parts."

"But we're the latest," Gariff said, cheerfully.

"I suppose," Kabor responded. "Jhinyari?"

"Doubt it," Nud said. "That would be a stretch."

Kabor acknowledged with a quick nod.

"Did you see any metal at all?" he continued. "There might be bits of it stuck to body parts or just lying around. Jhinyari would be wearing armor."

"Really?" Gariff said.

"No metal that I could see," Nud said. "I think these were just regular bog bodies."

"Well, maybe not," Gariff said, ever the optimist. "You never know." He started over the Crossing towards his cousin as he spoke. The Stout nearly lost his balance on a wobbly stone while recounting his story about how a decapitated head "winked" at him as it rolled over, before sinking into the murky pit. He went on to describe grisly details about blackened appendages and rotting corpses, all the while holding onto his hat in the wind. With all of his grand talking and wobbling about, he forded the creek with the grace of a pig on hind legs. Nud, on the other hand, bounded across effortlessly, shortly after.

Gariff was prone to exaggeration at times, especially when he became excited about something. Kabor should've known his cousin was making up half of what he said. Nud was not one to complain though, nor would he spoil Gariff's fun. As far as the Pip was concerned, as long as Gariff didn't mention the flickering stone, he could say whatever he wanted to in order to astonish his cousin. Kabor soaked in Gariff's words like they were whispers on the wind.

The trio headed for the Mire Trail at that point. Kabor listened intently to his companions' tale and probed for more details, especially about what remnants of clothing still clung to the bodies, and if there were any other unusual items or signs of structures nearby. Gariff accidentally spilled the beans about finding the bog stone, but Nud cut him off before he could say too much.

"So, where is this fancy stone, Leno?" Kabor asked. "Is that what you slipped into your pocket back at the Crossing?"

Damn… how does he do that?

"Stone-*s-s-s*," Nud said to the cousins. "Clean out your ears."

Gariff gave Nud a look.

The Pip fumbled through his pockets and pulled out some quartz crystals he'd picked up along the creek bank after rinsing off. There was nothing special about them, really, they just looked nice. Nud knew that, but Kabor didn't know that Nud knew that. They created the perfect diversion.

"Three diamonds in the rough," Nud told the two cousins. "You can each pick one if you promise not to tell. I want to go back and get more. Kabor, you first, since you're the ugliest and I feel sorry for you."

Nud held them up for Kabor to see. The Stout turned his head to the left and examined the three stones the way he always examined things, with a sideways stare and untelling eyes – dark and hollow looking. A long moment passed. He tilted his head and squinted. Finally, the cousin shrugged and contorted his face into a pained expression.

"They don't look like much," he said, shaking his head as he grimaced.

"Of course not, you can't see anything," Nud replied.

Gariff opened his mouth to speak, but Nud sent him a cold stare to quell his words. The Stout fell in line, scrunching his forehead as he struggled to hold his tongue.

Kabor shot back. "I can see well enough to tell you those aren't diamonds, you simple-minded duck!" He grinned. "But I like them anyway. I'll take this tiny nugget off your hands… *partner.*"

Naturally, Kabor grabbed the biggest one. Then he turned to Gariff. "Don't worry Cuz. I left the girly one for you."

Nud swung his outstretched hand over to Gariff, and raised an eyebrow. The Stout graciously took the smaller of the two remaining – an elongated tablet-shaped stone. Nud didn't actually care which one he took.

Kabor smirked. "That's the one," he quipped.

Gariff frowned. He'd passed the first test and held his tongue about Nud's true find. The Pip slipped the last stone back into his pocket for safe keeping, next to the *real* one. Nud's secret was still mostly a secret, but if Gariff's weasel of a cousin found out then everyone from Webfoot to the Bearded Hills would know too, soon enough. Kabor was a fast talker, a whisperer, and above all a shady dealmaker – all cause for alarm. All Nud could hope for was that he'd quickly lose interest and that Nud's find would be overshadowed by outlandish rumors of bog bodies and buried treasure.

"I bet artifacts are there too," Kabor remarked. "Good ones, well-preserved, not like the rusted-out junk from Akeda."

"Hey!" Gariff furrowed his brow. "Akeda has the best stuff."

"No," Kabor said. "I mean ancient. Really ancient. You should have brought back an arm or a leg or something. Where exactly did you go? Did any of the bodies still have bristly hair?"

Gariff answered. "We were just off the creek, where it starts to bulge out into little ponds. There's a section that's flooded – easy to spot, if y'know what yer lookin' for."

Kabor slowed to a stop. "I'm going to check it out, then."

"We're not going with you," Nud told him straightaway, not eager to return to the corpse pit. The Pip looked to Gariff. "Right?" When his friend didn't answer, he turned to his cousin instead. "Besides, you're not even dressed for it. That place is choked with flies like you wouldn't believe, and they're attracted to black clothes."

"Best to go in drier conditions," Gariff added. "The ground'll be more stable."

"Nonsense," Kabor said. "It's easier pickings after a heavy rainfall. You both know that."

"A new sinkhole could open right up under yer feet," Gariff implored.

"Who are you, my mother?" he replied. "That collapse has to be one in a million. I'll take my chances." Kabor started back towards the creek. After a few steps, he paused and then turned around to stare them down, sideways.

"Well?" he said.

Neither Gariff nor Nud budged.

Kabor shrugged and continued on his way without them. He took one last look over his shoulder, sputtered "Cowards!", and then slid his glasses back on his face.

"So long," Nud called back, content to let the little runt go rummaging through the boggy graveyard blindly and without them. *Maybe he'll fall in.* Nud shrugged his shoulders at Gariff and continued homeward, only to halt at the sound of his friend's grumbling. The Stout still hadn't moved.

"Ugh. What now?"

Gariff pinched his lips to one side. "C'mon Leno. Yer not still sore 'bout the flag incident, are ya?"

"What do *you* think?" Nud said. "I got slapped with three weeks of 'voluntary' service and, on top of that, a lashing. I could've done with just one week, if only I'd ratted out the rat. He deserved it."

Gariff's eyes shifted down to his feet, and then to his cousin in the distance. He must've known Paplov couldn't have taken the stunt lightly, being on the town council and finding the Webfoot banner in Nud's possession. Indeed, given the nature of the offence, Nud's grandfather had been unusually strict in his punishment. He seemed to think it was a black mark against Nud's future in local politics. "They'll never forget," he'd said. *They* being Paplov's esteemed peers – the other council members, not to mention the lord mayor.

"What heat did *he* get for it?" Nud asked.

Gariff's silence said everything.

Nud folded his arms. "That's what I thought. He has it coming, you know."

"Everyone says that," Gariff grumbled. The Stout raised his head and looked Nud over. His grumpy face turned apologetic, and the two narrow slits beneath his brow widened into the darkest brown eyes.

"Kabor doesn't mean any harm'n it," he said. "He just does it in good fun."

"Fun for him, you mean," Nud said, shaking his head. "I didn't even want him to take the banner down. It's not like I was encouraging him. And I told him not to do it… I *told* him *not* to. You know the connections – Town Hall, the mayor… Paplov."

Over the years, Gariff had done more than his share of apologizing on behalf of his younger cousin. Granted, Kabor's parents *were* lost in a caravan raid when he was very young, and so Gariff's family had taken him in. Plus, he couldn't see very well. The two combined had earned him more than his fair share of sympathy. Nud had to admit Kabor had it rough, but he also made it a point that Kabor was not to receive any special treatment from him. Kabor wasn't the only one who'd had it rough. Still, Nud couldn't help but to acknowledge that taking the town flag the way he did, when he did, was rather gutsy. And there was a certain thrill to it all…

"It's a wonder he didn't get caught climbing up that pole in broad daylight," Nud said, "right under their noses."

Gariff smirked and let out a reflective chuckle. "He never gets caught."

"Yeah, well, he will one day," Nud remarked.

There was a long, awkward pause between them. Nud knew exactly what was rolling around in Gariff's skull. Finally, the Stout let it out.

"I gotta go after him, Leno," he said, shaking his head. He slumped in a display of self-loathing, then turned to follow his cousin. The burly Stout started back towards the Crossing.

A couple of half-hearted complaints later, Nud followed.

CHAPTER IV

Second look

Nud felt more than a little queasy about returning to the gruesome scene.

"One body, or a whole bunch of bodies jammed together?" Kabor asked, sweeping his gaze over the sinkhole. It looked a lot wider and had completely filled in with murky water, to the point passersby wouldn't have noticed anything different about the spot by looking at it – just another muddy pond.

"How the heck should I know?" Nud replied. "I saw one part of an arm, one part of a leg, a head, and a torso – could all be the same person." He discreetly checked his pocket. The bog stone was still there.

"Gross. How do you think they died?"

"I don't know," Nud recalled the expression on the severed head, "…drowned, maybe." The Pip grinned when he saw Gariff's cousin swatting at the flies around him, moreso when he started to slip because of it.

"Whoa!" Kabor nearly took a dive into the sinkhole.

Gariff grabbed his cousin's arm and steadied him. "Watch it," he said. "I knew this was a bad idea."

"Oh, c'mon," Kabor retorted. "Where's your sense of adventure?"

Gariff grimaced, then backed away from the hole, dragging Kabor with him.

"Let go," Kabor said, wrenching free. Despite his protests, he was definitely more careful after that.

The three friends spent the middle hours of the afternoon poking around the site as best they could manage, without getting too wet or too muddy. Kabor attempted to fish unseen body parts out of the deep spots with a stick, to no avail. Gariff carefully dug along the edge of the sinkhole, testing the ground with every step as he felt through the wet earth. He pulled up river stones and all kinds of rotting vegetation, but no body parts or artifacts. Nud showed Kabor the tangled mess of tree roots, now submerged, where he'd found his bog stone, but without mentioning the bursts of red light that drew his eye to the spot in the first place.

After much slushing and mucking about, nothing grand turned up. Near the end of their search though, Kabor did happen to stumble upon a slim post in the ground. Nailed to its top was an orange ribbon with writing on it. Kabor adjusted his spectacles; his eyes looked three times bigger with them on.

"H-M-E 2-2-6," he read aloud.

Gariff winced and rubbed the back of his neck.

"I know," Nud said to Gariff. "Damn." He'd seen posts like that one before. Over the years, more and more had been popping up throughout the Mire and surrounding territories.

"What?" Kabor said.

"Already staked," Nud replied, defeat in his voice. "Probably for a mineral rights claim."

"We don't know the boundaries, though," Gariff remarked.

"True," Nud said.

Kabor shrugged, then yanked at the stake.

"Stop," Nud blurted out, but he was too late. Kabor had pulled it out of the ground.

Nud shook his head in frustration. "Put it back. Do you have any idea the administrative processes people have to go through just to stake a claim? And taking it won't change anything." Paplov had unloaded a pile of claim approvals on Nud recently, so the Pip knew just how tedious the paperwork could be. Plus, he'd learned to appreciate all of the careful mapping and measurements required to put that post exactly where it had to be.

Kabor raised an eyebrow, and enunciated every syllable: "Ad-min-is-tra-tive pro-cess-es?"

Nud huffed. "Shut up. We could all get in big trouble for what you just did."

Gariff's eyes darted between Nud and his cousin, worry engrained on his face.

"Oh ya?" Kabor taunted. His eyes narrowed. "Watch this."

"NO!" Gariff shouted, but nothing could stop his trouble-making cousin. Without hesitation, Kabor tossed the wooden post high up into the air, towards the creek. It crashed through the branches.

A flush of anger washed over Nud. *No consequences for him, of course.* He squeezed his eyes shut, trying to contain his irritation. *But more paperwork for me. And I hate paperwork.* Fuming on the inside, a distorted buzzing welled up in the back of his mind, like nothing he'd felt before – it pushed against his skull from the inside. Pressure mounting, Nud buried his head in his hands.

Gariff noticed. "Leno, you all right? Err… it's just a post."

Steady… steady… No…

"I'm losing it," Nud said, "I can't hold it back."

Nud heard Kabor's voice. "Hold what back?"

Suddenly, the pressure released.

A loud SNAP! sounded from the creek. Nud jolted back and opened his eyes, just in time to see the prospecting stake whiz past Kabor's head. It rifled into some brush.

"What the heck?" Nud braced himself on a crooked alder, feeling dizzy.

"Odd," Gariff remarked, scrunching his brow.

"Huh?" Kabor said, oblivious. He shot Nud a sideways glance as he squirreled his glasses away.

Gariff explained, hands waving and pointing. "The stake just flew into the bushes there, overhanging the sinkhole." He took a long look at his cousin. "It's like she flung right back at you… What are the odds?"

Kabor eyed his cousin suspiciously, then made his way over to the brush to poke through the branches, careful not to topple into the slop-filled pit. He retrieved the wooden stake. "Humph. What are the odds of it happening twice?"

"No!" Gariff cried again, grasping for the stake.

Kabor dodged Gariff's attempt, then whipped the signage back towards the creek on a low arc. This time, it flew clear of any trees and landed with a plunk. The steady current caught the stake and carried it away.

Gariff's eyes met Nud's. His shoulders slumped, in full knowledge that the Pip was less than impressed. And Nud knew that Gariff harbored some kind of inner desire that the pair would get along better, someday. *Not going to happen,* Nud thought.

As annoying as Kabor was though, Nud was actually more concerned about how the stake had boomeranged back the way it did in the first place, especially after such a long pause.

"How does that even happen?" Nud asked, prompting Gariff.

The solid-built Stout shifted his weight back and forth, unease in his stance. His squinting eyes scanned the tree-tops. Gariff had no explanation to offer. His cousin broke the silence.

"It's a bit gusty up there, that's all," Kabor said. "The stake got stuck in the branches for a second, then fell. The wind bowed a branch, and then the branch snapped back to hit the stake just right while it was in the air." He paused. "The stake flew into a springy branch – so what, big deal."

Scratching underneath his hat, his eyes still searching, Gariff shook his head. "It didn't look that way to me." He paused for a long moment. "But what else could it be? I can't think of any other way."

"That doesn't even make sense." Nud peered into the suspect branches overhanging the creek. The entire incident felt a little unnatural and the fact that freshly unearthed bog bodies lay nearby didn't help matters. A chill rode up Nud's spine. His stomach tightened.

"Do you think it has something to do with the bog bodies?"

"What d'ya mean?" Gariff replied. "Are you talking about ghosts?"

Kabor snickered.

"Never mind," Nud said, "we should leave now," and then he made up some other excuse for departing, "…or we'll be crossing the Mire in the dark."

Kabor scoffed. "You're worried about nothing." He waved his hand dismissively at Nud. With a nonchalant gait to his step, Gariff's trouble-making cousin started off to the next pond, by himself again.

Gariff sighed a heavy sigh as he watched Kabor leave, then shifted his gaze to Nud. "Just let'im go and get it out of his system," he said. "We'll just wait here." He lowered himself stiffly to sit on a log.

Sore himself, Nud took his seat on a nearby tree root. "Yeah, okay. I could use a break anyway."

*

The two friends sat and stared into the murky water, a stone's throw from where the staking post had been pulled. Between them, they agreed a hasty departure was the best course of action, but their reasons differed. Nud'd simply had enough – it'd been a hell of a day already. Gariff had already grumbled on and off throughout the afternoon that, with the time wasted, they could've made a quick dash to the Akedan ruins for some "real" treasure hunting. Shamelessly, he made one final pitch for it.

"We can still get there," he insisted, "instead of poking around here in the mud. It'd be worth it. Kabor says there's secret stairs in d'em ruins somewhere, with a heavy stone door at the bottom openin' to an arm'ry. The finest blades ever smithed came out of Fortune Bay, they say." Gariff puffed out his chest. "Someday, they'll say the same about d'Hills."

Nud rolled his eyes. "What are we going to do with a bunch of rusty old blades?"

Gariff shrugged in a way to suggest he was about to name a long list of fantastic things, but instead he listed a bunch of boring things. Nud wasn't convinced. Besides, trouble followed Kabor like his very own shadow, causing Nud to wonder exactly what was in store for them if they actually did find those stairs. It suffices to say he wanted no part of the rascal's scheming.

"There's got to be something good down there," Gariff went on. "Cuz seen those stairs on a really old map, Leno."

Nud huffed. "He can't even see his hand in front of his face."

"Well… ya… but he can sorta see his hand *beside* his face."

Nud conceded that much. His cousin could read, after all. "So, where did he get the map?"

"It was in a box of notes n'letters n'such," Gariff responded. "Property of the oldest, grizzliest Hill Stout you ever saw. The ole man was ready to pass on and he gave it up for nothing but three dirty jokes. And they had to be good ones."

Nud scoffed. "If he'd asked for clean jokes, Kabor would've been in trouble. And let me guess: he's dead now, making the story impossible to confirm."

Gariff winced slightly.

"Well, where's the map?" Nud asked. "Cough it up, let's take a look."

Nud had seen a good many maps and drawings of what Akeda used to look like. There were even maps portraying the old Abindohn settlement that preceded it. Akeda was once a first-rate staging ground for the defense of the bay, settled on its north shore by survivors of the old world. Those who'd once lived there abandoned it long before Nud's time – Paplov's too – and moved farther north along Dim River to establish Harrow on the shores of Dim Lake. According to legend, they destroyed their own city before leaving it behind, and gave up seafaring altogether, although Nud also heard that their descendants continue to build magnificent watercrafts that grace the lake they now call home. As far as he could tell, no one really knew why the Akedans abandoned their city, so readily and without a fight.

Gariff gazed at Nud with that apologetic expression again. *Oh no.* Nud rubbed his own face with his hands and shook his head. *Don't tell me.*

"Haven't actually… uh… seen'er yet Nud," Gariff said, confirming Nud's suspicion. "I was sorta hope'n Kabor'd bring it along."

The Pip continued to shake his head, then sighed. *Typical Gariff.* Then he scanned the woods. "KABOR!" he hollered.

Nud jumped to his feet when Gariff's cousin appeared out of nowhere.

"I thought you took off," Nud said to him.

The scrawny Stout shrugged. "Changed my mind and doubled back."

Gariff rose and regarded his cousin, expectation in his eyes. "Do ya have the map, Cuz?"

Kabor gave him a blank look.

"You know, the one we talked about?"

"Oh, that one." Kabor shook his head. "Nope. I keep it hidden away, back at the Flipside."

That sealed the decision to head for home. They left without telling Kabor about the flickering stone that day, and by the time he found out, it didn't really matter much. Nud was right about one thing though: he'd definitely want it for himself.

CHAPTER V

Mire Trail

After Nud's fourth "crossing" of the day, the trio finally clambered up the creek slope and met the Mire Trail, heading home. Until mere weeks ago, light watercraft and mucky portages were the only way in or out of town. They had no worries though.

Two weeping willows marked the entrance into the bog. The trees' serpentine roots spread along the ground and curled in and out of the watery mud. The smell of algae and wood rot saturated the air. Beyond the trailhead ran a corduroy road edged with eager poplars and heavy border stones. Along it was the Handler's Post – a dilapidated old shack with a faded sign over the door that read "Guaranteed Dry," where one could pay for a ride into town. The place was empty and overgrown with long grass that'd been trampled on.

As the three plodded on, the terrain unfolded and flattened into a shallow waterscape, spotted with grassy tufts and old standing deadwood that crackled and knocked whenever the wind blew. Pools of standing water mirrored the evening sunlight, splotching with orange a never-ending blanket of pale green moss that stretched out from the trailside to the horizon. It was the largest single section of actual bog in the so-called "bog lands" – the unofficial but common name for the network of wetlands encompassing Webfoot. Soon, a half-submerged sun would set the blanket ablaze with orange fire in the west.

"It's awfully late for startin' the bog-pass, isn't it?" Gariff asked.

His voice wavered ever so slightly, betraying a hint of concern, and the words he chose were just another way of complaining that they'd spent too long rummaging around the sinkhole. The Stout was far from the cradle of his beloved Bearded Hills and uncomfortably close to the fireside ghost stories of his youth. And although the bog was safe, as far as any of them knew, it just wasn't smart to be out and away from town late at night. Paplov would've never allowed it, had he known.

"We'll have daylight to spare on the other side," Nud replied, "unless you care to break for a swim?"

Gariff shook his head. "I don't think so. I don't have yer webbing, or love of leeches on my arse."

"No, you certainly don't have webbing," Nud said, stalling for time while spinning a respectable retort, "and as for the leeches... I'll have to take your word for it." Nud turned to size Gariff up, and immediately seized upon the Stout's compacted expression.

"You're too backed up to stay afloat anyway – you'd sink right to the bottom," Nud said. "You need to let some loose." After squatting in the bushes off the creek for the better part of half an hour, Gariff had returned with only a grunt and a sour expression to show for his efforts.

Kabor took one look at Gariff and broke out laughing. The sturdy Stout's scrunched face made the accusation hard to deny.

While Kabor chuckled on, Nud whirled around Gariff gracefully, leading a phantom partner by hand and waist: "Care to dance at the bottom of the bog... with the *Bog Queens?*"

"There's no such thing as bog queens," Gariff said. He turned to his cousin: "Right?"

Bog queens really were not something to joke about. Nud would've stopped there, they all should've stopped there, but Kabor picked up right where Nud left off. His knack for digging up little bits of information and putting them together came in handy from time to time, and it just so happened that he knew the rest of the legend even better than Nud did. What better time to enlighten his cousin than in the wake of a bog body discovery?

"Actually," Kabor began, in the voice of a noted poet, "on this very road and on an evening just like this, the men of Fortune Bay and their families fled their homeland, on a heading north, to Dim Lake. A brutal Jhinyari warlord pursued them fiercely, and his minions even managed to cut off their retreat on the other side of the bog. The men and their families were trapped. With their silvery blades, the Jhinyari slew men where they stood defending their families. They cast the women into the bog and conspired to steal the children for slaves."

Kabor made sideways glances to his left and right as they strode, and then behind, as if to make sure no one else was within earshot. He cleared his throat and continued, in a whispered tone.

"Once the mothers understood what was happening, and

saw that their plight was hopeless, each leapt into the bog willingly with their children in their arms, and swam under the moss to a watery death. They believed it an act of kindness."

"Is that true?" Gariff asked. He looked to Nud for confirmation. The Pip shrugged.

"Oh, it's true all right," Kabor responded, "if *The Diviner* says so, then it's true. And he said so."

"So then what?"

"Well… then a great *Leviathan* was raised from the bog," Kabor spread his arms in a wide circular motion to emphasize the sheer size of the beast. "It appeared as a giant white whale. And the thing spoke to the last men standing, weaving words of great knowledge and unsurpassed wisdom…"

The promise of the great beast's epic words hung in the air, but Kabor held his tongue. He glanced over to Gariff and took a deep breath. The three plodded on, listening intently to nothing but their own soft footsteps and the evening twitter of birdsong among the grasses. The storyteller's lips remained silent.

Gariff's brotherly impatience with his cousin erupted. He swung his arms to his side vehemently. "Well, what did it say?" he said, as riled up as Nud had ever seen him, "W-H-A-T did the white whale tell them?"

In stride, Kabor shook one finger at Gariff. "Now the men swore an oath never to repeat the words spoken by the Leviathan that day. But I can tell you this much…"

Kabor halted sharply, dramatically, and with a strong grip took Gariff by the shoulder.

"As the men fought on in desperation, the Leviathan made a deal with them, a deal that no one will speak of, even today, a deal that only desperate men would ever make. The beast, now satisfied, returned to the murky depths under the mosses.

For a moment, the fighting stopped and there was nothing but an eerie silence, broken only by giant bubbles that rose to the water's surface and burst into the air."

Kabor added a pinch of rasp to his voice and raised his arms high over his head as he spoke the next words.

"Then, as the orange sun dipped below a luminous green horizon, out of the bog arose the dead mothers, in vengeful fury, and many other dead things dredged up from the bottom of the bog along with them. Together they entangled the Jhinyari, each with a grip like wet swamp grass, and dragged them down, one by one into the murky depths, until those few that remained finally fled in terror."

Kabor paused for effect before continuing with the tag line. He must've known that he had Gariff right where he wanted him, for he relished in the moment. Gariff said nothing as he glanced at the water-soaked mosses and tall tufts of grass that lined the trail, and then down to the muddy ground at his feet, kicking away small bits of dried mud with oversized boots.

The ending that Kabor devised had a dreadful spin to it. "It is said that the undying mothers still haunt these wetlands, and if they happen to discover children not in the company of adults on the Mire Trail at night, they grab them and pull them down under the moss for mercy's sake, lest the Jhinyari get hold of them."

As if on cue, a few fair-sized bubbles broke the surface of the bog waters right in front of them. Although commonplace to those accustomed to the bog, the unnatural timing of the event sent Gariff marching ahead at a quickened pace.

Kabor and Nud exchanged a few animated glances and smirks. *We got him good… we got him good.*

*

Well past supper, the three hiked on. Nud's legs were spent and he thought they might collapse under his own weight if he had to walk much farther. When his stomach growled, the hollow noise sounded as though it'd come from a deep chasm. His good friend Gariff, encumbered by all of their gear from the failed trip to the ruins, dragged his heals as much or more than Nud. And simply grunted whenever Kabor tried to make small talk.

The Bearded Hill's most notorious delinquent was getting bored with his dreary companions, and so reverted to a time-honored tactic more fun for him – unadulterated mockery. Gariff and Nud were too tired to counter.

Kabor made fun of their clothes, their hair, the way they walked and the way they talked. He explained to them exactly why they didn't have girlfriends, in less than kind words, and wondered openly why they smelled so bad. All in the course of about half a league.

For once though, his distinct blend of humor – that being pure, unconstrained ridicule – was not totally unwelcomed. Kabor's insults actually made the pair laugh as he shifted focus from one to the other, sometimes even killing two birds with one stone, so to speak, with a double slam.

Gariff seemed especially happy to be distracted from the "Mothers of the Bog" story, despite being hardest hit by the flurry of insults. In the end, Kabor lifted their spirits over the last leg of the journey just enough to carry them into town with a chuckle.

Nud was the first to spot the long wall that palisaded Webfoot. A passing memory brought him back to something Paplov had said so many times before, pointing to the struc-ture with his walking stick. Nud repeated those grand words in Paplov's voice.

"Behold the great wonder of the Mire," he proclaimed, "the Wet Wall of Webfoot."

"A great wonder it's still standing," Gariff retorted, "You Pips should've used stone to build your wall."

"Oh, I don't know Gariff," Kabor grinned, "there's something charming about a twig fortress."

"Those *posts* are solid," Nud contested.

"Is that so?" Gariff asked. "Then what are they made of?"

"Oak," Nud replied.

"Actually, I think they're cedar," Kabor said.

"Whatever," Nud responded. "Probably the sturdiest you'll ever see… in a place like this."

Gariff scoffed. "Parts of it are nearly leaning into the water."

The posts were, for the most part, set vertically and bound together with rope made from a common swamp grass, but spaced so as to keep the larger, dangerous sorts of wildlife out while allowing small fish and game to pass freely. As a further deterrent to anyone or anything that might try to climb over, a dense array of thin, sharp spikes jutted out of the wall's base. One slip while attempting to scale its slime-covered surface could mean instant impalement and death. Gariff was right though. Some sections had seen better days.

As they passed under the arched gateway into town, Gariff's eyes scanned every post from bottom to top and tracked every beam overhead. Every contact received a scrutinizing look.

"I don't care what you say, Leno," he remarked. "The whole thing is crude, makeshift and easily undone. Fire, wind, the slow heave of winter ground – they all take their toll. You can't depend on a damn thing to stay still around here."

And then he summed it all up with an uncalled-for comment. "Who even wants to be in a bog to begin with?"

Wha… Nud's thoughts swirled so quickly he could hardly follow them. Contrary to what outsiders might say, bog lands are not dull and dreary places. They're full of life, color and variety. He couldn't believe that Gariff might suggest otherwise. *It's about delicate balance in the bog, not stability and strength like life on a rock.* Nud blurted out the only thing he could think of.

"You Stouts can't use wood to build because there are no trees left in the Bearded Hills. You ripped them all out of the earth until you hit bare rock, and now you're ripping out the rock."

Kabor chuckled at Nud's point, despite himself. The Pip didn't stop there.

"Your bricks and stonework would just sink to the bottom of the bog and decorate the halls of the bog queens."

Kabor liked that even more. He knew it would put his cousin on edge.

Gariff, however, dismissed Nud's comments as unworthy of serious consideration. He stubbornly held his ground and stuck to his point. As they continued into town, the Stout found more and more ways to criticize Pip architecture and construction. Everywhere he looked, something laughable or on the verge of collapse was just waiting for him to point out. Gariff's eye for structural detail was like no other – a product of his bloodline, no doubt. For centuries, his kin proudly carved caverns out of rocky hills and built towns out of heavy, squared-off stone blocks.

"You're totally inflexible," was all Nud could say in the end. "You're just not cut out for bog life. Not at all."

Before Gariff could respond, Kabor changed the topic. "How about we sneak in a few bites at the Flipside before calling it a day?"

"Beats cold leftovers," Gariff replied, straightaway. Perhaps the hint of home-cooked pippish stew blending into the night air had put the two Stouts over the edge.

Surely, Paplov expected Nud home at a reasonable hour. But… it would be leftovers for him too. He turned to the cousins. "Maybe just for a short while."

They couldn't pay for the food, of course, but their little round friend, Bobbin Numbit, was sure to slip them something delectable.

CHAPTER VI

Journey to the Flipside

The sweet, yet pungent aroma of peat-fires was already strong by the time Nud and the two cousins passed Webfoot's outer ponds on the main road in and caught sight of the first of the watergrass homes. As evening gave way to twilight, a pale orange sky backlit the thatched dwellings. Out came the glowflies, fiery sparks riding a gentle breeze across a sea of mire rushes.

In the distance, a red reed door whipped open violently. Two children dashed out of the hut, the smaller one yelling fiendishly at a slightly larger, laughing version of himself. Their yard was little more than trampled reeds and a scraggly birch tree with a dangling swing rope; their cone-topped hut little more than yard materials standing erect – woven grass and mud over a stick frame, splashed with shutters dyed in bright red, blue and yellow. Apart from the openings, the little hut looked as though it had grown out of the small mound it sat upon. The modest dwelling was inviting, if not elaborate, and Nud didn't care what Gariff might've thought of it.

Off to either side of the road, watergrass homes sprung up haphazardly over the mudflats, occupying nearly every hummock big enough for three Pips to stand on. A convenient web of muddy trails connected each and every conceivable shortcut from one worthy location to another: hut to hut, hut to tree, tree to tree, everywhere to boulders, everywhere to main paths, and back again every which way. The neighborhood was mostly home to the more traditional Pip families who followed the old ways, and secondarily to young couples just starting out who couldn't afford a premium lot in town.

The trio hiked on past wild rice farms, stands of smoke weed, the salamander ranges, the glowfish farms, and a row of covered longboat docks. Beyond the junction to Everdeep Pond – a rather affluent neighborhood – they passed Ling's Boulder, which brought them to respectable Wetwood. Farther along the main thoroughfare, the three hungry travelers veered east onto the high road to Drytown and started up the long hill. Even before catching sight of the inn, the smells of spit-roasted turtle and waterfowl filled the air. Twin trails of smoke from the inn's kitchen and hearth came into view, streaking grey across the faded sky.

At long last, by measure of tired legs and empty stomachs, they crested that final hill. The Flipside was a fair sight to behold, a beacon of civilization in the backcountry, with orange lanterns lit all around. Fine aromas circulated in the night air. A fair sight and a fair listen as well, with lively music and merriment spilling out onto the streets.

CHAPTER VII

Interlude – Natural-born story tellers

The wind is picking up and the treetops are whipping. The air grows soggy in the grove.

Ah yes… known far and wide for the fine fare served. How I miss my old taste buds. The inn's unsurpassed reputation among high appreciators of the culinary arts is something to admire; especially for such an out-of-the-way place. But in fact, because of it. More than just a few rare and unique delicacies still grace the menu, I am sure. Such flavors would not be processed quite the same by my new palate. No, not at all.

"The Flipside," I will say, is a fitting name for Webfoot's local watering hole. Loved by out-of-towners and despised by half of the town's permanent residents, the inn tends to attract what the locals would call *suspicious company*. Trappers, prospectors, rangers, boggers, and shady merchant folk, to name a few, could be found at the inn's tables or sitting at the bar.

If a bog queen happened to drag her twisted body out of the murky depths one day and slither in through the front door, few in attendance would so much as raise an eyebrow at her fashionably grim entrance, unless she promptly announced "drinks are on me."

Before the page I scribe begins to dampen in this drizzly weather, here is what to expect of the various folk likely to be lounging within the Flipside – big and small, respectable and not, genuine and scheming. I'll start with the Pips.

All you really need to know about Pips is that they pay acute attention to detail and, under normal circumstances, have the sharpest of memories. This lumbering form of mine, for better or for worse, has retained that mental acuity, so you can consider my ramblings as near record to the actual events. Keen memory, in part, is what makes us natural-born storytellers. You see, we actually *remember* all that happens, unlike some others (who will remain nameless). We do not *know* everything though, or necessarily make all the right *connections* that could be made, so the pristine pictures in our minds are not always as complete as they could be. Fortunately though, Pips tend to be *creative* as well in making such connections, and for coming up with quick solutions on the fly. Pips also have an extraordinary talent known as "recall" that allows them to essentially relive past experiences.

I just realized I wrote "us" and "we" throughout my description of Pips. Habit, I suppose, and at times I still count myself among them. But I was never quite as carefree as most, and there are times when I feel as far removed as one could be from such soft-fleshed creatures, so fragile and naïve in the world.

Stouts are very different than Pips. Hardworking and staunch, they are builders and planners by their very nature, with a stubborn streak now legendary. The younglings learn every practical matter there is to know about stone, metal, earth and hidden treasures. Adults, it seems, simply use that knowledge day to day, and slowly master their skills. Stouts think their way through every task with clever resolve, but sometimes I wonder if they remember anything about the journey.

Old-worlders and their descendants, on the other hand, seem to learn everything about everything and then forget most of it, except what gives them power. As such, they rule nearly all of the lands and do as they please, often with reckless abandonment.

Outlanders are the creations of old-worlders who dabbled in manipulations now locked away in deep mountains. Wide varieties were set loose upon the lands, at a time when the original Akedans thought themselves near extinction. Most are fiendish, but many are not; some are primitive, while others are sophisticated. For a precious few, the blood of leviathans courses through their veins, while for others it's the blood of beasts. This makes them unique and invaluable in many respects, but to some with the Outland Wars still fresh on their minds, it makes them difficult to trust.

Elderkin, the last to note, are not likely to be found at the Flipside. An offshoot of old-worlders, they are seldom seen beyond the confines of Gan and Deepweald Forest. They are the long-lived keepers of old-world knowledge.

Speaking of such, where is that ranger anyhow? It is getting dark and I am without a lantern. I asked him to bring writing supplies – how does that not include a lantern? How does one write in the night without light? When I find him, he is liable to get a piece of my mind. More to come about Webfoot and the Flipside, just as soon as I am set up for the night's undertaking…

CHAPTER VIII

A walk on the wild side

Stained in rich hues, the canvas canopy above the inn's jam-packed veranda depicted a green and yellow bullfrog, lying flat on its back under a table. Eyes closed, he wore a long and content grin upon his face. The frog's hands rested over a well-rounded, tender white belly. On that majestic paunch was balanced an equally majestic flagon, overflowing with golden suds.

"Built by Stouts, y'know," bragged Gariff Ram. As he nodded his head vigorously, his tattered hat slipped down over his eyes. That was only the beginning. "They dug deep and spent days pumping out ground water before finally hitting something solid under that hill o'muck – and that was just fer the footings."

The Stout wasn't far off the mark and Nud felt compelled to nod back in agreement. Webfoot's Flipside Inn was one of the sturdier buildings in town: two full stories tall and not on a lean. Mortared stone quarried out of the Bearded Hills formed the first level, and the second was rough-hewn timber cut straight out of the living heart of Deepweald, back in the days before logging restrictions ended that enterprise. Red clay roofing tiles kept the rain out, and a small stable with a thatched roof stood as a separate building on the south side.

Apparently, Gariff wasn't done gloating. "That inn…" he went on, pointing with one hand and scratching his scruffy chin with the other. "Now there's something – unlike yer precious twig fence a ways back… y'know, the one that protects this town from toothless water-rats, wounded geese and fat-bellied pike – now *that* there inn's something that won't fall over when you rest a hand against it, when the wind blows, or when there's a firm knock at the door."

Gariff kept talking, but Nud stopped listening to him. Instead, he tuned his ears to the melody playing inside over the buzz of fifty conversations and the tinkling of eating implements. Meanwhile, Kabor's gaze drifted from his cousin to the rooftop dormer windows. He whipped out his spectacles, fumbled to put them on, and gawked up at the guest rooms.

Gariff paused his narrative. "Kabor!"

The bespectacled Stout jolted in place, then swung his gaze to his cousin.

Gariff crossed his arms and glared at him. "Stop peeking at the 'Red Rooms.' Did y'even hear what I was saying?"

Nud couldn't help but to hazard a look as well, and maybe catch a glimpse of some fleeting silhouette, casually passing by a second-story window. *Nothing yet,* he thought. But the night was still young and shaping up to be one of the wildest ever at the inn. Everyone inside and outside seemed to be having fun. The Flipside was the hub of activity in an otherwise humdrum town.

Kabor scolded his cousin, slightly irked. "You can't tell me where to look and where not to look." He turned his gaze back to the windows.

Gariff shot back, "Why don't you make yourself useful and look for a table instead?" He made a hand-waving gesture to the veranda and the wide picture window that looked into the great room.

Nud's eyes traced the cue. Even from where he stood, he could see a five-Pip troupe playing fiddle and reeds in the great room, bobbing wildly about the staging area as they sang and clapped, thumped and stomped. Smoke rings wrought of the local weed billowed up over the heads of the customers and hung there in a dense cloud. The sweet scent filtered out to the veranda through window screens set high in the wall, and mingled with the other scents of food and wood smoke.

Kabor huffed. "Fine." He adjusted his spectacles and then led the way across the veranda, which was full to capacity with patrons. Kabor wove through the crowd, bumping elbows and knocking tables. At the picture window, they stopped to peer through the glass.

Throughout the chamber, newly arrived laborers reunited with seasonal friends and coworkers – some over drinks, others over hearty dinners laid out in front of them. Near the stage, it was standing room only as tipsy patrons jived to the music, drinks in hand. Nud swept his gaze over the room. Every seat at the bar was taken by regulars, and the heavy wooden tables were all cluttered with bottles and mugs, save one hot seat next to the hearth. A barmaid quickly wiped it down before new clients took it. The roaring blaze added a fiery glow to the girl's hair as she took their orders.

"Who's she?" Nud asked.

Kabor homed in on her. "Oh, I know her." He smirked. "She's my new girlfriend."

Nud grimaced. "Yeah, right. How can you even tell from here?"

Kabor's response was quick and seamless. "I can tell by the way she sways when she walks," he said. "And the way she holds her head up high. I have my glasses on, by the way, in case you didn't notice. I met her a few days ago when we got here and… we really hit it off."

That sighting was the first Nud had ever seen of Holly Hopkins, as he would later know her name to be. Long, flowing auburn hair and slim as a reed, even her eyes smiled at the patrons. She looked to be around Nud's age…

"Wait a minute… she told me she was my girlfriend!" Gariff said, sounding irked.

Kabor clued him in. "She just said that so you wouldn't feel like a dork – it's called pity. Plus, she knows it makes me jealous. What a tease."

Nud turned his gaze to the cousins, eyes measuring one and then the other. "She's too beautiful for the likes of either of you."

"Beautiful?" Kabor said. "Yeah, I guess she's not bad."

Nud guffawed. "Not bad? C'mon. Compared to Bearded Hills girls, she's gorgeous."

Gariff's head jerked back sharply, eyebrows crossed. "What're ya talking 'bout? Stout girls are pretty."

Nud egged them on. "They basically look like Kabor, except *he* has less hair on his face."

"Bhaa," Gariff waved his hand dismissively. "You can't be afraid of a little scruff now…"

The two cousins shared a look and nodded. Kabor let out a mild chuckle. "I don't know, Leno," he said, shifting his gaze back to the Pip, "some of them look down-right handsome with braided chin hairs. Keeps their hubs warm on long winter nights."

Of course, not all Stout women grow beards, but many

are prone to significant facial hair – mostly in wisps. A minority proudly sport full-fledged, braided beards, beaded and dyed in bright colors. In the Hills, the most popular establishment for visitors has always been the "Friendly Muttonchops," owned and operated by a proud – and famously friendly – bearded lady.

When Nud looked to the table again, the barmaid was already gone. "If you two know that hostess, then what's her name?"

The cousins overspoke one another in response: "Elena," Kabor said. "Chariot," was Gariff's response.

Kabor's shoulders dropped. He looked to his cousin, jaw hanging and shaking his head.

"What?" Gariff said.

"Chariot?" Kabor replied. "What kind of name is Chariot? Did you mean to say Charlotte?"

Gariff only shrugged. "Maybe she likes horses."

The two cousins continued to quibble. As they faced one another, Nud saw that they shared precisely the same family nose – prominent, protruding and high-bridged. Soon, though, Nud's attention shifted back to the great room – the girl had just returned from the back hallway, carrying an overfull tray of appetizers and drinks. She shoved her way back to the table near the hearth, and promptly served the three men seated there: barkwood ale, marked by the distinctive, bark-wrapped serving cups used; glowfish bowls, marked by the distinctive way they are served – alive and flipping in a colored glass bowl; and rice or herb side dishes.

Gariff tapped Nud on the shoulder, eyes gauging as he stared through the window. "Those patrons of hers look a little rough around the edges, don't ya think?"

The Pip nodded. "Outlanders." Uncle Fyorn had provided

Nud with many wine-soaked stories from days long past, when he'd warred against the Outlands in his youth as a Kith ranger. His uncle and Paplov talked long into the night at times about the woodsman's adventures far and wide, beyond the bog and the gentle shade of Deepweald; beyond the Tri-towns, Gan and the long reach of Harrow. Those wars were long over now, but they'd left their mark.

"I recognize that one," Kabor said, pointing to the far end of the table. A particularly slick looking Outlander sat there, well-groomed and able to blend his fiendish looks with an air of refinement.

"Are you sure?" Nud said. Even with his glasses on, the Stout's vision wasn't that great beyond twenty or thirty feet.

Kabor nodded. "I've seen him in the Hills. He deals in… uh… *rare herbs.*"

They all knew what that meant.

"Cuz's right," Gariff said, squinting. "I've seen him too."

Nud happened to catch the Outlander's beady eyes sizing up the barmaid's shapely form, while she looked away momentarily to gather finished plates and cups from an adjacent table, and to balance the serving platter. He habitually stroked his chin-strip beard as he did so, smiling thinly at the girl's small words when she turned her gaze back to him. Nud couldn't help but think there was something sinister behind his shallow courtesy and cool, collected mannerisms. *He's one to watch out for.*

Nud felt his stomach gurgle in the aroma-saturated air. "I'm starved," he said, "let's eat."

"Come on," Kabor said. "We can steal around back and find Bobbin. It's busy and you beggars are too ragged to show your faces in there."

"Who cares?" Gariff said. "Half of those people are drunk as skunks anyway. They wouldn't so much as turn their heads if we walked in wearing grass skirts." He pointed to a party of rowdy Stouts on the table adjacent to the Outlanders. "And take a gander at that sorry crew. They look like they just rolled out of a mud puddle."

"I'm with Kabor," Nud said. Had they made their move a moment sooner, the Pip would have avoided an embarrassment. The barmaid caught him at the tail end of making eyes at her. Nud cracked an awkward smile. She looked away. Then he wondered how well she could see outside, through the glare of the window.

Kabor'd observed the whole interaction. "Keep it up, dream-boy," he told Nud. "The smoke is getting to your head."

"Wait… I changed my mind," Nud said, addressing the two cousins. "We should go inside. It's boring out back, and besides, we're not kids anymore."

The back area was mainly used for overflow seating when even the veranda was full and by patrons or servers on break seeking private conversation or a quiet smoke. Otherwise, it didn't see much activity.

"We'll never get a table in there," Gariff complained.

Kabor seemed up to the challenge though. "We'll see," he said, as he led the way in. Gariff huffed and dragged his feet, but they made it to the doorway nonetheless. Kabor halted abruptly. Nud and Gariff jolted to a stop behind him. The bespectacled Stout turned to face them.

"What is it?" Gariff said.

"Did you forget something?" Nud asked.

Kabor spoke with earnest. "Did anyone else notice that?"

"What, Cuz?" Gariff said.

"We all just flipped sides."

Gariff scrunched his face into a confused look. "Huh? What'dya mean?"

"At first, you wanted to go inside. Me and dream-boy here wanted to go out back."

"So," Gariff said.

Nud punched Kabor in the arm for calling him dream-boy again.

"Ouch," he said, rubbing it. Then he continued. "Now, it's me and *dream-boy* that want to go inside, and you want to go out back."

Gariff blinked.

Nud waited.

Kabor shrugged, eyes wide with magnification. "This really *is* the Flipside," he added with a smirk.

Nud groaned. "That sounds like something Bobbin would say."

Kabor folded his specs and put them away. "Must be something in the air tonight."

*

Soon the trio impaled themselves on all the smoke, music and chatter of an energetic night on the town. Pale yellow lanterns cast a dim glow inside the chamber. Many eyes fell upon them on entry – Pips, Stouts, Outlanders, and old-worlders alike. One giant of a man with a long, drooping face took an especially long look. He was the only one in the room with a booth to himself. Nud nodded a "hello" to him. He returned the courtesy with a half-smile, before sinking his eyes back into his giant-sized tankard.

Nud could barely hear Gariff's relentless pessimism over the blaring music. "See. No tables anywhere," he said. "Let's go out back. The – … anyway."

"Hold on," Nud told him. "Just give it a chance. People come and go all the time."

As they waited and watched, acrobats bounded into the great room from the back entranceway – an uptick in the night's entertainment. All heads turned to watch their antics. Checkered black and white from head to toe and wearing the sort of floppy-horned hoods a jester might cherish, they began to tumble. Some cartwheeled, some flipped and others simply bounced their way to the stage, and then bounded from one musician to the next when they got there. The band played on, pretending not to notice. The acrobats, unsatisfied that they were not able to disrupt the band, set their sights on the crowd. They flipped onto tables and cartwheeled through the startled onlookers. After a minute or so of spilling beer and knocking around plates, a great clang arose from the stage. The music screeched to a halt. The acrobats – exclusively Pips – all stopped at once and stared at one another. They nodded their heads and smiled as the crowd clapped and cheered them on. "More!" some shouted, "Show us more!" After a long pause, the musicians started up again, but this time the band instruments rang with dissonance and the lyrics became utter nonsense.

The checkered troupe gathered at center stage to form a pyramid, one on top of the other. Stacked as they were, the acrobats wobbled and swayed as the crowd "whoa'd!" and the fiddles screeched, all the while feigning to topple at any moment. At one point, their sideways lean was so steep, it seemed they would crush the percussionist. But they whipped back, vibrating into place like a lively spring. As soon as one of the onlookers at her table stood up to get a better view, everyone did. All eyes fell upon the tumbling Pips… all eyes save two that could barely see anything at all.

A gut feeling had Nud wondering what Kabor was up to. Sure enough, by the glint in his eyes, Nud could tell he was scheming. Gariff's cousin had spied a vulnerable long table. With the former occupants standing forward of it to get a better view of the action, their backs were to them. Kabor snatched Nud's arm and Gariff's too. He dragged them to the table, and with a nod and a look, he coaxed his reluctant cousin to grab an end while he grabbed the other. Nud's role was to move the chairs, despite a feeble protest on his part not to be involved.

Nud eyed their destination, and grinned. The clever Stout had discovered an open space created by a large group having moved two tables together. Promptly, they filled it. To complete the devious and covert operation, Kabor pilfered them each a near-empty tankard – for show, not for drinking from – and some near-empty plates, replacing those he took with items from the stolen table. If anyone noticed, they didn't seem to care.

Kabor, now settled and in his glory, stood on his chair like so many others and cheered with the crowd. He hollered at a particularly daring acrobat, who began head spinning at the top of the Pip pyramid, all to the tune of *Mighty Maelstrom* played at a progressively fast tempo.

As they sat gripping their stolen tankards, Gariff whispered to Nud. "Don't look now."

Nud discreetly took note of how the rightful owners of the table shrugged their shoulders and exchanged annoyed glances. One of them swung his gaze to Nud and stared straight at him. The Pip flushed, then casually looked away, tilting his gaze to the ceiling. But it was too late. Out of his peripheral vision, Nud could see the man gauging him. *He knows.*

Nud leaned over to Gariff. "I think we've been spotted."

Gariff grunted. "No guff, Leno."

Sure enough, the four old-worlders made their way over.

Two were stocky, with soiled clothes and rough looks, probably construction workers in from Abandon Bay. Another was thin as a rake, wiry, and well tanned for the season, with a black cap over long straight hair. He could've been part Scarsander. The first to speak was the rounder of them all, with a fat face and sweaty hair that stuck to his head in tight curls. His voice was loud and full of spit, his breath as sour as the house garlic sauce.

"Get lost, Frog-face," he said directly to Nud, clearly irritated.

Kabor glanced back over his shoulder and drew his attention. "What?"

"You heard me," the man said. "You stole our table, now get lost before I put you on the menu."

Kabor raised his voice over the music and loud talk. "Menu? No thanks. I'll have another barkwood though." He paused. "And bring some frog legs too." Kabor turned his attention back to the show.

The man, who looked to be middle-aged, picked Kabor up off his chair by the shoulders. One of the stocky brutes grabbed Gariff the same way, but couldn't manage to lift him.

That was when the giant stepped in, having totally misinterpreted the situation in the teens' favor. "No hurting littler Pipses, little mens," he boomed, stumbling and waving his tankard at them.

Nud dove under the table before anyone could get a hand on him, and rolled to the far side. But as he rolled, so did something else. His ears picked up on the sound – the unnerving clatter of some small object skipping along with him. Shuffling feet sent it skidding off in another direction.

Yes, it was the bog stone, sparking wildly as it bounced and zigzagged, lit up like some kind of half-crazed glow bug.

Nud scrambled over the sticky floor to get it back, knocking legs and bumping tables. Heads turned and patrons gasped. Nud got stepped on, and one curious person made a grab for his stone when it sparked up at her feet. Every time the Pip got near, someone kicked it further away along the grungy floorboards. Finally, a ricochet sent the bog stone spinning against a wall. Just as Nud closed in, one of the stocky men they'd stolen the table from grabbed him by the scruff of the neck and hauled him up. The gem flashed and was kicked away again.

This time Nud didn't hear the giant's voice, but he did notice the giant tankard that struck his captor over the head. Ale sprayed everywhere. The man's grip let loose. Scrambling again, Nud searched for the light of the stone. It was gone. His heart raced. *I have to find it.* Adrenalin shot through his system.

Nud's eyes darted about the room, searching frantically. The place was in full chaos, the confrontation over the table had erupted into an all-out brawl.

The giant shouted as he spun in circles with some brute and the skinny man clinging to his back. They knocked over patrons, dishes, cups, and chairs. Gariff broke free when someone smashed a clay flagon over his captor's head. The Stout then swung a chair at the round man with curly hair holding his cousin. He clipped him squarely in the knee. The curly man fell back onto a chair, which collapsed under his heavy weight. Kabor squirmed free and bolted into the havoc.

Fueling the fray, Pip band members switched to pipes and played a spirited tune, fraught with dissonance once again. That much was comical. They must have conspired with the acrobats, who took the opportunity to add to the mayhem by bounding on and off furniture and brawlers alike, teasing patrons with pokes, pulled hair, covered eyes, slaps in the face, stolen food and pinches before leaping away. One acrobat received a square punch to the nose for his antics. He responded by pulling the offender's pants down and kicking him in the rear. The man stumbled onto the lap of a well-rounded Stout woman gnawing on a chicken leg, her wispy scruff soused in grease.

Then Nud spied his hard-earned prize. *Of all the luck.* That blasted Outlander with the thin beard held his stone. Its light painted the fiend's face with a pulsing red glow. The man's stubby horns made him look like a slick devil.

"That's my stone!" Nud cried. Heart pumping, he charged through the crowd at the Outlander, who was about to slip the bog stone into his vest pocket.

The Pip slapped at the Outlander's hand. The stone went flying. Flying and sparking in a high arc. Nud dashed and dove to catch it. With his arm fully stretched, he snagged the gem in mid-air and rolled out of his dive as smooth as any acrobat in the room. The Outlander made to follow, but got caught up in the pushing and shoving. Bog stone safe in hand, Nud scuttled along the floor, underneath the ruckus, and bee-lined to the nearest exit. As the Outlander turned his head this way and that way, eyes searching, Nud slipped out of the room. He backed up against the foyer wall, hidden from line of sight. Gariff and Kabor met him there in short order. The bar fight raged on without them.

Nud wiped sweat from his forehead. "Phew. That was close." The Stouts nodded like they were twins.

"Our work here is done," jibed Kabor. He was the first to start chuckling as they stumbled out the door and onto the veranda. A second later, they were all laughing and slapping their thighs. Behind them, the fight continued to build. Outside, patrons viewed the skirmish, some with amusement, others with disapproving looks on their faces. One older woman commented, "What a bunch of idiots" and shook her head. A grizzled-looking Pip with unusually large fore-arms remarked, "I'm getting a piece of this!" and hobbled off towards the door. Others made faces and exchanged gasping words.

Gariff breathed a heavy sigh. "Can we go around back now? Before we get into real trouble?"

Nud swept his gaze over the fighting inside. "Yeah, I'm ready to flip sides again."

Kabor, holding his chest to catch his breath, nodded in agreement. "Me too."

At last, the trio stole around back as originally suggested. The path was cobbled and unlit, lined with tall pines that blocked out any and all light. The fresh scent of resin spiced the air, and fallen needles softened their steps. Gariff and Nud stumbled along, while Kabor passed like a ghost from one end of the path to the other, unseen and unheard.

"Looks like we have the place to ourselves," Kabor said when the two caught up. The back area was open and airy, with ambient light spilling in from a covered passage that connected the inn proper with the kitchen house. A dozen empty, rough-cut tables occupied the cobblestone patio. Gariff strode over to one, let his pack slide off one shoulder, then the other, and thudded down on the heavy bench beside it.

"Kabor, light us a lantern," Gariff commanded. "Leno, you get moving and find Bobbin, and make it snappy – get back here with some food before I eat my hat! I'll hold the table."

Nud rolled his eyes.

"Never mind that. It was yer blinking rock that got us here this late in the first place," Gariff stated bluntly, carelessly. "A little flash here, a flicker there, next thing I know yer mystified." The Stout wiggled his fingers at Nud in true magician form. "So, the least you can do is put a rush order on our grub, thank-you-very-much!"

Kabor reached for a lantern. "What do you mean by blinking? My rock doesn't blink." He swung his gaze to Nud. "What's this about blinking?"

"It just sparks easy," Nud replied. "And Gariff meant 'blinking' like 'Where's my blinking hat?'" *So much for secrets.*

"Flint?" Kabor said.

Nud shook his head.

"Quartz?" he asked.

Nud kept his mouth shut, contemplating how he might answer to squirm out of this new predicament. *A liar knows a lie when he hears it though,* he thought. The Pip shot a glance to Gariff. The Hill Stout's blank look did nothing to help Nud's cause.

An unexpected voice cut through the awkward silence. The voice – rugged, older and distinctly country – called out from the shadows. "Blinking rock, aye? Now that's something I'd sure like to see. How 'bout we have a looksie?"

CHAPTER IX

Seekers

Mid-morning, head pounding and muscles aching, Nud slowly pushed himself upright on his hammock. He sat slumped, on the edge of it. When he shifted his legs, caked mud crumbled off his pants and scattered over the wood-plank floor. Still in his clothes from yesterday, Nud was in dire need of a bathhouse visit. He waited a long minute for the vertigo to stop swirling the room around him, and debated whether or not he should just sink back down into his hammock and pull the covers over his head. He could smell his own breath – terrible: a fatal mix of barkwood ale, fish, and ashes. The Pip let out a wide yawn, squeezed his eyes shut, and massaged the back of his neck. He could hear Paplov rummaging around outside the hut, in his workshop again. *Probably fletching.*

Suddenly, Nud gasped. Dread jolted him into action. Frantically, he patted his pockets. *Not there.* Hammock jostling and ropes creaking, he tossed his pillow and blankets aside, searching, feeling with his hands. *Dried mud... more dried mud.* The chunks he found broke into pieces when he squished them. His thoughts raced. *I didn't lose it, or trade it for a drink, or give it away.... Did I?* Nud wasn't exactly sure what he might've done in his stupor. He glanced under the hammock and spotted the quartz decoy. *Not there either.*

Finally, running one hand underneath the hammock he felt a hard, irregularly shaped object through the canvas. Keeping that hand on it, he slid the other under his sheets, then pulled the stone out. He rotated it in his hands. *Looks about right.* Nud waited… and waited…

It sparked. The Pip let out a huge breath, and then eyed the bog stone for a long minute before slipping the find back in his pocket, where it belonged.

Grateful to have avoided disaster, Nud stood up and shuffled over to the study. He plopped down on his grandfather's favorite chair. Through the window of the hut and the open shutters of the workshop, he spotted the old gaffer. Paplov had just notched a newly-made arrow and was reaching for his exact duplicate of Uncle Fyorn's bow – the original model, bought years ago at an estate sale in Doncaster. Precisely how the old farmer had come across such a fine piece of equipment in the first place was still a mystery. Anyway, that meant the batch of arrows Paplov was fussing over were for his uncle, and that he was about to test the draw on one of them. Nud's grandfather fashioned a single type for the woodsman, the kind that'll take down a deer at a hundred feet.

After slinging the bow on his shoulder, Paplov picked up a second arrow – for reference – and scrutinized the pair of them, peering down the shafts and then examining the ends with a magnifying lens. Then he balanced them on a scale. Paplov muttered to himself as he did so, and although too low to hear, Nud knew the words: "Dead even." Next, his grandfather would be sure to try the new arrow out on their target, hanging on a tree out back.

As Paplov exited the workshop for the laneway behind their property, the antics of the previous night swirled in Nud's memory. He struggled to recall what'd happened. Everything was a blur – an unfamiliar sensation for a Pip. For the first time ever, his "perfect" memory was fractured.

Slowly though, pieces came back to him. Eyes relaxed as he sat, images from the night before began to form in Nud's mind. *Mer – that was his name.* The rugged prospector had kept a bone pipe tightly clenched between his teeth the whole time, shaped like a whale. *Mer Andulus.* Smoke had pulsed out of his nose and mouth whenever he'd spoken. *What was he saying?…*

Another image flashed – rocks of all kinds strewn atop a patio table, a worn leather pack, and… *maps. Lots of maps.* The prospector kept saying something about the "mother lode," and he'd gone on about some kind of… *What was it? Ancient tree gum?* Then he'd preached about what sounded to Nud like some weird combination of witchcraft and geology that would lead him to… to… *The mother lode, of course.* It was all very confusing.

A familiar thud sounded outside – the thud of an arrow hitting the target.

Nud got up and drew the curtains, then slipped his precious find out of his pocket. In the dark room, the spark ignited instantly – bright and burning red. He gazed in wonder: *What is this thing? Should I ask Paplov? – No, he'll say it's dangerous and take it away.* Nud paused. *But Fyorn, on the other hand…*

Paplov called loudly from outside, snapping Nud out of his trance. "Quite the batch this round." *He must've spotted me earlier.* Nud parted the drapes slightly and peered through the gap, just in time to see Paplov amble past the window. He was admiring his own handiwork as he headed for the door.

Hastily, Nud went to shove the stone back in his pocket, but fumbled it in his hands. It flickered just as Paplov shouldered the door to the hut. The hinges creaked. Nud felt a blood rush, then dizzy… his thoughts spun in a frenzy and wound tight, his forehead throbbed.

"Good grain," Paplov remarked, about to step in.

The building tension in Nud's mind discharged all at once. The window to the hut popped open. A rush of air blew past the teen and forced the door shut, knocking Paplov backwards. It sucked the breath right out of Nud's windpipe.

"Wha?" Paplov said.

Nud squirreled the stone away. "Are you all right?" he called.

Paplov turned the door handle again, and this time stepped in slow and steady, peeking around the door's edge as he did so. His brow was crossed. "Why did you slam the door?"

"I didn—"

"It's not funny. You could've seriously hurt me. I was holding one of the new arrows right in front of my eyes." He demonstrated, squinting as he looked down the shaft.

"I didn't," Nud said, "the window opened…"

Paplov dismissed him with a scoff, then looked about the hut and sized up the situation. "Oh." He shrugged when he saw that Nud stood nowhere near the door. "Maybe it was the wind, then."

"I felt the air get sucked right out of the place," Nud responded.

"Mind boggling. I'll have to look out for that. A good lesson anyway – don't stumble around the yard looking down an arrow shaft." He shook his head. "I should count my blessings."

"Did you hit the bullseye?" Nud asked.

"And why is it so dark in here?" Paplov placed the arrows down on the eating table, walked past Nud and opened the drapes. Then he turned to his grandson. "Bullseye, of course!"

Nud went to the table and picked up an arrow to examine the fletching. "Do you have a few extras to spare… for target practice?"

Paplov ambled over, then replied with a variant of the same answer he always gave on the topic. "Regular arrows are best for that," he said, "They'll keep your aim honest." He never allowed Nud to practice with the arrows he made for Fyorn.

Nud pressed him this time, "But I can shoot from a lot farther now than ever before. If I adjust my sighting for regular arrows, your seekers fly hi—" Nud stopped himself.

"How do you know that?" Paplov said.

Stupid. Not the cleverest of mornings for Nud; not at all. The young Pip knew it was wrong to be sneaking Paplov's true-strike arrows onto the range. There was definitely something weird about them though. Nud didn't even try to forge an answer.

His grandfather let the misdeed pass. He stroked his chin. "You're adjusting your aim for distance? Hmm. Well,…" With one sharp nod, he declared the solution. "Just try aiming at the target as though you were half the distance."

"Easier said than done," Nud argued. "I don't know exactly how far away I am when I shoot. I adjust the cant of the bow based on… I don't know, what feels right?"

Paplov sighed, then took a long minute to think things through, as he often did before coming to even a minor decision. "Well, now that you're of age, maybe your Uncle Fyorn will see fit to take you hunting with him. He can let you in on a few secrets."

"Really? With seekers?"

"Of course with seekers! What else? He taught me a thing or two about hunting when I was your age, that's for sure."

Paplov's words caught Nud off guard for a moment, until he remembered Uncle Fyorn's lineage. Still, it was hard to picture a Paplov that looked young compared to his uncle.

The old Pip said, "It's time we made you enough deepwood arrows to get you through a good, long deer hunt."

Nud grinned. "Uncle Fyorn really knows a lot about hunting… and nature. Doesn't he?"

Paplov smiled back. "Fyorn knows a great many things about a great many things."

Nud thought of Mer's theory about the origins of his bog stone. "Trees especially, right?"

Paplov contemplated for a moment, then answered. "I suppose."

"Ancient trees?"

"What? Ancient? Well… I don't know. I guess. You'd have to ask him, Nud."

Uncle Fyorn was the most well-traveled person Nud knew and the only person he could think of who might know more about the mystery stone than the prospector Mer. Except maybe the Diviner, but the Diviner spoke in riddles and lived way out in the bog where there are no trails. *Fyorn would definitely keep my secret,* Nud concluded. *And I bet he'd know exactly what to do with this bog stone.*

"Are you planning an extra trip to Fyorn's?" Nud said, innocently.

"Well, I did just get back," Paplov replied, "and I already have more deepwood than I know what to do with, after that wicked windstorm. Probably enough for months. I even had to charter a pack lizard at the Handlers' Post just to get it all into town, without you there to help out."

Nud ignored the jab. "But… uh… do you have enough for the both of us?"

Paplov stared at Nud with his mouth half-open, eyes begging for an explanation.

"What I mean is," Nud went on, "I was thinking about maybe taking up woodcraft like you. I'd like to learn more about the arrows, especially… and the carvings you make too. Have you ever made… uh… a lantern?"

Now that was just about the lowest trick in the book, but guaranteed to work against someone old and sentimental like his grandfather. Anyone who knew Paplov well enough also knew his passion for the hammer and chisel. And he always brought up passing on his skills to Nud. His grandfather had many hobbies, but working the deepwood was the only one he ever made time for. He might not have been the most skilled fletcher in Webfoot, or the fastest, but he was the only one who worked the deepwood.

"Oh?" Paplov smiled at the notion, then gave his smooth beard a tug. "Hmm," he said, with a thoughtful nod of the head. "I don't know much about lanterns out of wood. They're usually made of metal and glass."

His grandfather paused. Nud held eye contact, expectant. Paplov lowered his head briefly.

"But," he continued, nodding slightly as a grin began to surface, "you could certainly get started with woodcraft easily enough. You already know more than you realize."

Nud carefully studied the arrow that he held, running the shaft between his thumb and finger. Paplov glanced out the window to the workshop.

"I have a few more arrows to get done today," he said.

"Does that mean yes?" Nud asked. And to seal the deal, the next words that rolled off his tongue hit the air with such sincerity that no grandparent could ever refuse them. "I just want to be as good as you someday, that's all, and maybe trade with Fyorn like you do… someday."

Hearing his own words, as noble and utterly convincing as they were, Nud nearly believed them himself. Shameless.

Paplov stared down at the lone arrow on the table, then slowly bobbed his head a couple of times. He looked older than usual that morning, as if he'd had an "age spurt" the way young children have growth spurts.

"Tomorrow I'm to have morning tea with the new lord mayor to discuss some political matters." Paplov put his hand on Nud's shoulder. "Then in two days I'm off to Turnsby, and I'll need you to come along with me to help out with the documents."

"Oh," was all Nud could say. The young Pip let out an exaggerated sigh.

Paplov kept talking. "I'll need you to learn those documents and cite relevant passages as they come up in conversation."

Easy. Nud nodded.

"Not just memorizing either – I need you to *know* what it all means."

Not so easy. "O - kay," Nud said, drawing out the syllables.

Paplov smiled with his eyes. Warmth seemed to radiate off his face, as he added: "If we don't get held up in Turnsby, with your help, we can drop in on Fyorn's cabin a day or two after that… if you like. He's been asking about you."

"Great!" Suddenly, Nud felt rejuvenated.

Paplov clapped his hands and held them together. "Then

it's settled," he said, his tone upbeat. "But only if you help me finish off enough arrows to make the trip worthwhile. That ole woodsprite was hoping to get them early anyway. Asked for bright orange feathers on them this time… must be going blind."

Paplov laughed, then put his arm around Nud's shoulders and led him to the workshop. When they got there, with a grin on his face that stretched a mile wide, he passed his grandson a handful of shafts. "You can get started on these."

CHAPTER X

The lizard handler

Paplov could be stubborn about getting his hiking in, but it'd been raining for two straight days. So, on the Council's tab, Nud reserved a "blue-tail" for the first leg of their journey. Travel to the Stout town of Turnsby would be easier on the old gaffer that way. Blue-tails were the only reliable mode of transportation into or out of town during the wet season. Year by year, more and more corduroy sections had been laid over the worst parts of the Mire Trail, but there were still plenty of soft patches on the beaten track to contend with.

While packing arrows in the workshop with Paplov, out the open doorway Nud caught sight of one Mer Andulus strolling up the road to their hut. He wore the same tans and leathers as that night at the Flipside, and a floppy hat reminiscent of Gariff's monstrosity. The bearded prospector chewed his whalebone pipe as he strolled towards the gate. A thin stream of smoke trailed over one shoulder, up into the fresh morning air. Both hands gripped the worn, leather straps of his backpack as though they were suspenders.

"Just a sec," Nud told Paplov. Then he darted out the door and jogged to the twig gate at the end of the yard. Light drizzle feathered his face on the way, coating it with a warm, thin film. When the prospector approached Nud, he looked a little soggy himself.

"Gidday-gidday," Mer said as one long word, out of the corner of his mouth. His voice was fully animate – nothing like the tired old coot Nud had him pegged for when the Hill Stout first emerged from his shadowy seat on the Flipside patio. His weary eyes with the bags underneath were a testimony to hard living, and his weathered cheeks to an outdoor lifestyle. "Glad to see yer up and about." He pulled the pipe out from between his worn teeth, and used it as pointer. "On my way yonder to yer bog, to stake our interests. Any chance you can get yerself together? We can swing by and pluck yer partners out'a their soft beds at the Flipside."

"Is that all you're bringing?" Nud said, motioning to the prospector's pack. A wooden handle stuck out the top.

Mer patted the weather-beaten canvas on his back. Metal jangled inside. "Pick, hammer and shovel," he said. "The rest is already out there." He laughed to himself, until he started to cough.

Nud couldn't help but smile back. "Sorry, but I'm off to Turnsby today on a diplomatic errand." Now *that* sounded important.

With a squint of one eye and a slight rise of the chin, Mer gave Nud a long and measuring stare. He cleared his throat. "Ahem. Horses won't be seen for another two weeks, give or take. Are ya taking a lizard, or flip-flopping?"

"Blue-tail," Nud said.

"Yep. What else," Mer responded. It was not a question.

Nud went on, "I'll be back tomorrow. But then shortly

after I'm off to visit… an Elderkin associate." He knew the wording would come off even more important-sounding.

Mer raised a suspicious eyebrow at the mention of Elderkin. He slipped the pipe stem back into his mouth, chewed it a little, and then shrugged, with a look like "that figures" on his face.

Nud asked, "What are you going to do out there, in the bog?"

"Well," Mer said, "everything we discussed, I s'pose." He stroked his tangly beard. "You don't remember, do ya?"

"Well…"

Mer snorted smoke. "I worked six summers with a frog-faced old-timer by the name 'a Clop. He remembered every-thing to the N'th degree, 'cept all the stupid things he did after a few barkwoods."

"Oh."

"'Oh' is right. Let me remind ya's. I'm off to check on that spot where the ole glowing tree spit turned up – lookin' fer staking posts to see what's claimed by HME and what's not – bog iron claims, I'm think'n."

"HME?"

"Harrow Mining and Exploration – they're just about everywhere in the bog lands these days, according to the town clerk, Old Remy."

"I know him," Nud said. Paplov relied on Remy for any-thing to do with maps.

"Problem is though," Mer explained, tapping the side of his head with his pipe, "half the claims records are locked away in that thick skull of his, so's I have to go find the stake posts myself. Remy only seems to know where they're s'pose to be, but where they're pounded into the ground is what counts. Interest'n, he says this one's the first claim south of the trailhead."

"Really," Nud said.

"You bet. By the way," Mer went on, "we're going equal splits on the finds, 'cept you and Gariff get a double share, 'case you don't remember that either."

"Okay."

"Okay is right. And don't forget you promised everyone a treasure hunting day."

"Who's everyone?"

"Well, myself fer starters, but I might not make it. The two Stouts, the well-rounded smiley Pip, as you might say, and the girl you were making googly eyes at. That's everyone."

"Oh… O - kay." Nud's knees shook a little because none of this sounded familiar.

Mer said, "'Til then, keep that gem o'yours close. I wouldn't bring any more attention to it, if I was you."

Nud patted his pocket and verified that the bog stone was still there. "I will," he promised.

Paplov broke in, calling from the hut. "Nud, you ready?"

"Well, alrighty," said the prospector. "Catch'ya at the Flipside. We'll keep it fast and loose 'till then." He turned to go.

"Wait," Nud said.

Mer halted. He looked back over his shoulder.

"Nud?" Paplov called.

"In a minute," Nud shouted back. He regarded Mer. "Can you swing by the Flipside on your way out anyway?… to pass some news to Bobbin – the round one." Mer gave Nud a slow nod. "Tell him to be ready to hit the trail in a few days, right after my Elderkin… meeting. Bobbin can tell Holly and the cousins."

"Gotcha covered," he said. "And while I'm out and about in loon goop, I'll keep an eye on the trail and an ear to the Handlers'

Post – they know who's going in or out of town." He raised a hand in salute. "Go easy," he added with a nod, eyes smiling.

"Go easy," Nud replied with half a wave. The words felt strange, borrowed. Nud could never own them the way Mer Andulus did.

*

Turnsby lay cradled between two rivers, a full day's hike away. Any delay would see Paplov and Nud on the trail at dusk, which is never a good idea in the open wetlands or along the forest edge.

When the lizard handler finally arrived at the hut, Paplov took the seat up front with him, while Nud climbed aboard the rear amidst the strapped-on baggage. "Wyatt" was a real bogger, dressed only in tattered shorts and a wide-brimmed hat – no shirt. He wore a sheathed knife on his belt. The wiry Pip's long bones looked as though they might punch through his leathery skin at his elbows and shoulders. He didn't seem to care about the drizzle. Nud doubted he would've blinked if it rained newts.

"How do you keep the flies off," Nud said to him. "The midges must eat you alive out there."

Wyatt glanced back and flashed Nud a one-tooth smile. "Bugs don't bug me anymore," he said, "only snot-nosed little boys do."

Snot-nosed? I'm almost sixteen!

Paplov chuckled at the look on Nud's face, and louder still when, out of some kind of self-conscious reflex reaction, the young Pip happened to wipe his nose with his shirtsleeve. Nud's grandfather leaned over to whisper something.

"Don't mind him," Paplov said. The whisper was loud enough for the bogger to hear too. "Old Wyatt's just sore."

"Damn right I'm sore," Wyatt shot back. "Eleven years locked up in Harrow is enough to make anyone sore."

"You were a prisoner?" Nud said. "How did you get out?"

Wyatt rubbed his bristly chin. "Well, they let me go when I finally gave them what they wanted – a secret I swore I'd never give up."

"What?" Nud asked.

"Are ya sure ya want t'know?" he said.

Nud nodded.

"The one I'd sworn it too 'disappeared' – poor bastard. They told me I was next. I never gave 'em any more than the half of it anyway."

"Is that true?" Nud said.

Wyatt scoffed. "'Course it's true." He shook his head in frustration, then turned his gaze to Paplov. "Look at that, a snot-nosed kid calling me a liar." He glared back at Nud. "Are you calling me a liar?"

Nud responded with a string of rapid head shakes.

Paplov interjected, "Harrow'll come looking for that other half, Wyatt, once they figure it out."

The old bogger didn't answer. He just kept his eyes to the trail and handled the mount. It was common knowledge that the youngest of the riding lizards – the so-called "blue-tails" – were paired to the oldest, grumpiest handlers. That was certainly the case with Wyatt. Not to say that young riders make better handlers. Young blue-tails can be difficult to control and tend to go off on their own or flip over, whereas older red-heads are so worked in, even a novice can handle them.

Although the topic had grown stale, a question still burned inside of Nud. Asking Wyatt another question felt a bit like pulling out that last snaggletooth of his, but Nud did it anyway.

"When you were in Harrow, did you see any other prisoners? I mean, anyone you knew, like other Pips… or someone?"

Wyatt exchanged a knowing glance with Paplov. Nud didn't know exactly what it meant, but it meant something.

"Nope," Wyatt said, with a wide shake of his head. "Not a one from the Tri-towns."

The handler kept to himself for a time, from Everdeep cut-off through to Wetwood and past Ling's Boulder. He finally loosened up by the time they reached the watergrass homes. The first bit of gossip out of his mouth concerned a crazy story about a glass trinket with a firefly trapped in it, waved around by some party-boy at the Flipside a few nights back. "I was there," Wyatt said, "and with my own two eyes I saw this mud-coated Pip holding it over the pretty girls' heads, begging for kisses. Then I heard he got a slap instead, from some girl. Half the town is talking about it." Nud shrank down between the traveling bags, knowing the muddy Pip could only be him. He felt his cheeks and tried to remember the sting.

If Wyatt's story checked out, Nud had managed to contain his secret for little more than half a day. The headcount of those in the know had to be substantial then: two friends from the Hills; one Webfooter who worked at the busiest establishment in town; a pretty girl from Turnsby he'd never seen before who also worked in the busiest establishment in town; a traveling prospector who'd been just about everywhere and whom Nud had never seen before; and a tavern full of patrons from lands far and near.

Soon, the conversation migrated to politics – it always did with Paplov. As the blue-tail strode along, Nud could see that the handler kept himself in tune to the lizard's every sway and step. The subtle calls, the slight taps on the sides of the lizard's neck, the pushing and pulling of the reins – it all blended together in complex ways to form one simple command: "GO STRAIGHT." At times, the handler would grunt as he squeezed his bony ankles into the lizard's sides. And every so often he'd follow with a string of frustrated remarks, pull a fish out of his sidebag, and pitch it well ahead. Our mount dashed at the offering, scooping up the morsel in its bridled jaws, mid-stride. As they rode on, Nud noted that whenever the lizard began heading off-course or became a little testy, the handler would squeeze. Whenever that wasn't enough to set her straight, he'd toss her another fish. They didn't teach details like those at the riding school Nud attended – all reins and whip.

By the time they met the misty bog, the morning air felt heavy, still and silent. The riders were alone on the Mire Trail that morning. The slow rhythm of the lizard's stride and gentle lurching after bait had Nud nodding off before long.

*

Nud jolted awake to violent shaking and Wyatt's angry shouts. The young Pip bounced and jostled with the luggage around him. Without warning, the blue-tail darted off the Mire Trail. Into the greater bog they went, bounding over uneven ground and splashing up stagnant water. The handler's fish incentives flew from the sidebag as Wyatt reared back on the reins with both hands. The lizard zig-zagged from hummock to hummock. Its pretty blue tail detached in the commotion. The thing twisted and writhed over a patch of thick moss.

After firm coaxing, a few long tipsy moments, and a plethora of cursing, Wyatt managed to wrestle the tail-less mount to the trail again. He swung his gaze back to the twitching blue-tail, and swore a blue streak as it sank into the water.

Wyatt wiped the sweat from his forehead. "Phew," he said,

when the lizard was nearing calm again. He spoke partly to Paplov and Nud, but mostly to his mount. "She'll get us to the Outland no problem, just you wait and see, with time to spare, I'll wager." His tone switched to reassuring as he patted the lizard's nape and stroked her neck. "No worries, girl." Then his eyes shifted between Nud and Paplov.

"Everyone all right?" he said. "Lose anything?"

Paplov gave Nud and the gear a quick once-over. "All good," he replied.

"Well," Wyatt admitted, "something's got the ole girl spooked. I've run this route many a year and none of my lizards have ever been so skittish. Might be a good idea to make arrangements now for safe passage on the way back."

Paplov nodded. The handler kept on past the Handler's Post at the edge of the bog and brought the travelers to the Outland Trail, as promised. That was as far as Paplov would agree to be ferried. Nud's grandfather had claimed it would be bad form to show up on a blue-tail. Riding lizards had been outlawed in Turnsby, ever since one young Stout had gotten himself eaten and another trampled, all in a span of two spring months. On top of that, the full journey would be costly — more than the town was willing to pay out, so any farther would have to come out of Paplov's pocket.

Before Wyatt turned back, Paplov arranged for the old bogger to meet them at the Handler's Post for the return trip, but not to wait in case they were delayed a day. "No problem," Wyatt replied. "I can always take on another rider. I'll just keep showing up until you get here."

*

Nud and Paplov made the rest of the journey on foot, as Pips normally travel. They didn't talk much along the way, each lost in their own thoughts. With about an hour to go before meeting the Dim River, Paplov finally started in on the diplomatic particulars of the visit.

"We have important work to do today, you and I," he started. "This evening, at Lord Mayor Otis' manor, I am to debate Turnsby's proposal to extend their agricultural region by draining a sizable portion of our wetlands. In return, they are suggesting a minimal lease fee and reduced prices for some crops. But they want the option to increase rates due to the heightened mineral exploration activity in the area as well, claiming that if a mine springs up on their property, the cropland will be devalued and they won't realize the projected future gains. I'm not giving in to that one – if a mine springs up the property value will increase substantially along with it."

Blah blah blah, Nud thought. He'd reviewed the documents in detail the night prior, and was well acquainted with the particulars of the mission. He didn't need more coaching.

He glanced up at the standing deadwood, and his eye caught something moving. "Look!" he said, pointing. "Is that a white raven? Over there. On top of that old dead tree."

Paplov looked up and nodded in acknowledgement. "Norwin's Breeze, lucky. I've seen that one around these parts before. Anyway, as I was saying…"

Blah blah blah. Paplov just kept talking.

"…Lord Mayor Undle and the Webfoot council are mostly in favor, but they feel the lease fee is too low and it was pointed out that the reductions—"

"Can ravens really talk as good as Gariff says they can? He says they can sound just like a person." Nud eyed the majestic bird as it hopped from one branch to the next.

"Yes, yes," Paplov replied, his tone dismissive, "Gariff is right. Some are fantastic talkers."

Paplov halted for a second, and tapped his left hand to his forehead. "Where was I..."

Blah blah blah, thought Nud again. *I don't care. I don't care.*

"Oh yes," Paplov went on, "it was pointed out that reductions in crop prices were not at all quantified; it wasn't clear if the reduced prices meant that you had to buy through the town's common market – which is always more expensive – or if they applied when buying directly from the farmer, the way most sensible folks go about business. At any rate, it's our job to ensure that Webfoot gets—"

"Are there really white ravens at Dim Lake too?" Nud said.

"Maybe," Paplov replied, again dismissively, "not that I've seen... As I was saying, we have to ensure that Webfoot gets good—"

"Gets a good deal," Nud finished. "Can we get a raven like Uncle Fyorn's, except white?"

Paplov raised his voice. "NO!" he said. "We're NOT getting a raven." He fixed his eyes straight ahead and pursed his lips. "And NO about getting a good deal. Well yes, I mean..." Paplov seemed a little flustered.

"Nud, you're almost sixteen now, and you can already sign documents in my place as aide and successor. Like so many others in this business, you seem to have more authority than the smarts to use it."

Nud wasn't sure how to respond to that. He blinked.

"It's time to WAKE UP," Paplov impressed, "PAY ATTENTION, and GET INVOLVED in what's going on around you. You're too young to... you're too young to go out all night like that. And even when you're not too young, you still shouldn't. I don't plan to do this forever, you know. I should have been done years ago... I thought I was done years ago, until..."

Paplov's head was shaking as he spoke; no, it was quivering. His hands were quivering too, and he continued to quiver for a long minute after his words trailed off, after he stopped short of saying *It*.

Nud's grandfather bowed his head slightly and held it that way, looking very old again. *Yes, he is aging in spurts,* Nud thought. When next he spoke, Paplov's voice was low and it wavered a little.

"Nud, you are the one who's going to inherit these responsibilities." Paplov found an inkling of his stern voice again. "You are the one who needs to learn how to take care of the future. It is *your* future, not mine. My legacy maybe, but you have to live with it, day in and day out. Sooner or later, I'm free of it. Gone." He waved a hand. "Bye-bye. And Harrow, well…"

Paplov shook his head and let time pass before calling again upon his diplomatic voice. He started over. "Back to the task at hand," he said. "We have to ensure that Webfoot gets good REP-RE-SEN-TA-TION in the deal-making process. It isn't just about getting the best deal, or even a good deal. A deal that is too good for Webfoot is likely poor for Turnsby, and that fact will carry forward into the next negotiation to whip back at us like a stinging branch – it has its own… memory, and that can have undesirable consequences. Everything needs to balance out. In the long run, this is about building good relationships, acting honorably, and having faith in the good folks you are dealing with – in this case the Glebe Stouts. Honor and faith are the pillars of trust, and trust is the foundation of good relations."

"What if you're not dealing with good folks?" Nud asked.

"Then you tread ever so carefully," Paplov responded, like it should've been obvious.

He was right. The agreement with Turnsby was meant to be long standing, and it influenced Nud's future more than his – Paplov wasn't getting any younger.

"Can't someone else just handle it?" Nud asked.

A heavy, disappointing silence lingered between them for the rest of the hike.

All Things tangled from the Outside in,
All Things joined in Purpose.
All Things bent to the One Design,
Until the Chains are broken.
—The Diviner

CHAPTER XI

Trouble in Turnsby

Before long, the wooded wetlands fell out of sight behind them and the two travelers came upon lush fields of young wheat on gentle, rolling hills, fresh with the passage of new rain. The dirt road cut through bright green pastures dotted with grazing cattle. The way ahead rolled alongside cornfields, sprouting vegetable gardens, many a farmhouse, and many a barn. Stretches of the Dim River gleamed in the distance. Diamond-bright flashes marked the division between a nest of craggy hills on this side of the river and the ghost pines of Whisperwood on the other side.

An hour later, Nud and his mother's father had journeyed well into the Flats. They sighted the ferry dock to Turnsby and the curtain wall that rose above the opposing shore. The pang in Nud's stomach reminded him dinner would be late.

The Stout town lay nestled between two southbound rivers, before they merged into one, and the Dim river crossing could be likened to a side door in. Nud and Paplov reached the dock just as the ferry bumped the pier. Its waterwheels came to a grinding halt and a scrawny Pip jumped out to tie her in and lower the ramp. Local farmers were the first to spill out of the boat. With heavy steps, they led mule-drawn carts and carried sacks of leftover wares after a long day's sell at the market. In the midst of the crowd, a handful of bearded prospectors, bearing sturdy packs, chatted one another up, minds surely bent on the promise of gold or other earth-borne treasures from the Outlands. When all had passed by, the new load of passengers – far fewer in number – paid their griffs and boarded.

The ferry's return crossing began by reversing the two horses on their treadmills to spin the waterwheels in the opposite direction. Nud watched as the beasts clopped along, each step propelling the barge across the slow, strong current of the Dim, waterwheels slapping and sloshing the water as they spun. Soon the Pip's gaze turned to the river itself. The bottom, in particular. Nud leaned over the rail and peered into the watery depths at the shadowy forms that resided there: submerged logs and rocks mostly, and the broken skeleton of a sunken dory, like those he'd seen in Abandon Bay.

When the barge reached the other side, Nud and Paplov disembarked and headed for the gatehouse. Paplov provided his name to one of the guards there and handed over his letter of intent, complete with the official wax seal of Turnsby pressed into the upper left corner. He also produced his diplomatic colors, which granted him access without a fuss and without the usual toll. Paplov told the guards Nud was his diplomatic aide – likewise no papers or toll required. The old Pip left a gratuity anyway.

When they were out of earshot, Nud asked, "What was the tip for?"

Paplov waited another ten steps before answering. He kept

his voice low. "The ferry only runs until twilight. If I'm ever stuck and need to get across, it doesn't hurt to have a good rapport with the guards – they can call the ferrymen to make another crossing."

The town layout was an inviting one, emphasizing greenery and openness in a park-like setting. Turnsby Lane, the main cobblestone throughway, ran from the east gate across town to the west gate. Lined with pink and white crabapple trees at measured intervals, it was wide enough for a coach to make a complete turn. Each tree had a small walled garden around it, and the sweet bouquet of apple blossoms scented the air. A series of cascading gardens also lined the road, putting on display all manner of shrubbery and seasonal flowers.

Sleek passenger boats with Pip rowers glided along the boat way parallel to the road, passing under numerous bridges that connected the common part of town to a neighborhood of stately homes. The network of narrow canals linked "anyplace to everyplace" throughout, with the flow of water regulated by floodgates and locks at the river junctions. The main east-west line fed into a southbound canal that eventually opened into the turbulent Lower Malevuin – a tricky run to navigate, even for those familiar with the waters.

Stouts, Pips, old-worlders and the occasional Outlander came and went as they made their way along the sparsely populated main street. As his eyes darted about, Nud was reminded that Glebe Stouts are generally taller, slimmer and fairer than their Bearded Hills cousins, but as far as he knew, they were no less resilient or "of the earth". Their particular blend of affinity for the land simply draws them more to farming and stonework than mining and metalwork.

As they crossed a grand and decorative bridge about midtown, the roads became busier, but the smell of the river never quite left. Nud slowed his pace to take in the sights – so very different from the middle of a bog.

"I really like how the Glebe Stouts built their town," Nud said as they arced over the south canal. "Gariff would like it too. It looks sturdy, but not so barren as the Hills... and the water's all... organized."

"Has a nice feel to it, doesn't it?" Paplov said.

Nud nodded.

Paplov paused. He seemed to engage in a moment of reflection. "You should know though," he remarked, "that during the famine years and the long winters that accompanied them, the skilled hands of Hill Stouts built this town and everything in it. Back then, common foods were traded for gold. Many worked themselves to near death just trying to feed their families back home in the Bearded Hills, while perfectly good food spoiled in the cellars of hoarders."

Nud had learned about those years in his lessons with the Diviner. Everywhere in the Land, life had dwindled: crops, animals, and people alike. Even the bounty of the sea couldn't be counted on for sustenance. Everywhere, that is, except lush Turnsby and the ever-fertile Doncaster Flats. Deepweald remained somewhat impervious, as the story goes, but during that period, the Wild Elderkins would let none pass into their realm. It was even worse than the desolation that hit the Star Sands, or so Nud was told. Hearing Paplov's words said that way, Nud finally understood his grandfather's caution in dealing with what appeared to be simple, hardworking folk. When it comes right down to the very essence of getting ahead in life, all bets are off with regard to decency. Nud changed the subject.

"What are Pips best known for?" he asked.

Without pause, Paplov responded. "The culinary arts, weaving, diving and river boating... those sorts of things."

"How did *we* survive the famine?"

Paplov's head jerked back. "You mean Pips? That was long before even I was born." He stroked his beard as he walked. "That first item on the list, I suppose. Webfooters always had to be creative about what they ate. The Pip diet is a varied one."

"But food is just about everywhere, any time of year," Nud said.

Paplov laughed. "You only know that because it has been hammered into your skull since you were just a newt. Few Stouts, if any, see the natural world the way we do. Food is grown or raised in a field and comes served on a plate to most, complete with knife and fork; or from the market; or is hauled up out of cold storage."

Nud shrugged. "I guess so."

The pair kept up a brisk pace through to the west side of town. Each time they passed a water fountain, Nud felt the urge to kick off his shoes, cannonball in and wade through the ruffled water. Three grand fountains graced the main throughway as they entered the Westgate Market, each three levels high. On top of the first, a bird spouted water from a long, curved beak; the second showed a whale, spraying water from its blowhole; and the third – the largest and most spectacular of the three – dominated the market square. Even from a distance, Nud could clearly make out its cascading assortment of spinning waterwheels.

Seeing the fountains triggered something in Nud – a memory. No, not quite, but something like a memory. It stopped him in his tracks.

"Nud?" Paplov said.

The mark on Nud's arm suddenly tingled with electricity. Shapes began to form in his mind. Images, scenes: *Stouts…*

*thin... drawn... war cries... weapons clanging... attack...
attack!... chains.* He swung his gaze to Paplov.

"The Bearded Hills planned to attack."

Paplov's head flinched back slightly. His eyebrows drew
together. "Attack?"

Nud nodded. "During the famine. They were plotting
to overthrow the mayor, and they wanted to force the Glebe
Stouts to work for them instead, as *slaves*."

"Slaves? Glebe Stouts?" Paplov shook his head. "Preposterous."

Nud felt the tingling rush coming on again. He squeezed
his eyes shut. Scenes about Turnsby's past swirled in his mind
and shifted like a cloud of dark smoke: *gardens... torn up...
fountains... toppled... statues erected... massive statues... sea
creatures... leviathans!* All at once, the images dissipated.

"The fountains... they were going to be destroyed."

"Enough." Paplov grimaced. "What game is this?"

"I... I don't know, exactly. It's not a game."

Paplov put his arm on Nud's shoulder. "But Nud," he said,
sudden concern in his voice, "the fountains were built *long
after* the famine." After a brief pause, he started walking again.

Nud rubbed his forehead, took a last look around, and
then followed. "Oh," was all he could say as he caught up.

The pair strode in silence for the last stretch, with Paplov
clearly disturbed by Nud's outbursts. The young diplomatic
aide tried to sort out in his mind what'd just happened, but
he came up empty. He knew there was something called "false
recall" that happened to some Pips – a kind of memory disor-
der, but he didn't know much about it.

Before long, the faint but distinctive smell of coal-smoke
carried on the air as they made their way through Westgate
towards the Helmfast Inn. Paplov politely declined the last
of the merchants trying to unload their wares – peddling

everything from tools and spices to furs and tapestries. Paplov came to the front door of the Helmfast, all oak and wrought iron. It was arched and set in a wall of black, polished stone, and edged by ornate carvings of climbing vines. He pushed it open.

Inside, the curtains were almost completely drawn and the foyer was dimly lit by lanterns. The air felt heavy, saturated with lush smells of carpet and fabrics, with hints of crushed, dried flowers and apple-scented candles added – in stark contrast to Nud's airy hut. Paplov approached the innkeeper, standing behind a high desk, and once again produced his letter. The Glebe attendant was a round, red-cheeked and pleasant-looking fellow, seemingly content to be in the thick of midlife.

"Lord Mayor Otis' aide dropped by this morning to reserve our best room," the man said. "It has a balcony overlooking the market square. There will be dancing and entertainment later tonight. We have a performing troupe in from Dennington – theatre and songs."

"Very nice," Paplov said, adding enough intonation to sound thrilled. Nud knew he wasn't.

The Stout's hands soon were busy gathering paperwork and a quill as he chatted on about last year's show. Motioning to an inkwell on the desk, he handed Paplov the quill and then the paper. "Please make your mark at the bottom so I can validate your attendance with the mayor, Councilor Leatherleaf."

"Thank you kindly," Paplov replied. Nud's grandfather carefully studied the document he was about to sign, and only when satisfied returned the paper with his mark.

"Streets are a little quiet this evening," Paplov remarked.

The innkeeper's cheeks inflated with air, and then he puffed it out slowly. "Yesum. Been quiet for days. As soon as the shadows start getting long, most everyone packs up – ever since the incident on the Outland Trail. Not tonight though!"

Paplov raised an eyebrow. "Incident?"

"Haven't you heard?" The innkeeper's eyes went wide. "Well, the whole town's talking about it. One of many lately – a bad batch of low-life slave traders from the Outlands, I say. And that's not all. Merchants and other travelers raided just outside of town, and traders raided *inside* town walls just the day before last, right out there under my nose, at dusk. Bandits." He gestured to the door. "Unbelievable." He shook his head.

Resting his elbows on the desk, the innkeeper leaned forward. He rested his chin on his hands and shifted his gaze to the narrow slit of light from the window, where the drapes didn't quite meet, and to the market square beyond. His jaw dropped slightly as though about to speak, but no words came out.

"And the incident?" Paplov reminded him.

The innkeeper looked confused for a moment, then straightened up and slapped his forehead.

"Oh yes, pardon me," he said. "I got sidetracked. There hasn't been a lot of outsider traffic since a few days ago. Three, no four, or two. Two days. Mostly just locals about town. It's making for a slow start to the season." He reached under the desk and produced two sets of keys.

"I see," Paplov said, as he took the keys handed to him.

"One for each of you," said the innkeeper.

For a moment, the two men just stared at one another.

"And…" Paplov prompted.

"And…" echoed the innkeeper, eyes wide and inviting, palms open to suggestion.

"The incident," Paplov said.

The Stout slapped his forehead again. "Oh yes, the incident, pardon me. A most foul murder, theft, and kidnapping – and good upstanding Glebe Stouts they were, falling victim that is – up your way near the split, so I hear. The whole town's talking. Outlanders, I say."

Paplov tilted his head to Nud, eyebrows raised in all seriousness: "We best keep our heads up and our ears pricked." He turned back to the innkeeper. "Thanks for the tip," he said, and flipped the man a griff.

Despite the lizard incident, they'd made good time and so could afford a short rest in their chamber before changing into more formal evening attire.

The night's itinerary was to begin with dinner at the lord mayor's house at dusk, over which Paplov would no doubt engage in the usual polite conversation. Meanwhile, Nud could focus on enjoying a much-needed meal after such a long day of travel, politely nodding when prompted, and sipping last year's sweet summer wine from the local vineyards.

*

As dusk set in, Nud and his grandfather crossed the canal over the private bridge to Turnsby Manor – the mayor's residence. The evening began on a high note. The stately home was warm and aromatic on the inside, from an afternoon of cooking. The gracious mayoress greeted them in the foyer, and a gracious staff led them to a holding chamber for drinks and polite gossip, before moving on to the main attraction. Nud's culinary visions seemed not far off the mark – a hot lamb meal as grand as anything he could have hoped for began to unfold. Dimly lit lanterns and scented candles on ornate chandeliers set the ambience of the dinner chamber. Nud helped himself to a fair portion at the mayor's table before anything more than greeting words came his way. He'd barely noticed the building tension in the air.

Now, Lord Mayor Otis Dagger was known to be a cantankerous and irritable sort, but Paplov was quite masterful in the art of diplomacy. As a councilor, Nud's grandfather was adept at building up a trusting relationship in short order, able to break the ice quickly and establish common ground. The way the old gaffer got along with people, Nud often made the mistake of thinking he was catching up with an old friend when, in reality, he'd just met the person.

As Nud heaped a second helping of lightly-steamed fall greens onto his plate, the mistress of the household leaned forward from across the table, smiled at Nud and near whispered: "You carry the same look in your eyes as your mother did." She had the gentlest voice.

The woman's mention of his mother caught Nud off-guard. The young Pip finished chewing what was in his mouth, and swallowed. "You knew my mother?" Most people avoided the topic altogether.

"Briefly," she replied, "though I would have liked to have known her better." The mayoress' gaze was full of compassion. "Your mother had a warm heart and bright eyes filled with wonder and excitement," she went on. One of her daughters smiled shyly at Nud from across the table. She had a plain, friendly look to her.

"Yes, she did." Nud recalled the warmth most of all. He sipped his red wine. "Thank you." Then he scooped up another mouthful of the greens.

The mayoress straightened back into her seat and shot her burly husband a loving smile before sipping more white wine, while he downed another red. That was when Nud noticed the mayor's stern demeanor, and that his wife's smile had been wasted; to reciprocate might have broken his face. Nud decided to clue in, ears tuned to the conversation.

"Harrow wants the Malevuin Bridge dismantled for larger vessels to pass," the lord mayor told Paplov. "Doncaster too." He shook his head. His tone was harsh. "They already have us floating across on the Dim side."

"Oh?" Paplov said.

The bridge over the Upper Malevuin River on the town's west side was a landmark in the region, that stood as a tes- timony to the town's pride and sense of accomplishment. Intricate and overdone in every detail, the bridge received enterprising parties from Fort Abandon and the Bearded Hills, plus business-minded travelers from as far west as Dennington, and in days past, the Star Sands. The Doncaster bridge, on the other hand, was simply practical, used mainly by farmers and ranchers with land on both sides of the river, or those traveling between Fort Abandon and either Gan or Harrow who didn't wish to pass through Turnsby.

"Naturally, the whole town is up in arms," Otis went on. "And who will they blame? It could cost me the next election."

"Most certainly."

Mayor Otis scowled at Paplov's response.

Nud's body tensed as he fixed his gaze on the mayor. The man's anger was palpable. And as his irritation grew, Nud watched and sipped more wine. How Paplov could remain so calm on his end of the discussion was beyond Nud, given his often-vocal dis- dain for Harrow and the suspicions he harbored surrounding the disappearance of Nud's parents. Although he'd been careful to keep any such mention of Harrow to a minimum over the years – for diplomatic reasons – the topic managed to creep up every so often. For the most part, they'd simply moved on with their lives, or at least they convinced themselves that they had.

"Do you know what it costs to run a ferry?!" Mayor Otis raged. "And who wants to wait?! Let Dim Lake pay, I say!" Fists clenched, the toe of the mayor's shoe tapped loudly against the floorboards. He raised his voice. "And the ferry that we do have is treacherous in the winter… treacherous. No one wants to use it." Otis shook his head vehemently. A moment later, he stopped. His shoulders dropped. He rubbed his face with his hands.

"What can I do?" he continued, deflated.

Paplov sighed. "Harrow takes what Harrow wants."

Otis nodded, slowly. Then his lips pinched as the anger inside him welled up again. He grimaced, then ranted on, loudly and with renewed fury. "I was trying to say 'there is just no negotiating with Harrow'… before you interrupted!" The mayor's face turned beet red, and the purple tie around his neck looked so tight it seemed his head might pop off.

Paplov's comment wasn't an interruption though. Otis had clearly paused long enough for him to inject a comment. Nud opened his mouth to defend his grandfather, then stopped himself. *Not my place,* he decided.

"I apologize, lord mayor," Paplov said.

What? Nud's head started to throb. *He's buckling under?* The young aide didn't know why it bothered him so much.

The mayor waved a finger at Paplov. "And you're next, you know," he added. "Harrow has spies all over your bog looking for some damned ancient battleground. They'll do anything to find it. And what do you think will happen once they do?"

What? Nud had heard similar talk before, but this time it really hit him.

Nud burst out. "What is Harrow doing in our bog?" The adults ignored him.

Still, the implications of the mayor's heavy words bred

like wildfire in Nud's mind. As they hung in the air, he thought of the sinkhole and the bog bodies, and he thought of the claim post they'd found. *What does Harrow want?* Nud closed his eyes, and he began to see images of the bog all dug up. *Workers – hundreds. Buildings. Soldiers.* Thoughts of the impending destruction of his habitat ignited and multiplied. Consequences pressed against Nud's inner skull, and mounted. They mounted until he thought the bone there would burst open. Suddenly, the stress let go. He opened his eyes. Around him, the lanterns and candles in the room all flickered.

"Oh my." The mayoress put a hand to her chest. "Is there a draft in here?" She rubbed her shoulders to ward off the phantom chill.

Nud glanced to the mayor. More worked up than ever, the Glebe Stout lifted his right hand a few inches from the table, followed by a controlled, yet powerful slam to the hardwood top. Nud didn't think the man's face could turn any redder, but it did. *Crimson.* He became so angry he started to shake.

Paplov, on the other hand, remained fully calm. He made curious glances at the lamps and the candles before his gaze fell back to the mayor. He looked the man in the eye. "How do you know this? How did you learn about Harrow's intentions with regard to the bog lands?"

The mayor seemed to shake off his anger, at least momentarily. He rested his elbows on the table and leaned in towards Paplov. He spoke in a hushed voice. "A friend in Harrow, about our size," he explained. "He works in the entertainment and culinary industries – organizing events, catering and such. He hears things."

Nud couldn't hold his composure any longer – the visions: the torn-up gardens, the fountains toppling, the bog dug up…

"We can't just sit here and take it!" Nud said. This time, the adults took notice. "Why doesn't someone stand up to Harrow?" The words just spewed out – there was no way to contain them. But really, Nud didn't want to contain them, not anymore.

"Nud! Mind your place," Paplov scolded. In the midst of his interjection, the room went dark.

The diners gasped, followed by a long hush.

In good time, Mayor Otis rose from his chair, in the dark. "A moment," he said, fumbling for a match. He lit the nearest lantern and cranked up the brightness dial.

"Ah, good," Paplov said. In the newfound light, the councilor shot Nud a stern look, and then turned his gaze back to the mayor, in the midst of igniting the next lantern. "Please excuse my grandson," Paplov said. "He seems to be a bit off today. Clearly he is out of line."

"No, you are," Nud said. "Why doesn't anyone else see it? Harrow—"

"That's enough out of you!" Paplov said. "Mind your tongue or… or I'll… you'll… regret it."

Nud clenched his jaw. The muscles there tightened. He glared at Paplov, and Paplov glared back. Nud opened his mouth to speak, about to say something he'd probably regret.

That is when the mistress of the household reached up to her husband, standing next to her. She gently squeezed his arm, and tilted her head slightly towards him. And when the mayor swung around, his eyes locked with hers. An unspoken kindness passed between them. Any tension left in his face washed away instantly.

Nud swallowed hard on the words about to flip off his tongue. The timing suddenly seemed wrong, inappropriate, like he'd be interrupting a good thing. Mayor Otis lowered his head and let out a loud heavy sigh, then sat down beside his wife. The redness in his face had dissipated into faded patches. He eyed Nud with a measuring look.

"The boy is passionate, I'll give him that," Otis said, "and with enough hot air to blow out all the lights." He swung his gaze to Paplov. "He'll make a fine politician, some day." Everyone laughed. Everyone, that is, except for Nud.

The mayor went on, "But such words are easier said than done – something experience has taught us both."

Paplov nodded his head. "Indeed."

"I suppose they are one in the same with Harrow – want and take," the mayor said. "We were told to 'take the bridge down your way or we'll take it down for you.' That was the negotiation."

Biting his upper lip, Paplov shook his head and sighed. "Harrow takes what Harrow wants," he repeated, "always has, always will. There is little anyone can do about it. Glebe Stouts will know that whatever happens isn't your fault."

"Indeed," Otis said. The mayor finished his wine, then topped up his glass and Paplov's. Then Otis smashed the table again, but lightly. His voice boomed. "Give up the swampland, Paplov, or we'll…"

"Give it up for you?" Paplov said. They both laughed, for no real reason that Nud could discern.

Makes more sense when served with wine, Nud figured.

Mayor Otis raised his cup to Paplov. "Our negotiations will take a more civilized route, no doubt."

"Certainly," Paplov said, raising his own cup to the mayor's.

And with that, every smidgen of tension between the two fizzled. But it would take more than a toast to drown Nud's emotions on the matter. He dispensed with his wine glass and reached across the table to help himself to a pint of ale. Paplov chose to ignore Nud's indulgences, and Nud returned the favor by containing any further outbursts.

"I take it you have full authority in the matter before us?" Otis asked Paplov.

"Of course," Paplov replied. "I have been fully briefed and empowered by our own lord mayor and council, and I have all the necessary paperwork to prove it."

"Very good." Otis motioned to one of his daughters. Paplov looked to Nud. The young Pip got up, gathered his carrying bag and fumbled through its contents. Eventually, he produced the relevant documents. The mayor's daughter came to meet him and Nud handed them over to her.

Now Nud hadn't expected official business to be conducted at the dinner table itself, but with those words, the dealing began. Paplov and Otis filled and refilled their cups as they spoke of economy and risk, of present and future value, of obligations, balance, taxes, who had devoted what forces to the security of the Tri-towns, the upkeep of the trail, and the dibbing up of the many concomitant roles and responsibilities that went along with the simple leasing of a parcel of land.

Nud kept an ear to the conversation, but also made small talk with the missus and her three chatty daughters. The youngest acted very strangely. Giggling, saying weird things and making weird faces. The middle one wasn't much different. Both were easy on the eyes, but Nud tried to avoid topics that led to input from those two, which mostly resulted in some kind of teasing. Instead, he focused on sensible conversation with the missus and her eldest daughter, Oda - a few years older than Nud.

Eventually, the spirit of a deal was hammered out and the two diplomats rose from the table. Mayor Otis steadied himself, one hand on the chair next to him, then reached the other hand out across the table. The two shook on it.

After a half-pint of ale and a generous serving of desert, Nud retreated to the mayor's study with Paplov and Otis where they worked out the finer details. Nud was responsible for recording and witnessing the agreed upon arrangements. The mayor's assistant – Oda – performed the same duty. All Nud had to do was listen, write, retrieve forms from Paplov's carrying bag, and quickly draft up any understandings settled upon, organizing their wine-soaked notions into coherent and well-meaning sentences.

As negotiations drew to a close and all involved took to packing away their things, Otis' daughter – the assistant – made her way over to Nud, smiling pleasantly.

"Will you be joining us later tonight at Westgate for the dancing and entertainment?"

That was unexpected. Apparently, not everyone was afraid to be out at night.

Nud wondered how he might avoid stepping on her delicate toes, and then replied, "That sounds fun."

Oda was friendly, and she was not bearded.

CHAPTER XII

Good company

The journey home was cold, wet, and tiresome. Nud had stayed up all night feasting and dancing with Oda and her sisters. Mayor Otis had warmed up to his grandfather considerably after dinner, behaving like his new best friend before the night was through. They'd shared stories about all the deal making and underhandedness on the political scene lately, then raided the wine cellar and sang songs until daybreak.

Paplov, too stubborn to call for a coach, would never have made it to the Handlers' Post without falling over. Nud carried everything just to get as far as they did, and the lizard handler filled in the rest. He met them halfway after they didn't show up at the post on time, despite their arrangement. Old Wyatt had heard the same rumors that the innkeeper made mention of, and he was worried the pair might present a tempting target for would-be bandits, or worse.

Wyatt looked like a drowned rat by the time he dropped them off at home, past nightfall. Paplov and Nud were equally drenched. Nud's grandfather tipped the old bogger generously and thanked him profusely.

Nud slept dead to the world that night. It wasn't until mid-morning that he rolled out of his night sack and lumbered to the study. There, he found Paplov resting in his favorite chair, sipping tea and slowly digesting a biscuit and a book. He was still in his night robe. A heavy wool blanket lay folded over his lap. The tea was a special blend, steeped from young five-finger leaves he'd insisted on picking just outside of Turnsby before they'd left. Paplov claimed the remedy soothed his throat and eased his aches. Nud slumped into the chair opposite him.

A few nibbles of biscuit and the occasional handful of wild berries were all his grandfather could keep down. Without looking up from his plate, Paplov quickly went over Nud's duties for the day – getting himself together and dropping by Town Hall to file the land lease records from the negotiations in Turnsby. Nud acknowledged what he had to do, but there was something else on his mind.

Paplov must have sensed it. Aware of his promise, he sighed heavily when he shifted his gaze to Nud. He stared for a long minute with those tired eyes, as though weighing something within. Then he smirked, and without cause for concern, he bade Nud to gather the arrows made, his wits, and some good company. Rather than wait on Paplov, Nud would make the journey to his uncle's cabin with friends instead, come morning the next day. "It will be fun," Paplov told him. "A trip to remember." At even the slightest sign of resistance from his grandson, the old Pip insisted that he wanted Nud out of the hut until his ailment ran its course.

"Fyorn's eyes'll light up like fireflies when he sees some fresh young faces for a change," Paplov said. "I gather he's getting plenty tired of that ole coot he sees in the mirror every day, with only one other old coot's company to look forward too." Paplov began to laugh, but his laugh became a cough. He had choppy words of advice for his grandson, rolled in with a request: "Give him my best <cough>; keep <cough> one eye <cough> on the water and the other on the tree-line; and no <cough> laggards."

Paplov shut his mouth tight, filled his cheeks with air, and did his best to muffle an oncoming flurry of coughs. Nud took the opportunity to blurt out something that should've been said years ago.

"Last time I went… there was something not right about the forest," he said.

"Ahem. Not right?"

"I thought it was a tree at first, but…" Nud trailed off. He didn't know how to describe what happened.

"But what?" Paplov said.

"It moved."

"Pardon?" he wheezed, trying to suppress the inevitable.

"It moved," Nud replied, "and not just a little. It came at me. It was gnarled and crooked, with jaws and teeth and…"

Red-faced, Paplov raised his hand, shook his head, and then began to cough-roar at the notion. The act cleared his throat, temporarily. His voice was scratchy.

"Oh really?" he said, swallowing. "Boogalies too? And did you hear the flip-flap-flopping of their floppy wet feet? Maybe they were in the trees."

"It wasn't like that," Nud said.

His grandfather coughed again, pounded his chest, and took a minute to regain his composure.

"Maybe you *are* having false recalls," Paplov said. "One thing's for sure, Uncle Fyorn doesn't miss a beat, especially in his own woods. And he never, ever mentioned anything to me about talking trees."

"They chased me. I didn't say they could ta—"

"I meant *walking* trees," he grumbled, "...or whatever <cough>. You just have a vivid imagination."

Nud glanced at his branded wrist.

Paplov caught on. "That has nothing to do with anything," he said. "Looks like a rash. Better get it checked out – the Diviner probably has an ointment or some other remedy that'll take care of it. Did you scratch yourself against something up in that attic?"

Nud's eyes went wide. *That was four years ago.*

"Yes – I know you used to go up there, despite being told not to." Paplov hesitated. "Rashes can be stubborn. They can persist for years. Does it come and go?"

Nud shook his head, while Paplov took a closer look. He muffled another cough.

"Ahem. That mark has been there just about as long as I can remember, so no worries. You know, I'd say it was smaller years back <cough>, but you've grown since. Your stubborn little friend probably just grew right along with you."

His grandfather's explanation seemed ludicrous, but the young Pip had learned to expect that much – the man was old and out of touch, after all. Nud sunk into the chair even further and rested his head on one hand. *Why bother pursuing the matter?* Paplov had no real answers to offer, only mockery and half-disguised criticisms.

*

The rest of the day Nud spent at Webfoot Hall where he met up with Old Remy and filed the lease records Paplov and Mayor Otis had agreed upon. The grizzled old Pip sat by himself on a wooden chair in a cluttered corner of the administrative wing, stacks of paper and rolled maps strewn everywhere. Remy was the only one in Webfoot who understood the filing system, if you could call it that. The man's head was unusually small and shriveled, with only a few tufts of white hair that sprung forth from the scalp. Frog-like, his bloodshot eyes bulged out of their sockets.

Old Remy reminded Nud that Council still had to sign off on the final documents before they'd be official. While he was there, Nud brought up the topic of mineral claims in the bog. The clerk provided the young diplomatic aide with a claims map and the forms he'd need to stake a claim. He even told Nud he could have them free of charge, but Nud paid the normal fee anyway. Remy also mentioned he'd have to cut his own claim posts.

That evening, Nud packed what he thought he'd need for a trip to Fyorn's. He also pondered the circumstances. Going to Deepweald without Paplov just didn't seem right at first, but as night drew nearer the idea grew on him. It could be fun, like Paplov said. Nud came to the conclusion that he could combine two excursions into one. What possibly could be better after visiting Fyorn than a treasure hunt? And maybe – just maybe – Nud and his friends could get a start on a real mining claim.

Nud debated which cloak to bring and whether or not to bother with boots. He chose the heavier of his two cloaks, despite the fact that the weather was warming up. It would keep the bugs from biting through the material in the evening, on their way home, and it would also show better to Holly. And oh yes, Holly definitely would be invited. Nud could only hope that Mer remembered to make that point clear when he passed on his message to Bobbin at the Flipside – Stout memories are so unreliable.

Boots… Nud hated wearing them. The return trip could be problematic though, with biting insects nipping at his toes near sundown. He decided to carry a light pair in his pack. Nud hooked his shortbow in as well, unstrung, in case his uncle had time for target practice. Nud expected a lighter load on the return trip, since Paplov already had a full stock of deepwood. As for the stone that Mer had referred to as some form of light-emitting, ancient tree gum, Nud wrapped it in leather to hide the flashing and stuffed it into his pocket.

*

The next morning, Nud skipped breakfast to save time. Fully burdened, he made his way to Paplov's night chamber to bid him farewell. It was empty. He stumbled in the dark to the study, and found his grandfather asleep in his favorite wicker chair again.

Now Paplov never would've let Nud go to Fyorn's without him, were he not sick, and adding time for treasure hunting afterwards would have been a tough sell. Lately, there'd only been time for work, one kind of training or another, and chores. It was suffocating. Not to mention the recent dangers to travelers that everyone was talking about.

This trip is freedom, Nud decided, as he watched Paplov slumber.

The old gaffer jerked when Nud touched his shoulder ever so lightly. In the dim light, the spittle that ran down from the corner of Paplov's mouth was barely noticeable. Nud spoke with a hushed voice.

"I'm off to Uncle Fyorn's now, okay?" he said. "And then some treasure hunting."

Eyelids pumping, Paplov turned his head towards Nud and murmured something unintelligible.

The young Pip took that as a "yes," whispered a soft good-bye, and left Paplov sleeping as he set out to town. And that is how, without so much as breakfast, Nud was out the door and down the road in no time flat. Making up for the lost meal would be easy enough: plenty of wild forage could be found along the way, even that time of year – sour moss berries that had wintered well and bitter catkins, for starters.

Nud picked up Gariff first, already hard at work with his kin – it was a family business. His "Pops" liked to get out early and accomplish as much as possible: "before the bugs woke up," as he'd say. With both hands grasping the sturdy wooden handle of his shovel and leaning all his weight on it, Gariff's father spoke with a gravelly voice.

"Come to steal away my best worker?"

"I'm not go'in anywhere," said a cousin.

Gariff let out a series of short grunts. "Don't make me laugh." He was in the midst of lifting more than he should. He couldn't even see over the blocks he was carrying. The stumble in his step didn't deter him. And when he unloaded, he looked up at his father like a hound waiting to fetch. All he got was a lecture.

"Why didn't ya tell me earlier?" Pops said to his son.

"Never plan yer day around a Pip," said an uncle. "Don't ye know that?"

Gariff shrugged his shoulders. Pops rubbed the beard on his chin, thick and grey-speckled, then sighed. "There's no arguing that point. Ahh, go on," he said. "It's nigh summer. Just be back in town before dark. Got it?"

"Got it!" Gariff replied.

Pops grunted. A hint of annoyance infused his voice. "And bring Kabor wit'ya this time!"

Gariff brushed the dirt off his shirt and pants, took his hat off to give it a shake, and then placed it firmly on his head. According to him, Kabor hadn't left the Flipside, so they headed there next to round up the other three.

When they arrived at the inn, they met round Bobbin first, who just happened to be tidying up the foyer. As Pips go, he was a bit of a novelty. In the right light, the splotches of color along Bobbin's neck matched the pattern of a devil's paintbrush, replacing with a slash of red the usual muted green or brown markings that appear on most Pips. Although a few years younger than the rest, he made up for that deficiency through sheer entertainment value and – being the only child of the more-than-generous Numbits – by virtue of the palatable benefits he extended to his friends. Bobbin habitually raided the kitchen on their behalf.

"Hello Leno! Hello Gariff!" he piped as the two entered. "Mer told Holly who told me all about the treasure hunt and the claim staking. Are we leaving today?"

"Right away," Nud said. "I have to stop at my uncle's first though."

"What?" Gariff said.

Bobbin grabbed a damp cloth and went to the bar to wipe it down. "Is he the important Elderkin you were supposed to meet?" Nud and Gariff followed.

"That's him," Nud replied.

Gariff mumbled something under his breath.

Nud pushed a stool in place. "Where's Holly?"

"We don't serve holly here," Bobbin tootled. "The berries are toxic."

Gariff winced and shook his head. "Here we go."

"Don't worry, *Loverboy*," Bobbin said to Nud. He tossed the cloth behind the bar. "I'll find her. She's excited about going. Give me two shakes to get some food together too. We have to eat, you know."

Loverboy? Nud felt his face go flush. *What does he mean by that?* Gariff chuckled and Bobbin wore a goofy look from ear to ear.

"Shut up!" he told Gariff, and gave his friend a shove. The Hill Stout didn't budge – like trying to move a tree stump.

Gariff turned to Bobbin. "Have you seen my *busy* cousin?"

"I didn't know you had one," Bobbin replied, putting the spirits in order.

"Too busy for work, that is," Gariff said.

Bobbin stopped what he was doing. "Oh, *that* kind of busy. I haven't seen him at all this morning. He's probably still sleeping."

With the great room in good order, the young Numbit ran out back to the cookhouse to pack as much food as he possibly could carry, and also to find Holly.

Gariff left to fetch Kabor, leaving Nud by himself near the foyer.

It was too early for the breakfast crowd. The greeter's desk was vacant, the hearth gloomy and lifeless. Nud swept his gaze over the great room and immediately felt a sense of loss, as though he'd just missed his own birthday party. The place didn't look quite right so empty, so calm. It was too quiet, and too tidy.

The floor had been swept and the tables wiped clean, and extra chairs stacked up to one side of the stage. Windows were open, but even a fresh morning breeze could not hide the layering of smoke, ale-soaked wood, and hints of smell like old clothes left too long in a pile.

Nud's stomach began to churn. He couldn't stop thinking about Holly. He wanted to remember everything about that night at the Flipside… at least he thought he did.

Just then, Holly entered the great room, alone and carrying

a book. She wore a loose shirt and a form-fitting skirt, putting her lean athleticism on display.

"Hello, Holly," Nud said, trying to sound chipper. "You look… good."

Holly smiled. "Thank you, Nud. And good morning, what brings you here so early?"

"Plans have changed," Nud told her, "We're going treasure hunting *and* visiting my Elderkin uncle, all in one day."

Holly's eyes went wide. She spoke with hushed enthusiasm. "Really? That's even better than what Mer told me." Then her eyes narrowed slightly, as though suspicious that Nud was hiding something. She tilted her head.

"What's your uncle's name?" she asked, ears pricked for the answer. Her slender jaw hung slightly open with anticipation.

"Fyorn," Nud replied.

"Fyorn," she repeated. Her olive eyes shone. "That's a really nice name." Holly repeated the name musically, teasing out the syllables with inflection. "*Fy*-orn." Dreamy-eyed, she raised a hand to her chest and ran her fingers along the beaded necklace that she wore. Nud recognized it – the same necklace she'd worn that night when he first saw her.

Holly granted Nud a mischievous smirk and a gentle shoulder nudge. Her voice was playful. "You tried to kiss me," she said outright.

"I… err… sorry. I don't even remember the part about kissing girls—"

"Girl-*ss*," she said, glaring daggers and emphasizing the "s."

Nud fumbled his words. "I mean…"

Disaster.

"Great. How nice for you," she stated flatly.

But Nud didn't think she really meant it.

"Humph." Holly pressed her temples. "I have to put my book away." She turned to go.

"Ahh… What book is it?" Nud asked, his attempt at damage control.

Holly paused and shot him a sideways glance, nose slightly in the air. "Elderkin legends," she replied. "Your friend Kabor helped me to track it down. He's quite resourceful *and* good company. Does he ever mention me?"

That was *not* what Nud wanted to hear. "He told me that you were his girlfriend. And then Gariff said the same thing."

"Oh, isn't that interesting." Holly shrugged and left Nud standing in the great room alone, again. Nud sighed heavily and shook off his carelessness as best he could. Then he took a seat and unfolded the claims map to study it more carefully than he had at the hall – and without Old Remy breathing down his neck.

*

Gariff was the first to return, and he was fully laden. His adventuring gear had already been packed and ready. Kabor followed soon after, and then Holly, minus the book.

The burly Stout eyed Nud's map. "What do we have here?" he asked, peering over the Pip's shoulder. Kabor and Holly shuffled over to have a look as well. Nud explained to them everything that Old Remy had told him.

"I can make the claim posts on the fly, no problem," Gariff said. "I just need to know what to put on them."

Nud asked, "Do you think you'll be able to figure out *where* to put them?"

Gariff scratched his scruff. "I have an idea. I can bang them into the ground where I think they should go, but Mer should be the one to verify that they're placed right."

Holly lifted her shoulders, as though to hide her neck. "Do we really need him?"

"Sure do," Gariff replied, nodding. "Like I said, I know enough to get us started… maybe, but we'll need a professional to go over everything. There's lots to know when it comes to prospecting, if you want to do it right."

Nud said, "Where the heck is Bobbin? He's sure taking his sweet time."

"NUMBIT!" Gariff roared. His voice echoed back.

From the cookhouse, their well-rounded friend squeaked back politely. "Coming," he called. Moments later, he repeated his assurance: "I'm coming… just a minute…"

Bobbin's jolly red face eventually bobbed into the great room; arms fully laden with everything he'd need – lots of food. His pack was so stuffed he couldn't close it properly. Holly went up to Bobbin and starting fussing with it. She quickly became frustrated with his lack of organization.

"Don't worry," Bobbin said. "It'll be a lot less full on the way back. Even half way there…"

"Not if you fill it with Fyorn's maple candy," Nud said.

Bobbin's eyes lit up.

Holly grunted as she pulled hard on the straps, sealing the pack tight. Then she spoke in a stern voice. "The last thing he needs is more candy." Bobbin's face went sour.

Despite all the antics and minor setbacks, Nud's friends, old and new, were eager for an adventure that morning. Together, they set out for Deepweald Forest.

The day promised to be a fine one for travel – cool and foggy so early in the morning, but before long, the sun would burn through the mist and a good breeze would blow up. That would keep the bugs down and spirits high.

Interlude - Some great thing

Once, I was much like a typical flesh-bearer, awake at dawn and asleep after nightfall. But now that I am scaled and bark-skinned, sleep is more of a seasonal thing. So, I have no qualms about carrying on after sunset and into the dawn, and all the next day again and the day after that too, if need be. The real night for me is long and cold and goes by the name of "Old Man Winter." Not to say that you will never see a Green Dragon about in the winter months – it just doesn't happen very often.

No worries then, plenty of time, everything will be recorded before it's too late… if I hurry. All must be scribed before that Wilder druid's perfect storm arrives. I hear he's on his way. The winds are howling tonight; it's the fury from the east he's been waiting for so patiently, all through the summer and into the fall. So many colorful leaves will be blown to oblivion if this keeps up.

You might recall that early on, one of the first comments I made was that this tale is "the beginning of the end for some great thing." I suppose all beginnings are the beginning of an end of sorts. What begins and never ends? – sounds like a child's riddle. Maybe that all eternal Time is not a bad answer, but even Time is so constrained. Then so must everything be… well, almost everything…

It is coming. I can feel the surge through my heartwood. In all the days I was my former self – my flesh-and-blood self – I believed this saga began with the coming journey, the outing from the Flipside that I am about to tell tale of. But now that I am tapped into the Hurlorn consciousness, and as I near the very end alluded to, I know better. This part I speak of next is more of a tipping point than the beginning of an end.

My involvement was inevitable, really, and integral to the progression of a cycle that I had no idea even existed. I had become an important cog in a great wheel without even knowing it. It's the little things that the Hurlorns seem to pick up on, the subtle ways that can make all the difference when you sum them all up. I am sure that the stubbornness of the Lenokin family played a crucial role, as did an engrained independence streak and an overwhelming sense of civic duty. The ability to negotiate a deal factored in as well. Contacts also had to be an indispensable part of the grand scheme. But more importantly, it was the interplay of these factors on the great undertakings of my time, hanging in the balance, that made all the difference, together with the right combination of means to adapt to whatever came of them.

As so often seems to happen in life, the chains of events looped in on themselves. In a sense, the beginning and the end are ever entangled. Recognizing such things for what they are is important to a Hurlorn.

CHAPTER XIV

Friendly passage

Gariff obsessed over the prospect of buried treasure, and as the party of five made their way out of town, he kept everyone's wandering minds focused on the "real purpose of the trip."

"Never mind 'Fyorni,'" he told mostly Nud straightaway. "Fyorni" was his pet name for "Fyorn." And "don't waste yer time on Elderkin fancy" – whatever that meant. Nud's personal favorite: "Save yer energy for diggin'." Gariff's booming voice drowned out anyone who tried to get a word in edgewise, which was unusual for one so amiable. Not even Holly chose to take issue with the Hill Stout, not on that topic, which was unusual for one so contrary.

As Gariff yammered on, excitement bubbled into every word and every breath, and that was all before they'd even reached the gate out of town. Once beyond the tall, cedar archway, he seemed satisfied to have said his piece. For a long stretch, Nud took simple pleasure in the grinding rhythm of their footsteps and the fading voices of the wall guards, chatting endlessly about town gossip and the weather.

But the Stout wasn't quite done talking yet. "Do ya's think we'll find the 'mother lode' that old prospector was rambling on about?"

Kabor took him on. "Mer's a bit delusional." A wolfish grin began to form. "Do you really think a bunch of frogs are sitting on a gold mine? I mean really, we're talking about a *bog* here."

"Not gold," Gariff countered. "A *ruby* mine. And why not?"

Holly set them both straight. "Put it together dimwits – he said blue sapphires. Don't you two remember?" She lowered her voice and roughed it up a little. "It's the sto-wo-wo-wo-wone of des-tiny."

Mer doesn't sound anything like that, Nud thought, with a slight shake of his head.

"Whatever," Gariff said, sending Holly a dismissive wave.

"It's not whatever," Holly said. "It's *blue frikken sapphires... blue sapphires... blue sapphires...* get it?" She flicked Kabor in the ear.

"Ouch!" Kabor said. "Why'd you hit *me*?"

"You were closer," she said playfully, and giggled. Then she turned her gaze to Gariff. "Boggers and whatnot have been scouting the place forever. I see them all the time at the inn. Don't you think they would've found everything there is to find by now?"

"No," Kabor answered, on behalf of his cousin. "Take Leno's little mud hut, for example. He could be sitting on a stack of gems half a league high and he'd never know it."

"Wait a minute," Nud contested. "Which side are you on, Kabor? You can't be on *both* sides of an argument."

Holly flicked Kabor's ear again.

"Ouch!"

Holly chuckled. "That one was just for *you* being *you*."

Kabor feigned retaliation. Holly skipped out of reach.

Nud was still hung up on Kabor's derisive comments about his home. "I don't live in a mud hut. It's sticks and, well, *fired* clay. And boards. And lots of things…"

"Cuz is right," Gariff cut in, "ya gots to know the grounds. Mer knows the ground better than most Stouts, and most Stouts know the ground better than any Pip, even if they've been rollin' around on it fer fifty years."

Kabor chuckled. "And even if the Stout *is* a little delusional," he added.

Holly frowned, as if something not quite satisfying was on her mind. "I don't see why we should split equal shares with Mer."

Bobbin, strangely silent since they'd left, suddenly chimed in. His voice sounded muffled.

"We shoul'ge just share wi'sh everyone," he said. Bobbin was already snacking on a bun, thick with butter. No one really minded his naïve comment.

Nud regarded Holly. "It's more complicated than you might think."

"Leno's right," Gariff said, nodding with agreement.

"Mer knows the process and he knows the competition," Nud went on, "and he can help us secure the rights so there are no mistakes, no oversights, and so we don't get scooped. It'll be tricky because HME is already in the area. I'm sure Paplov could help us too. All we have to do is convince him."

Holly's eyes were aglow. "Will we be rich?"

Nud shrugged. "If we get the claim staked right and the paperwork in on time, then maybe, someday."

"Look," Bobbin said, pointing straight up, "a sailboat."

They all tilted their gazes upwards. Slowly, the teens came to understand Bobbin's interpretation of the soft boundaries of a sail and the puffy outline of a boat's hull, set against the true blue backdrop of the surrounding sky. No one mentioned anything for a long minute. They just stared up into the sky where the lonely cloud sailed on a chance current of air. Nud's mind drifted right along with it, dreaming of untold riches. *I could finally get some answers*, he decided. *I could pay for an investigator and finally find out what happened to my parents. I could pay informants, offer bribes. I could even visit Harrow and find out who or what was behind their disappearance.* And if Nud's parents were being held captive – the same way Wyatt had been for so long – Nud could have them rescued, or begin a campaign to pressure the Iron Tower into releasing them. *Shame Harrow in front of all Theia.*

Holly broke Nud's trance. "Nud… *Leno*, how long can we stay at Fyorn's?"

"Pffaaa!" Gariff protested before Nud could answer. "Half an hour, tops. We have a claim to stake and treasure to hunt."

"Let's start by getting there early – well before noon," Nud said. "It's still a bit of a hike. That'll give us maybe three hours to visit and the same for treasure hunting and claim staking. We need to get back before dark."

"What?" Gariff's eyes went all squinty. "You're not pulling that one on me again."

"We'll see," Nud said.

Without warning, Holly darted ahead. "I have to run," she called back to the others. The sudden need to burn off energy came as no surprise – normal for any Pip. Kabor started into a jog, then changed his mind and reverted to walking.

"I can't run with you, I'm eating," Bobbin proclaimed, his

tone apologetic. He'd just taken the last bite of bread and was already probing his pack for more.

"Hold up," Nud said, and started after Holly by himself. She kept a tight stride and it took a good minute to catch her, after which they jogged together for a stretch. The waddling Pip and the two cousins in their wake continued along at a hiking pace.

Huffing between short sentences, the Flipside girl began to make small talk with Nud about life at the inn. And as they passed the first stand of deadwood, the two Pips slowed to a fast walk to better accommodate their budding conversation.

Holly started off talking about the regulars she encountered on a weekly basis at the Flipside, and then turned her focus to their coastal neighbors in the South.

"And a good number of the merchants from Abandon Bay are very well-to-do," she said, "and some of the wildest partiers – they can go all night."

She paused. It was Nud's turn to say something.

"Really?" he remarked, trying to sound interested. Her necklace caught his eye again – a string of pearls with a leaf pendant, red and green. He gestured to it. "That's nice. Where did you get it?"

"Oh, this?" Looking down at her chest, Holly placed her hand on the necklace and rolled the pearls under her fingertips. "Do you like it?"

"Yes, I do," Nud replied, "very much. It looks like… it's very familiar… can I take a closer look?"

The two teens halted. Holly turned to face Nud, directly. She gathered her long hair, pulled it up and away, then casually leaned in so that Nud could garner a clear view of the necklace. A feeling of awkwardness set in. The necklace – it hung quite low on her, and her shirt could be revealing when she took on a certain stance…

Holly, on the other hand, appeared to be completely free of any inhibitions whatsoever. So, in the end, Nud just sighed and went with it. He stooped for a better look.

"Ahem… Ahh… Hmm," was all that came out as he studied the necklace, and her to a shameful extent. On closer examination, the necklace was just as Nud had thought. Each bead was actually bell-shaped, which he recognized as the tiny flower and winter leaf of the leatherleaf plant. The dangling leaves on the pendant, of course, were the leather leaves themselves.

"Yep, that's it," Nud said.

"What do you mean?" Holly asked.

"My mother had a necklace just like it. Those beads look like they come from the leatherleaf plant."

"Yes, I know," Holly said. "They're quite unique."

"Paplov talks about her necklace sometimes," Nud continued. "He says my father gave it to her – 'Leatherleaf' being her maiden name and all. It was supposed to be a family heirloom. I also recall a set of matching earrings – crystal and sort of bell-shaped."

"I have never seen the earrings," Holly said, "but they sound nice."

"I'll pick some up for you, if I ever see any," Nud said. They both straightened up. Nud's eyes met hers. "Wherever did you find it?"

Holly adjusted her shirt and let her hair fall over her shoulders. "Well," she began, "I get to talking to lots of people at the Flipside. Do you know Councilor Mrello?"

Nud knew Councilor Mrello all right. *Harrow's man.* Paplov was not fond of Mrello, and neither was Nud. Years back, he'd held a grudge against Nud's mother because she won the council position he'd petitioned for, which was Liaison to Harrow, even though Mrello had managed to produce a written recommendation from the Iron Tower supporting his application.

"I know of him," Nud replied. "The braggart that's always spreading his money around."

"He's the one," Holly said. "Some nights, he buys rounds of drinks for everyone in the Flipside. He's popular."

"I bet he does," Nud said, unable to hide his disdain. "But with who's money? Councilors don't get paid *that* much." Nud gritted his teeth. His face felt flush, hot with resentment. "Did he give you the necklace?"

"Well, sort of..."

Nud went quiet for a long minute, internalizing her response. *Where did he get the necklace?* Nud didn't like some of the answers that came up in his mind. His family's past dealings with Mrello and Harrow all came back in a flood of memories.

When Nud's grandfather reversed his retirement and returned to politics, intent on resuming the role he'd once passed on to his daughter, he made a great many accusations against Harrow connected with her disappearance. After all that'd happened, the Council ruled Paplov could no longer hold the position Liaison to Harrow – a conflict of interest, they said. And so, they assigned it to Mrello instead. But Paplov knew Mrello was crooked. He complained to the Council that the man lives well beyond his means, and insisted that Webfoot authorities investigate his spending habits and dealings with the Iron Tower. That investigation was stopped before it ever started.

As the thoughts continued to swirl, Nud's blood boiled in

frustration. His temples throbbed to the beat of his pounding heart. He squeezed his eyes shut.

"No, not again," he told himself, calling to mind the strange events that'd happened when he felt that same kind of rush before: the stake flinging through the air at Kabor, the door slamming on Paplov while he was holding an arrow to his eye, and the lights going out at the mayor's house. *Something is happening. I don't feel right.*

The sensation amplified. Nud opened his eyes and stumbled away from Holly, fighting the surge of emotions. He fought them until his mind began to clear, and then he fought them harder.

Nud heard Holly's voice – small and distant sounding. He felt her touch on his shoulder. Holly repeated herself.

"Is something wrong?"

Finally, Nud snapped out of it. "No," he stated, blinking. "I'm... o - kay."

Holly winced slightly. "Are you sure? You looked like you went into recall for a minute."

"No... not quite... not really." Nud tried to piece together the discussion they were having. "Where were we... oh ya. How did Mrello get the necklace?"

"Are you *really* sure you're all right?" Holly said. "You look a bit pale."

Nud shrugged off the comment. "I'm really sure."

Holly picked up where they'd left off. "Well then," she continued, "Mrello said he got the necklace in Harrow – it had been thrown in free with another deal, as sweetener. So, he got it for free."

Could it be? Nud wondered. *Of course it could.* The young Pip's mind reeled with more nefarious possibilities. *The words he'd used – a twisting of the truth?* It was almost a confirmation that…

Nud pressed his hands to his temples. He couldn't stay still. He started to walk. Quickly.

"Wait," Holly said. She jogged to catch up. "Leno, what is it with you?"

"Nothing. I'm fine." Nud turned his gaze to her. His words were abrupt, "Why did Mrello give you the necklace?"

"Well," she started, as if the explanation could go on all day, "he didn't really give it to me. He just *loaned* it to me. At first, I said 'no' of course – I didn't want to lead him on or anything, but he insisted there'd be no strings attached and I gave in because it's *so* pretty. He was hoping I'd just try him on for a while." Holly covered her mouth. "Oops," she giggled, "I meant to say try *it* on – Mrello made the same mistake. And then—"

"What?" Nud broke in.

"Oh," Holly said, shy and looking away. "When he gave it to me he said, 'If you like it you can try *me* on for a while,' and then he pardoned himself."

"I see." *Well that figures*, Nud thought. *That was no mistake.* "He was propositioning you."

"I don't think so," Holly said, and left it at that. They walked in silence.

Nud began to wonder about Holly and the company she keeps. He wondered if maybe he'd missed something about her that everyone else knew.

Before Nud could speak his mind, Holly had more information to offer about Mrello.

"He's *very* nice," Holly added. "I always get the best tips from him and Fort Abandoners, and he has lots of fun stories to tell." Holly giggled again. "I'm not sure if he's married or spoken for, but by the way he carries on, I suspect neither." Her comment opened the door to Nud's doubts, and the way she said what she said just fed the unsubstantiated notions rolling around in his stupid head.

"Holly," Nud said.

Anticipation ripened her voice. "Yes, Leno. Do you want to look at the necklace again?"

Nud shook his head.

Words popped into his mind and spewed out of his mouth before he had time to think about how dumb they were.

"You don't work… *upstairs* ever, do you?"

Holly's eyes narrowed instantly. Her voice was cutting. "Do you mean the dormer rooms? With the *red windows*?"

"Ahhh…"

"What's that supposed to mean, Leno?"

"Ah… I mean—"

"I *clean* up there, sometimes."

"Ahhh…"

The Flipside hostess had only one word to say about that. She made it good though. She made it sound like the last word she'd ever say to Nud.

"JACKASS!"

Holly stormed ahead, leaving the gulping Pip to wallow in a sea of loneliness and idiocy.

Nud glanced over his shoulder to see if the others had heard. *Of course they did.* Sure enough, all three of his friends had stopped dead in their tracks to gawk at them… to gawk at Nud, more like.

Why did I ask such a stupid question? Nud's pace slowed as he pondered that very thought, until the others caught up. Holly eventually fell back to hike with the group as well, but from that point onward, there was always someone between her and Nud, and if not someone, an invisible wall of indifference. She made small talk with Bobbin and Kabor, and all the while she wouldn't even hazard a glance Nud's way.

To break the isolation, Nud caved in and offered a few desperate comments to Gariff, playing up their prospects. Gariff's revving words in response were music to Nud's ears. The burly Stout did all the talking for yet another long stretch of trail. Nud's thoughts drifted as Gariff carried on, and he barely processed a word of it. He just liked hearing the sound of his good friend's voice.

*

In due course, the five arrived at the last strip of corduroy road that would bring them to the trailhead. Bulging hillocks welled up alongside the trail, matted in grass. After rounding a scraggly patch of alders that grew out of one of them, they caught their first glimpse of the upgraded Handlers' Post. As they closed in, it became apparent that the compound was unfinished.

Nud cringed at the shoddy sight.

"What?" Gariff said, noticing the change in expression. Then he glanced ahead. "Oh." A satisfied grin crept over his face.

The Handlers' Post looked as rickety as ever, and then some. Its newly raised walls were already leaning – truly a pathetic sight. The main "building" didn't even have a proper roof to speak of. On top of that, the doorway lacked a door and the windows were shutter-less – that much at least could be accounted for by the fact it was still under construction.

Holly smiled at a young guard as they passed, hard at work erecting a post. He was shirtless and barefooted, with leggings that only went down to his knees. A second guard sat on a log nearby, and a third individual banged away with a hammer inside the main structure, unseen. The young guard sent Holly a return wave, sporting a friendly smile. He couldn't have been more than two or three years older than Nud was, with a fresh complexion, bright green eyes and short-cropped, sandy hair. Tall for a Pip, by his amiable expression he seemed an easygoing sort. Near where he worked, a long spear, a weapon more for reach than for throwing by the looks of it, stood leaning against a wall – a wall that was itself leaning.

The shirtless guard called out to them. "Greetings," he said, addressing the group as a whole. He sounded very polite. "Are you good folks coming back this way later today?"

They all stopped, and Bobbin jumped in to answer.

"Yep," he said, but it was Gariff who took it upon himself to speak on the group's behalf.

"Yes, sir," the Stout replied, "Back by evening."

"Will you be here all day?" Holly asked.

"Sure will," replied the guard. "Where are you folks off to today?"

"Err… we're off to do some hiking in Deepweald," Gariff said. "And then we're off to Blackmuk Creek to… ahh…"

Kabor finished the sentence for his cousin. "What he means is… uhh… we're going to Blackmuk to catch some fish."

"Really sparkly fish too, yep, if you catch my meaning," Bobbin added. He winked at the guard, who then flashed him a confused return look.

"Fish, eh?" said the guard, feigned suspicion in his tone. "Where's your fishin' gear?" He rubbed his close-shaven chin and gave them all narrow-eyed, suspicious looks. Not *real* suspicious looks though – they were only for show… for jest.

"Something's a little fishy all right," he added.

"We use our hands," Bobbin interjected.

"A Pip might, but not a Stout," replied the guard, eyeing Gariff.

"He's so ugly, he scares them our way," Bobbin said, "… not much good for anything else."

Gariff raised one arm, backhanded, and shot the Pip a stern look of warning. The guard laughed outright.

"I'm the spotter," Kabor said.

"But your half blind!" Bobbin cried.

"So, let me get this straight," began the guard. "A blind Hill Stout spots the fish, and then an ugly one scares it towards three Pips who corner the fish with their hands and try to catch it. Do I have it right?"

Bobbin answered, his voice chipper. "Yep, that's about right."

"You're missing one part," the guard said to all. Then he winked at Holly and flashed her a smile. The next part he said only to her. "You must be the one who charms the fish if they get scared in the wrong direction."

Holly returned a confident smile. "It's true," she said, and shrugged. "They like me, poor things. Sometimes I even feel sorry for them."

Nud didn't appreciate where the small talk was heading, and he didn't understand why they were making up an elaborate story to explain themselves to the guard of a muddy trail. None of it was his business.

"We're rock-hounding mainly," Nud told the guard straight out, "and a rock-hound doesn't just give away his best turf."

"I hear you," he returned, satisfied. "Now here's something *you* need to hear, so listen up. Word is there's been some trouble on the Outland Trail that we don't need here." He looked to Holly, concerned. "So, if you happen to be going that way, be careful."

Holly smiled shyly. She turned her eyes slightly downward.

The guard addressed the group. "And if you come back this way late, you *will* be given a mandatory escort. You may even have to wait for one to arrive. This is by order of the lord mayor and, well, he's covering our fee, so it won't even cost none to ya… but gratuities are more than welcome, of course!" He grinned as though he was joking, but anyone could see the obvious pitch in it for a little extra take.

Nud caught Holly feeling outside her pocket for a coin.

"Thank you, sir," Nud told him, "but I don't think we'll be needing an escort. We'll get along just fine."

"It's *mandatory*," he repeated.

Holly smiled at the guard, nodded, and then turned to Nud. "Ya Leno-boy, it's *mandatory*… do you know what that means?"

Nud tried to ignore the jab. He addressed the guard directly. "We both know that such orders are never strictly enforced. Besides, no one that I know of has ever needed an escort before. That sort of thing is reserved for important diplomats or wary merchants, and is mostly just for posterity."

"Yep, that may well be true… but those are my orders and I plan to carry them out." The guard winked to Holly.

Bobbin, acting like a complete fool, started dancing about and singing.

"Let's go catch some sparkly fish,
Shiny, sparkly glowy fish.
We'll serve them in a crystal dish,
Snuff the spark and make a wish!"

That earned Bobbin a huge shove from Holly, that sent him flying. The guard broke out laughing.

"I think your big sister has heard enough," he said to

Bobbin. The Pip looked confused for a moment, but chose not to correct him.

On that note, the friends bade farewell to the guard and veered off the main trail, east to Deepweald, leaving behind the mire and the "Stick'n Twine Outpost," as Gariff aptly named it. Few travelers ventured the way they were headed, ever since a freezing over of relations with Fort Abandon – Gan's main ally and trading partner. The Elderkin, of late, mostly kept to themselves in the heart of Deepweald Forest, and didn't take kindly to uninvited visitors. Nud didn't know exactly how Paplov and Fyorn had become such good friends under such circumstances, but the old Pip seemed to be the exception to the rule, being a diplomat and all.

After a good hour-long hike, the wind rose up with a cruel bite to it. The five quickened their pace and soon crossed into the cool shade of Deepweald, welcoming them with its sheltering trees. Nud kept to the middle of the trail, steering clear of suspicious looking branches and tree hollows – a habit he'd gotten into. Treading deeper into the forest, the woodland trail seemed more confining than ever, overgrown and in dire need of clearing. Drooping branches loomed above their heads and many trees leaned heavily into the trail or had fallen across it over the years. Twisting roots curled out of the ground and threatened to trip them up, but at least they remained still.

By mid-morning, they'd climbed the long, rocky hill that brought them to the woodsman's territory. An unseen crow sawed out a warning and announced their arrival.

CHAPTER XV

A long overdue visit

Uncle Fyorn had hands as rough as pine bark and a grip like roots that could crush bare rock into rubble. He always extended that gnarly right hand of his to Nud first when visiting with Paplov, and the young Pip's hand always hurt when he shook it.

Nud caught a whiff of smoke on the wind as the party of five rounded the final bend of the woodland trail to Fyorn's log cabin, secluded in the wild.

With crossed arms and a stoic stance, tough old Uncle Fyorn was ready and waiting, as usual, garbed in his bushiest bush clothes with his sleeves rolled up. At first glance, he appeared exactly the way Nud remembered him – the unshaven lumberjack. But there was something different about his uncle that day. He was still long and spindly, with knurled limbs and a slim, solid trunk. Yet, as they marched over, he didn't seem to tower over Nud quite as much as he used to. And his wild dark hair had grown lighter and longer over the years; now tied back and fully tamed, away from his face. And his face, inquisitive and kind, was the same as always, except maybe thinner, more tanned, and showing a bit of weather. Fyorn's eyes shone the same hazel-grey that always seemed to blend in so well with Deepweald, a gentle shade of the sentient forest.

One question lurked behind those all-knowing eyes. At last, Nud would have to own up to what he'd taken so many years ago, and give the woodsman his long-awaited answer. Well, a partial answer anyway.

As the group neared, the woodsman acknowledged Nud with a quick nod, then addressed them all with a smile and a general "welcome," before exchanging names and greeting each one individually. His thick, outstretched hands reached for Holly first, this time. He held both her hands in his with the grace of a duke, and spared her the iron grip. Next was Kabor. A quizzical look came across the woodsman's face as he tried to make sense of the Stout's sideways glances, but he said nothing of it. He gripped Kabor's hand with unbridled enthusiasm, until he saw the Stout's knees begin to buckle. Next was Gariff.

"Brothers?" Fyorn asked, glancing back to Kabor and then to Gariff again.

"Practically," Nud said.

"Cousins," Gariff corrected. Gritting his teeth, the burly Stout held his own against the woodsman's crushing grasp.

When Bobbin's turn came, the young Pip didn't want to give up his hand.

"Hmm." The woodsman exchanged glances with Holly and Bobbin, rubbing his square chin. "Brother and sister?"

"Practically," Kabor said, still massaging his palms.

Holly huffed. "No!" But she couldn't ignore the wanting expression that spread across Bobbin's little round face. "Well... all right. Sort of."

Bobbin spoke up. "It's complicated."

Fyorn extended his hand to Bobbin. "Put'er there, partner," he said. "I promise I'll go easy on you."

Reluctantly, Bobbin obliged. Fyorn grinned widely as he gave him just a bit of a squeeze.

Nud was the last. Fyorn addressed him in his usual way. "Glad to see you, Sir Nud."

"Glad to see you too, Uncle Fyorn." Nud was no sir and Fyorn was no uncle, so they were even, in a sense. Nud extended his right hand and braced himself.

"Sorry about… you know," Nud said. He winced in anticipation.

The woodsman engulfed the aspiring diplomat's hand in his. And while Nud prepared for the worst, Fyorn simply shook his hand… on the firm side but otherwise a rather normal handshake, just like he'd shaken Paplov's in the past. But when the handshake should have been over, Fyorn didn't let go. A serious look came over him, and he raised his eyebrows at Nud.

"I… uh… got your message," Nud said.

Fyorn's eyes narrowed. "Then you must have something for me."

"I have your arrows."

"Is that everything?"

"You mean…"

"You know what I mean."

Holly was standing next to Nud. She whispered into his ear. "Leno, what does he mean?"

Nud shifted his gaze to her and shook his head. "Nothing," he replied, and flicked his chin at her. Then he looked Fyorn in the eye. "That's everything," Nud said. "I don't know where… *it* went after… it got swallowed… I couldn't get it back."

"Swallowed." Fyorn nodded his head slowly in under-standing, then breathed deep and exhaled with a giant sigh. "A most unpredictable thing, it was. Impetuous. Deft." Nud's uncle left the matter at that. Satisfied, he released his grip on the Pip's hand.

Not so bad, Nud thought. His eyes darted to his friends and back. "Paplov's under the weather, so he mentioned to bring some good company along for the trip… and I did. He said you wouldn't mind, and, well, here they are…"

"Good company?" The woodsman grinned, then addressed all. "I don't mind one bit. The more the merrier." He swung his gaze back to Nud. "I really hope your grandfather is back on his feet soon – all this rain lately is to blame, no doubt." Gesturing to round up his sudden guests, Fyorn pressed his top teeth to his bottom lip and let out an airy sound, some-where between a whistle and a loud whisper.

"Fvit-fwit," he called, pointing to the cabin with a dou-ble backwards flick of his thumb. "I was just finishing up an early lunch. Come on in and take a load off – the table is set. Cider's chillin' in the cellar and I just smoked a batch of specs this morning. That'll set you straight." Uncle Fyorn winked at Nud. "And there's maple candy, of course."

The woodsman went ahead and beckoned them to follow. Holly wedged in her first question. "How did you know we were coming?"

Nud's uncle was quick to reply. "Well, that's easy," he said, striding beside her as they made their way to the cabin. "It was the wind that told me, and the birds that cry out and take flight, and the insects that scatter, and the chipmunks that run up the tree trunks. These woods are like old friends that take in everything that happens, and I happen to know these old friends very well."

Bobbin fanned the air in front of his face. "I know the sensation," he quipped, "the wind tells all when Gariff is coming too…"

The offended Stout shot the young Pip a scornful look.

"Just keep your own wind outdoors," Kabor said. "It's a small cabin." He looked to Fyorn. "No offense."

Fyorn acknowledged the comment with a humbled smile.

Gariff chuckled. "One who is constantly eating is constantly—"

"Boys!" Holly broke in, like a stern mother. She shook her head at them all, then shrugged Fyorn an apology on their behalf. "Forgive them. They're nitwits."

Uncle Fyorn opened the cabin door. A warm waft of dry air invited them in. Inside, the space felt more closed in than Nud remembered, but no less hot with its sturdy woodstove on a low burn.

They'd entered the kitchen, which was also the bedroom, the dining room, and the living room all in one. Behind the door, they hung their cloaks on wooden pegs, next to an assortment of gear and outerwear also hanging there. Gariff hung up his adventuring hat too, and then he and Nud set their packs down on the floor, careful not to nudge a masterfully fashioned longbow tucked away in the corner. Bobbin shrugged off his own deflated backpack, far less stuffed than when they'd left.

Gariff swept his gaze over the room. "Great place ya gots here, sir," he said, sizing up the structure. He grabbed a support and tried to shake it. It didn't budge. "Simple, but practical… and solid built." Next, Gariff stepped to the kitchen table and gave it a hard knock. "And this here table, well, it'll just about last forever." The maple slab was heavily marred with stains and nicks. Five covered plates and five goblets had been set on the table, along with utensils, one dirty plate, and one goblet half-filled with cider – all made of wood.

Kabor headed straight for the table while Nud scooped water from the woodstove's reservoir and poured it into the washbasin. All three Pips used it to clean up. Over the washbasin, a small window overlooked the path to the cabin. The late morning sun shone through the dusty glass, diffuse and skittery.

"Please, grab a plate," Fyorn told them. "They're all the same." Kabor had already taken his seat.

Holly chose a seat across from Fyorn's abandoned spot. Bobbin went to sit beside her, but Nud squeezed in between the two of them. Fyorn served fish with cider and maple candy. The fresh meat melted in Nud's mouth and the candy was sweet and fresh. Time and again, Uncle Fyorn made his rounds as the boys made busy with their forks. He paced the length of the table with a jug and topped up their cups with cider as they chewed. Unlike the others, Holly only picked at her food. The moment Nud's uncle sat down; she had a question for him.

"Hope you don't mind me asking, but how old are you?" She topped her question off with a coy smile that only she could get away with, after such an off-the-cuff question.

Fyorn popped his last piece of fish into his mouth as he contemplated his reply. When he was done chewing, he asked her something: "How old are you?" he said, "if you don't mind *me* asking?"

"Seventeen," she answered.

"Sishteen," Bobbin corrected. A piece of fish slid out of his mouth and stuck to the bottom of his lip.

"Well, I'm *almost* seventeen," Holly said.

"Can I have some more fish, please, Uncle Fyorn?" asked Bobbin. "This stuff is great! Tastes like meaty candy. We could serve it at the Flipside. Can I have the recipe too?" He looked to Holly. "Sixteen."

"You can have more fish," Fyorn said. "As for the recipe… it's a bit of an experiment every time."

Holly flashed Bobbin an annoyed glance, then stopped everything and fixed her steady gaze on Fyorn as he drank his cider and swished it in his mouth. She studied him patiently. When it seemed as though the woodsman might skip the topic altogether, she made sure to keep it alive.

"I hear that the Elderkin never die," she said.

Fyorn gulped down the liquid, lowered his goblet and grinned kindly. "You are relentless, aren't you?"

Holly nodded, gazing up at him with sparkling eyes, her hair tousled from the wind and falling onto her shoulders in waves of rich, reddish-brown.

"Mr. Numbit says I'm *really* good at finding people out," she boasted. "He says I make them feel comfortable, like someone they know, and for that they open up to me… and maybe leave a fair gratuity."

"Well, Holly," Fyorn responded, "I think your talent works quite well out here too – I feel quite comfortable and at ease." He snickered momentarily. "And you certainly are getting the scoop on things, with that attitude."

Holly smiled as she soaked in the compliment. Fully captivated by the Elderkin's presence and the attention he gave her, even her eyes seemed to grin. She arched her back and leaned forward against the table, resting her elbows on the wooden slab and cupping her chin within her palms. Her shirt rode up her back a little, revealing her lean torso, splotched with dabs of muted green.

"As for your question," Nud's uncle continued, "unfortunately, we – the Elderkin – are as trapped as all of you, in these decaying bodies. None of us expect to live forever. In fact, I've seen Elderkin lose their lives by the hundreds in the Outland Wars."

Fyorn lifted his goblet, took another swig of cider, and set it down again with a knock. "I'm afraid, Holly, that Elderkin are just like everyone else, except some have found a way to rejuvenate – to renew their lives again and again, and live longer."

Kabor interjected. His knowledge of history always impressed Nud. "The Elderkin weren't the only ones to make such a discovery," he added. "The old-worlders of Fortune Bay who banished the Elderkin for dabbling in such arts ended up doing exactly the same thing, didn't they?"

Fyorn winced slightly. "Almost true. Sorry, what was your name again?"

"Kabor," said the Stout.

The woodsman sighed and rubbed his day-old stubbles. His look was ever rugged and wild, but when he spoke, his voice took on an air of sophistication.

"To give you a sense," he began again, "after the *Grey Revolt*, those who were exiled from Fortune Bay entered Deepweald and founded the Hidden City. With only simple, natural means at their disposal, they continued their outlawed studies and invented a way to pass longevity to their unborn children, although they themselves went to their graves just as their parents did before them. As you mentioned, Kabor, others also learned how to cheat death to some degree, but it was for themselves and not their offspring, and at great cost. That, however, is another story."

Uncle Fyorn shifted his gaze to the small window above the washbasin. A narrow beam of sunlight caught his eyes. In that brief moment, a bright amber ring burned around his pupils. He turned his attention to the Flipside hostess sitting across from him.

"I hate to disappoint you, Holly," he said, "but Elderkin rejuvenation does not apply to me. You see, I am only half-Elderkin – *Wild* Elderkin as they say, as are all the tribes of this forest. The full-blooded ones, the *High* Elderkin, only live in Gan. I'm afraid that I'm nearly as old as I look."

"You basically look like someone from Abandon Bay, in his middle years," Holly said.

"Interesting you should say that," Fyorn replied. "My father was from the bay area."

Holly seemed to be in danger of finding out more about Nud's uncle and the Elderkin in one day than Nud had learned over the past ten years. Not that he hadn't been interested, or attentive… he just never thought to ask such things. Paplov usually did all the talking.

The woodsman leaned forward, placing his own elbows on the table and folding his hands together. Streaks of earthy brown and dark green stained the sleeves of his shirt. Heavy leather patches covered his elbows. He whispered to Holly, but they could all hear his words.

"One-hundred and two," he said, then pulled away with an apologetic grin.

With gaping mouths, all those present looked Nud's uncle up and down, trying to justify the years in him. But Fyorn didn't look much older than Gariff's dad who, strong as he was, always seemed tired and overworked, with big black bags under his eyes. And he looked far younger than Paplov ever did – rougher maybe and certainly more weathered, especially now, but definitely not older.

"You really are an old coot then, aren't you?" Nud said,

"just like Paplov says." The teens laughed and shook their heads in disbelief. Fyorn offered a humble nod.

Bobbin and the cousins finished off the last bits of maple candy and slurped up the final drops of backwash remaining in their cups. Nud slipped some maple candy into his pocket for later, and then requested a few minutes alone with his uncle to discuss the business of the day. Everyone seemed eager to do some exploring. Bobbin strolled over to where Fyorn sat and thanked him for his courtesies. Not to be outdone, Kabor and Gariff thanked him profusely on their way out the door. Holly lingered back.

Nud and his uncle shared a knowing glance, then Nud turned his gaze to Holly. "Fyorn and I have some private matters to discuss," he told her, "town business."

"I won't tell anyone," she said.

"I know that," Nud replied, "but there are rules... You don't want to get us in trouble, do you?"

"No," she said, shaking her head. "But who's going to tell?" Holly paused, let out a sigh, then turned to Fyorn.

"Thank you for the lovely meal," she said.

"It was my pleasure," Fyorn replied. "Now mind the woods and keep an eye on those boys. Make sure they don't stray too far."

Holly shot Nud a stern glance, and then out she went, carrying with her the responsibility of "the older sister." Nud witnessed his friends racing to the creek before she closed the door behind her. The Elderkin ranger and the Webfoot representative finally sat alone at the table, just like Fyorn and Paplov used to always do.

"Your friend Kabor," Fyorn started, "does he have the *shadow vision?*"

"Something like that," Nud replied. "He has trouble

seeing straight on. Don't let him fool you though – he sees more than he lets on."

"Hmm." Fyorn stood up and closed the window shutters, eclipsing the daylight. "It could be that he makes up for what he can't see some other way."

Nud shrugged. "I suppose."

After sparking up a lantern and adjusting the brightness, Fyorn glanced to Nud's backpack. "So, how many arrows for me today?"

"Oh yes, quite a few," Nud announced with pride. "And some fine ones at that. Two full score of arrows, plus another two." He shrugged and couldn't help but laugh over his next words. "I don't know why you need so many… you must miss a lot."

Fyorn scoffed. "That's something Paplov would say." A long silence passed between them. "So, how was Turnsby?"

Uncle Fyorn listened intently as Nud spoke about his official visit to the Stout town with Paplov, the land-lease deal, and Harrow's meddling. The woodsman shook his head angrily when Nud mentioned Harrow's demands regarding the Malevuin River crossing.

"Unbelievable," he said, disdain in his voice. "Taeglin is a buffoon. He never listens to anyone."

"Yet the Council and all the neighboring territories just give in to his every whim," Nud said. "It's pathetic. No one is willing to take action."

Fyorn grunted. "Action comes at a very high price. Unfortunately, Taeglin is a very powerful buffoon."

They both bit their lips and shook their heads.

"Have you heard about the raids in and around Turnsby?" Nud asked. "There was a horrible murder along the Outland Trail. The entire town was buzzing about it."

Nud's uncle nodded his head in acknowledgement, and then offered his own observations.

"Let Paplov know that Wulvers are not to blame. One of my Kith brothers stopped by on his way back from Whisperwood – the packs there are too busy fighting amongst themselves. But one of the nomadic Outlander tribes has set up camp on a tributary of Wellspring Creek, northeast of Old Akeda. They're a nasty bunch – thieves, slavers, and worse… you name it. Apparently, Gorbag the Torturer runs the show – if you can believe that. I think he's been killed about ten times now. A new one just springs up out of their ranks to take his place, every time. They're the bandits likely messed up in your raids. One more note: the council might catch wind of a small band of Scarsanders that slipped past the border guards, last seen skirting the northern edge of the Bearded Hills. Tell Paplov they don't pose a threat – just a few desperate runners, that's all. Our sources tell us they don't have the scar."

"What about in the bog lands?" Nud said.

"Nothing I've heard. Why?"

"No reason… just our blue-tail acted up on the way to Turnsby."

"They can be skittish… do you know the reason?"

Nud shook his head, then reached into his pocket and felt for the bog stone, bundled in leather. Slowly, he began to unravel its cover. A muted flicker of light spilled out of the Pip's pocket for an instant, and lit up the space under the table. Fyorn didn't seem to notice. He'd taken the brief pause to stand up and stretch. Fyorn drummed his fingers along the old wooden slab, as though impatient.

"Well then," Nud's uncle said, "now that that's settled, how 'bout you take those arrows out back, Sir Nud? I'll look'em over in a jiffy. I just need to tidy up a bit first, before the syrup hardens on the plates."

Before Nud could reveal his find or say another word, Fyorn got busy collecting dishes from the mid-day feast.

Later, the Pip decided, and then re-wrapped the stone in his pocket. He grabbed his pack and headed out the door, to the workshop.

Fyorn's shed was nearly as big as his cabin and just a few steps away. Paplov had helped him build it, many years ago. Nud opened the door and stepped inside. The room was cool as the day and smelled of freshly stained wood. He set his pack down and casually glanced about. The place was exactly as he remembered it: a workbench cluttered with tools; wood planks neatly organized by size; big cabinets along the walls; and at the back, hanging animal pelts stretched onto boards, together with paddles for Fyorn's narrow river-crafts. Bins sat here and there, full of bits and pieces of hardware, and an axe leaned against the wall behind the door – a very familiar look-ing axe… *the axe*, in fact. The nicks Nud'd made hadn't quite disappeared in all the sharpenings since; abuses to the blade were many.

The young diplomatic aide stood under the trapdoor in the ceiling and stared up. It, too, looked smaller than before – square and boarded, with no practical way to get up through it.

I never should've ventured up there, Nud told himself.

The real world began to fade away…

CHAPTER XVI

The attic

Tap… tap… tap.

Nud recalled exactly the noise from the attic: crisp and regular, like fingernails on wood.

Tap… tap… tap.

Lying on his belly, the young Pip coughed and sputtered in a cloud of disturbed dust. With the back of one hand, he rubbed his itchy eyes. Winds howled over the rooftop as his vision slowly adjusted. The first thing he saw was a lone sliver of light. It shone in from the outside through a vent in the attic wall. He tracked its course. The sun's rays fanned out into a luminescent sheet, igniting dust motes like silvery sparks as it sliced through the darkness.

The attic itself was a huge, stuffy mess. Dusty junk spewed from every corner: broken furniture and countless old trunks, cords and ropes all jumbled and knotted, faded boots with holes in them, a cracked wooden shield with a tree sigil, and as many odds and ends as possibly imagined. The smell of a small, dead animal lurked in the air.

Tap… tap… tap.

Where is that sound coming from? Nud honed his senses, and waited.

Tap… tap… tap.

There it is again. The sound originated at the far end of the loft.

Tap… tap… tap.

Scratch… scratch.

Nud crept along joists and wriggled between rafters to get to the source. Along the way, he gripped the severed leg of an old wooden table and used it to clear the abandoned cobwebs in his path, drifting off beams and straddling old furniture.

Tap… tap… tap.

Scratch… scratch.

The sound led him to an old metal coffer in the corner on the far side, illuminated by light from the vent. Its dusty lid was spotted with handprints. The box had a caved in side-panel and a broken latch, black and pitted. Nud gripped the latch firmly. The metal was cool to the touch. He hesitated before opening the coffer – the rustling sounds had stopped. The attic had gone quiet. *Does it know I'm near?* Nud tapped the box with the table leg.

Tap… tap… tap.

The attic stayed silent. Then he scratched the box with the edge of it.

Scratch… scratch.

The silence persisted, dull and unsatisfying; like waking up too early in a strange house.

With one hand, the Pip raised the table leg and held it like a club, ready to strike. With the other, he undid the clasp. Slowly and gently, he nudged the lid up against the rusty give of the hinges – just a crack – and waited. *Nothing.*

He could hear his heart beating from the inside. The tension over his body pulled every muscle tight. He stopped breathing, and creaked the lid a little higher… higher… higher still. He tensed his grip on the club. His heart began to pound. *Still nothing…*

TAP… TAP… TAP.

"Aaah!" Nud yelped, and released the lid. It slapped down but not shut. Dust billowed up. He swung the table leg hard and smacked the lid tight, then scrambled backwards into a pile of moldy books.

But he didn't retreat. Instead, heart pumping wildly, Nud sat there on the pile of junk, eyes fixed to the coffer. It didn't move or make a sound. The wind gusted up again and branches scraped against the outside of the shed, then fell off into a hush-hush. He waited for the dust to clear.

Slowly, the Pip regained his nerve and crawled back to the coffer. He took a deep breath and flipped the lid open. This time, a puff of terrible smell rose up, oily like old fish, but with a metal tang to it. Nud shifted sideways so as not to block the light. Holding his breath, he stretched his neck out over the coffer to peer inside. Forgotten things, broken and useless, were scattered about its bottom and covered in a sticky residue. A thousand dead insects had gotten themselves stuck in there, and a precious few barely alive ones still tugged on their immobile parts. The tapping started up again.

Tap… tap… tap.

And the scratching.

Scratch… scratch.

A box within a box. Many and more unusual objects filled that coffer as well. Their strange designs Nud could not identify or even begin to imagine the purpose of. Some may have been tools after some fashion. Others had fleshy surfaces with oily threads sticking out everywhere – bits and pieces of broken creations not wholly natural. And amidst the clutter and sticky mess of tar was a shoebox-sized container made of dark wood. Clearly, it did not belong with the rest.

Tap... tap... tap.

Scratch.

Tap... tap... tap.

Scratch.

Tap... tap... tap.

Scratch... scratch.

The noises emanated from the dark wood box, more urgent than ever. Nud rested the table leg beside him.

It didn't occur to him that he should just leave the box right where it lay. And it didn't occur to him that history might one day paint a fairer picture of the past if only he'd done just that. The tapping intensified.

TAP... TAP... TAP.

The dark wood box was plain in its design and nailed firmly shut. Scorched onto the lid was a crude representation of the Hidden City of Gan – high towers fronting a misty waterfall. Nud yanked the box free from all the goo and stickiness underneath.

The Pip weighed the box in his quivering hands. It was heavier than it looked. He felt along the edges and found the lid to be a tight fit, with some kind of resin seal.

TAP... TAP...TAP.

"Aaah!" The vibration shot through him like a violent shiver. He fumbled the box. It dropped back into the coffer.

A long pause followed, and then the pattern changed.

tap... tap... tap.

scritch... scratch.

Submissive. Wanting.

tap… tap… tap.

scritch… scratch.

Like a cry for help?

Nud took deep breaths to gather up his nerves again. *It can't hurt you*, he told himself. *Whatever it is, it's stuck in there.* Muscles tight and jerkiness in every limb, he lifted the box back out.

tap… tap… tap.

This time, he didn't let the eerie vibration get to him.

Box in hand, Nud made his way back through the attic clutter to the trapdoor. With a loud thump, he dropped down onto the workbench. A bucket went flying and Nud's ankle twisted, but he held on to that box as though the fate of the world depended on it.

The tapping had stopped completely. Nud gave the box a slight shake. It felt like dead weight inside.

Then he heard talking – Paplov, on his way over from the cabin. He sounded hoarse, his voice on the verge of loss.

"Nud?" he rasped, and then cleared his throat. He mumbled something to Uncle Fyorn. Nud didn't hear all of it, but it started with "He better not be…"

Their footsteps drew near.

"Nud, are you in there?" Paplov said. "We heard something crash. What are you up to?"

Nud tucked the box under one arm and slid under the workbench. Then he dragged Fyorn's big ranging pack in front of him. He heard a click as the door handle turned, and gulped air to hold his breath. Someone stepped in.

"We're going out to fetch some dead wood," Fyorn said. "Wanna come?"

Nud ignored his uncle's call. He stayed hidden under the table, breathless. Whatever was in the box kept quiet as well.

"Humph." Fyorn's feet shuffled and his boots knocked. "I guess he's not in here after all."

Soon after they left, Nud quietly closed the trap door, pushed the table back in place, and then snuck out of the workshop. On his way out, he grabbed the hatchet beside the door. He wasn't exactly sure why he took it, but the thought crossed his mind that a hatchet might come in handy. It did… and it nearly got him killed.

CHAPTER XVII

An Elderkin perspective

"nud?" called a small voice, like a whisper inside itself. The faint sound twisted its way through a paradox and fell like hissing rain, only to drain away.

Nud did not respond. He could not respond. How can anyone respond to something like that?

The door to the workshop creaked open.

"NUD?" This time the voice slammed his ears and knocked him out of recall. There was a moment of blurriness, vertigo. Solid hands clamped his shoulders tight. The spin of the world began to slow; the image began to clarify. A part of a face came into view. Borrowed from the here and now, his uncle's hawk-eyed stare met Nud's own blank gaze. The woodsman was expecting an answer.

The arrows.

"I'm back," Nud said. "I'm here."

Fyorn knew all about Pip recall, so Nud didn't have to explain himself. Carefully, Nud's uncle let go his hold. Once assured that the Pip could stand on his own two feet, Fyorn tilted his gaze up to the hatch in the ceiling, then back down to Nud.

A tingling sensation swept across the back of Nud's neck. He swallowed hard, then shifted his gaze away, too ashamed to bear the brunt of the woodman's penetrating stare. Nud felt like a child, as though the incident had just happened, as though Fyorn had just discovered him cowering beneath the very workbench he now stood next to. Not that such displacement is unusual after recall; it just caught Nud out of sorts.

The Pip turned and casually shuffled towards the backpack, as nonchalantly as a guilty person with shaky knees could. Still in half a daze, Nud stooped over, yanked up the pack and ferried it back to the workbench. He undid the drawcord, without looking up. Lightheaded but determined, Nud hauled out the deepwood arrows and set them on the workbench in front of his uncle.

Fyorn picked up one arrow and brought it to eye level. He peered down its shaft and gave it a quick bend. Next, he tugged at the feather fletching and wiggled the arrowhead. Then he rested the arrow on one finger and found its point of balance. Finally, he wrapped his hand around the balance point and gave the arrow a gentle shake, as if to gauge the weight of it. He made a satisfied "hmph" sound followed by a satisfied nod. A subtle, impressed smile formed on his lips.

"Not bad," he said, and proceeded to inspect a handful more the same way, with the same results. "Not bad at all. Straight, solid and well-balanced… that's what I need. I like the blending."

Still eyeing the workmanship, he hit Nud with an unexpected comment: "I see now why you have not returned in so many years."

"Pardon?" Nud said.

The woodsman's gaze shifted from the arrow to Nud's arm. "The Mark," he said. "When did you receive it?"

"The Mark?"

Fyorn tapped the Pip's wrist twice with an arrow, put it down, and then picked up another.

"Your wrist," he added.

"Oh, *that* mark," Nud said. "It's nothing, really. Paplov says it's a stubborn rash."

"How long have you had it?"

"Since about… the last time I came here."

"I see."

Fyorn fingered through a few more arrows and lightly scrutinized each one with little more than a passing glance. Then he rested them on the pile and shifted his gaze to Nud.

"Let me have a look at that thing," he said, gesturing to Nud's arm.

Nud raised the limb and exposed his inner wrist. The woodsman gently took hold of Nud's forearm and held it steady, then applied that same examining look.

"How?" he asked.

"A tree's whipping branch hit me when I was running," Nud said.

"So, you were running through the woods and you swung your arm into a branch? Is that what happened?"

"Not exactly."

"I didn't think so."

Fyorn released his grip. "It's not a rash, Nud." Then he twisted his own forearm to reveal his inner wrist. Nud could hardly believe his eyes. He too bore the Mark, and like Nud's, the symmetry of the pattern was so fine and intricate it could have passed for ink.

"Such strange ways," Nud's uncle muttered, with a slight

shake of his head, as though rejecting a bad idea. A moment later, he was back to his usual self.

"Nud, thank you for bringing me the seekers," he said. "The craftsmanship… masterful, as always. And thank Paplov too for me, would you?"

"Sure," Nud said. "And you're very welcome, as always. You do so much for us, to keep us informed."

"Did you make any for yourself?"

"Not many," the Pip responded.

Nud's uncle scooped up half a dozen arrows in his rugged hands.

"Keep these for target practice. Next time you visit, I'll teach you a few tricks about archery. Deepwood has a special… quality to it. I'd do it now, but I don't like the idea of your friends running about with arrows flying through the trees."

"You're not *that* bad a shot," Nud quipped.

Fyorn frowned and handed the arrows over to the young Pip.

"I have something else for you to bring back as well," Fyorn went on. And without a moment's delay, Nud's uncle was off to the far end of the workshop where he kept his best stock.

Nud tucked the arrows away while the Elderkin rummaged through a large, wooden bin. A minute later, he was back with an armful of deepwood, neatly tied, which Nud stuffed into his pack until it bulged. The Pip pulled the drawcord tight around those awkward pieces sticking out over the top, and then tested the weight. Although not overly heavy, it would be cumbersome. Pips hate burdens, and Nud was no exception.

"I threw in two exceptional pieces of deepwood," Fyorn

said. "Paplov will know which ones. The thick one with the big burl on one end is destined for woodcarving, and the other one… well… I am not sure exactly what it's good for, but surely, he will find some use for it. I'd throw in more, but your pack is a little on the small side."

Nud acknowledged with a nod and slung the pack over one shoulder. He winced as the strap dug into his already-chafed skin there. Having finished in the workshop, they made for the cabin.

As Nud stepped out of the door, voices of child-like commotion filtered through the trees. And as he made his way along the covered walkway, Holly screamed.

The outcry jolted Nud. His body tensed. But the soft echoes of laughter that followed soon put him back at ease.

Once back in the cabin, Uncle Fyorn and Nud got to talking again. Many small matters the woodsman revealed as they put away the dishes that he'd set to dry. Pleasantries aside though, Nud still had a purpose to fulfill, and he'd spent half a day already just dancing around it. The others could be back any minute. *To heck with the dishes*, he told himself. The time had come.

"You need to see something," was all Nud said. He walked over to the table. At last, Nud pulled out his bog stone, unraveled the leather, and placed the curious find square in the middle of the slab. With the first flash of light, his uncle's eyes lit up as wide as an owl's. The man gaped in wonder at the trail of sparks that followed.

"How… wherever did you obtain such a thing?"

"Well," Nud started, "I was with Gariff on Blackmuk Creek and… well… I heard the wind blow up and a crow caw and… well… it made me look and then, well… I fell into a sinkhole full of bog bodies and… climbing out, this stone was just sitting there, caught up in some gnarly old tree roots, then—"

"Sinkhole? Bog bodies? Tree roots? What sort of tree roots? What did they look like?"

Remembering is one thing, describing, quite another. Fyorn seemed to get that.

"I was hoping *you* could tell *me* what it is," Nud said. And when the Pip tried to answer his uncle's questions and describe the event more fully, he fumbled every word. The woodsman put up his hand to interject, his voice calming.

"Enough," he said. "Clearly, it was not chance alone that brought this fanciful stone to you. Nud, I can tell by the way it happened that there are 'Wilder' forces at work here, and that it was meant to be… the Mark, the stone… everything – gift or bane, the 'Hurlorns' have chosen."

"Meant to be? Wilder forces? Hurlorns? What are Hurlorns?"

The translucent gem flashed a trail of red sparks, on and off like a firefly. Fyorn fixed his gaze on it. His voice was telling.

"I do not mean to say that what happened was meant to be in the sense of the greater cosmos or the grand scheme of things, heavens no. How could I even speculate on such a thing? I mean it in the sense of what might be the next best thing though… a higher consciousness in our midst, but it is just out of reach for most. We do not tap into it… not usually, but it is no less there because we are naïve."

The woodsman's mystifying words might have confused even the Diviner. Fyorn read Nud's puzzled expression like an open book. He let out a heavy sigh.

"I think it's time you learned something of Hurlorns," he said, "since they seem to have included you in their plans."

"Plans?"

"Yes, Nud, plans. Maybe 'designs' is a better word. Have a seat."

Nud took the middle seat, back to the wall, and Fyorn took his directly across from the Pip, the stone set to flicker between them. The woodsman rested his elbows on the table and sat forward, hands folded together, his thick fingers marred by fresh nicks and old scars.

"Hurlorns are far more than just trees," he began. "That much is obvious. The sages of Gan have studied the most common sorts extensively: 'Sleepers' they are called. A hold-over from the days when behemoths walked these lands and hunted them for food, it is generally believed that early Hurlorns were more like giant bugs than trees, slow moving terrestrial invertebrates that fed on swarms of insects and vegetation. They had no hope of outrunning or outsmarting the crafty predators that pursued them. However, over time, the early Hurlorns adapted. And they developed some interesting defenses nonetheless."

The light continued to flicker on and off intermittently as he spoke, with five or ten seconds of dormancy between every flash-stream. The strange illumination was becoming part of the background, part of what was normal.

"First off," he continued, "Hurlorns evolved ways to blend in with the forest by mimicking features of the vegetation they consumed – green and brown coloration and the ability to remain absolutely still, for instance. As time went on, they also developed ways to pass messages over distances and to warn one another of a predator's destructive path. The messaging became more complex over time, and the distances greater. Having become observant and thoughtful, Hurlorns began to record the knowledge they gained and share it amongst themselves so that any one of them could access the whole – the beginnings of the consciousness I speak of. It took millennia upon millennia to evolve the capability into what it is today."

Nud listened intently as Fyorn explained further.

"At some point," he said, "there was a kind of divergence. As the behemoths got better at searching, some Hurlorns became better at hiding, even taking on the physical traits of trees – exoskeletons like bark, appendages like roots and branches, long narrow bodies and even leaves of a sort. A portion gave up movement altogether – content to live out sedentary lives. Those ones are the Sleepers."

Fyorn shrugged. "Others, well, they continued to become smarter. It seemed to happen all at once, actually, according to the sages who look into the past through the natural record."

The stone flared up super-bright with Fyorn's last words, and then stopped just as abruptly. A long pause in activity followed, during which time Nud processed what his uncle was telling him. *The tree creature I saw was real,* he thought to himself. He'd known it all along, really. No words passed between them until, finally, Nud broke the silence.

"How would the sages know all of that?" he asked, skepticism in his tone.

"Oh, they have their ways," Fyorn replied. "Fossil records, for one. Perhaps brain cavity measurements, movement patterns – I do not know. I have to confess I cannot say how they disentangle the past to such detail, but I will say this: if given the luxury to study a problem for a hundred years, I imagine one might obtain a pretty good handle on it."

The Elderkin certainly had a point. Another bright flare-up occurred. Fyorn waited for the flickering to teeter off, before continuing.

"When prodded, Hurlorns tell a different story of their coming, more myth than fact if you ask me, but if looked at the right way, it pretty much lines up with what the sages are saying, although with a little more drama."

"Behemoths," Nud said. "What happened to the behemoths?"

Fyorn shrugged. "No one really knows." Then he smirked. "Perhaps their food outsmarted them."

Nud chuckled. "Why doesn't everyone know about them – the Hurlorn trees?"

Fyorn wagged a scolding finger at him. "Remember Nud," he said, "it's in their nature to remain hidden and to whisper secretly amongst themselves. You will never breed that out of them."

"Then why did a Hurlorn tree reveal itself to me?"

"You do not say 'Hurlorn tree,' Sir Nud... it's just 'Hurlorn,'" Fyorn corrected. "You can say 'tree' as well, if you like; that will not offend. They feel a close kinship with trees."

"Okay," Nud replied.

"Unless you're talking about *Spirit Hurlorns*, that is," the woodsman added. "They're totally separate... much more sophisticated... and 'trees' simply won't do for them."

"All right then," Nud said. "Are there any other kinds to worry about?"

Fyorn winced. "Only one. But there hasn't been one of those for... well... since I was about your age."

"What happened to it?" Nud said.

"The forest has many secrets," Fyorn explained. "Sometimes, the secrets are best kept that way."

He knows, Nud decided, *but for some reason he can't tell me, or won't tell me.*

Fyorn paused, pricking his ears to the sounds outside. Nud's friends' voices filtered in from a distance, confirming that none were near. Following that, the woodsman stood up and casually strode over to the lantern to dim the light. When back at the table, he furrowed his brow as he watched the bog stone flicker on. Arms crossed again, Fyorn just stood there and drew in a deep breath, as though to speak. When the words did come out, something in his voice had changed. He sounded different, more serious. For many and most, such gravity in tone would not be a strange thing. But for the woodsman it made all the difference. He'd never been so completely earnest with the Pip as in that moment.

"Nud," he said, "the Mark of the Hurlorn is something most often reserved for bearers of precious knowledge that the Hurlorns value, knowledge that must be preserved at all costs. It is received from time to time by great heroes and sages, and those that have performed some great service and proven their worth."

"I'm no hero or sage," Nud replied, "and I'm not sure who I've proven my worth to. I'm only fifteen and the aide to a diplomat of the smallest community anywhere."

"Fifteen," repeated my uncle, and then he raised one eyebrow. "Humph."

"You have a mark too," Nud said. "What *precious* knowledge do you possess that must be preserved?"

"Well Nud," he said, amused at the brashness of the Pip's query, "first you must understand that Hurlorns are known to mark their own as they see fit, and for the most part without any discernable rhyme or reason to it. Being obvious is not their way – that much I can vouch for personally. There are times though when, in retrospect, I can say that they saw something coming, and in their own way planned for it by selecting the talents needed to deal with the situation well in advance. I do not know why a Hurlorn chose to mark you, Nud. You are a most peculiar and unprecedented choice. I am sure the Hidden King would not approve, but something tells me he was not consulted. As for myself, the Kith are the exception. We receive the Mark as a matter of course to bind us to the Hurlorns and to our brothers who came before us. It is not so much for our knowledge of great things as for our services rendered. Our community is one in the same with the Hurlorns. We are joined."

The woodsman picked up the rough, amber-like gemstone. He wore a weighing expression as he observed it emit another series of flashes. Nud had seen that look on his face before when he spoke with Paplov, discussing delicate political situations and wondering what to do without setting someone off. He seemed to be deliberating. Raising the stone to eye level, he rolled it repeatedly in his hand – the one that bore the Mark – and he examined each facet one by one. Then something changed.

Fyorn suddenly tensed. His eyes widened, like fear. His head jerked up and the vessels in his neck bulged. He drew a frantic breath. The lantern snuffed out completely as wood all around the cabin began to twist and creak – the floorboards, the walls, everything.

"Uncle Fyorn?" Nud stood up and backed away from the table. The light itself brightened, almost burning. The heavy table slid. And Fyorn's arm... his wrist... the Mark there began to bleed. Blood trickled down and dripped to the floor. The Elderkin let the stone drop.

And it fell.

The next instant, a deeper darkness flooded the room with a chill like death in winter. Nud heard the stone clatter on the tabletop. His bones turned to ice.

A long minute passed, and then everything went back to normal. Dim, yellow light spilled forth from the lantern, and daylight filtered through cracks around the shutters on the kitchen window. The fire in the woodstove flared up and the warmth returned. The mysterious stone from the bog resumed its usual pattern of flicker.

Fyorn held his wrist tight in his other hand, blood dripping through to his fingers and onto the floor. His breaths were heavy and quick. Nud dashed to get something – a washcloth – and handed it to his uncle. With a concerned look on his face, the Elderkin accepted the cloth and wrapped it around his arm. Nud tied it for him, tight, then pushed the table back into place.

"Are you all right?" Nud said. He'd never seen Fyorn so much as flinch before in all his life.

His uncle nodded. "Everything is fine," he assured the Pip. Fyorn took a deep breath and exhaled.

"What happened?" Nud asked.

"I don't know really, Nud," Fyorn replied. "I don't know for sure. It was like… it was like a ringing; a ringing that became stronger and stronger until I was ready to burst."

Carefully, slowly, he took his seat. Nud sat back down across from him, grabbed the stone and returned it to his pocket.

"I know what you mean," Nud said. "I felt something like that too – before. Like a buzzing in my head. Weird things happened."

"They will not stop happening," his uncle warned.

Nud sighed. "Someone could get hurt. Should I destroy it then? Put it back in the bog? Give it to you?"

Fyorn waved his palms at Nud. "It isn't meant for me. That much is clear."

"What, then?"

For a long while, Nud's uncle just breathed, without answering.

"Can I get you some water?" Nud said.

Slowly, Fyorn shook his head. Finally, he spoke.

"This is your dilemma to solve, Nud. There is no second-guessing the Hurlorns, so just do what you need to do." He rubbed his wrist.

"Your friends," he continued, "they seem like a good bunch. Can you trust them to keep a secret?"

Nud wasn't sure how to answer that. He certainly didn't want his uncle to discover how careless he'd been at the Flipside. He just nodded.

"Good friends are important in the world," his uncle added. "May I see your stone again? Don't worry; I won't touch it this time."

Nud took the stone out again and held it in front of Fyorn. The woodsman gazed at it – into it, more like, all the while applying pressure to his wrist.

"A natural beauty in the rough," he said as the next flurry of flashes lit up the cabin. "I have never seen anything like this."

"I will have to find out more in Gan," he went on, "… Crimson Tower sages with access to the archives, perhaps. Best to keep your stone under wraps for the time being. As I alluded to, I suspect there is a deeper meaning to all of this. On the off chance you happen to find any other stones like this one, please do bring them here, to me, for safekeeping."

"Really?" Nud said, unable to conceal the disappointment in his voice. After all, he'd already planned a treasure hunt.

"If you're wondering about value," Fyorn added, "I'm fully certain the sages of Gan will offer more than a fair price for such rare wonders, after determining exactly what it is you've found."

That works, Nud thought. *Gariff will like that – a guaranteed buyer already.*

Fyorn nodded. "They might even cut and polish something like this to adorn the king's crown."

Nud said, "I have it on good authority that it's some kind of ancient tree gum."

Fyorn raised an eyebrow at Mer's assessment. "Ahh," he said, nodding in acknowledgement. "I'm not completely surprised to hear that."

The woodsman grasped Nud's hand and closed the Pip's fingers around the bog stone. "I don't know what more to tell you, except to say that what you've found is something unknown to humankind. I can tell you something more about the Mark though. Of that, I have done my own collecting for my own reasons, as you have seen."

Uncle Fyorn laid his left arm flat on the table, slowly undid the cloth, and showed Nud his wrist. The bleeding had stopped. His mark seemed to spread out radially from mid wrist. On the dark edges that defined the boundary, green tendrils curled up and out, then dove sharply into his skin, as though the image had been stitched on. He wiped the area as clean as he could, then shot a slight nod to Nud's arm.

Nud also laid his left arm on the table, the Mark fully exposed. His appeared faint compared to Fyorn's. From a central axis instead of a point, pale dots with fractured geometry branched out in elaborate looping patterns that curled in on themselves, smaller and tighter until they disappeared. There were no tendrils.

"According to the archives in Gan," Fyorn explained, "the Mark will grant you a choice at a time when choices do not exist, in true Elderkin fashion. You may choose, one day, to live among the Hurlorns – as a *Spirit Hurlorn* – or instead, pass on to whatever fate awaits you. It will be your choice. Those rare and unique Hurlorns who once walked the earth on two legs as you and I do now, who then cross over to become custodians of the forest, are the uncommon exception rather than the rule. They grow to become the keepers of our knowledge and history, captains of our forest guard, and may even become great leaders."

The idea seemed magical and wondrous to Nud.

"You mean… I can be a Forest King? A Tree King? King of Trees?"

"In a manner of speaking, but not so much a king. The King is in Gan, remember?"

Nud nodded.

"And there is no 'King of Trees.'" The woodsman shook his head and smiled. "Heavens no. But… in good time, among the Spirit Hurlorns one may grow to become *the Green Dragon of Deepweald.* I don't know how that happens."

"That's a myth," Nud said. He hadn't heard of Hurlorns before, but the Green Dragon was legendary.

Fyorn's eyes met Nud's with a steady gaze, his words unhindered by the Pip's doubts. "And when the day finally comes to cross over," he went on, "your former life must be abandoned. That is the oath taken to receive the gift of renewal. There is no turning back once you decide to follow that path."

Nud's uncle smiled, reached across the table and placed his hand on the Pip's shoulder, then patted it.

"And one more thing," he said. "You can just call me Fyorn now. You are no longer a child. You do not need a made-up uncle."

Nud couldn't help but to feel a little empty at the suggestion.

CHAPTER XVIII

Interlude – The way around

What does it mean to wake up in the morning? Are you the same person that you were when you fell asleep? – of course you are. Your memories tell you so and your body is still your body. But what if one day you awaken in a body that is not your own, yet you still remember everything about yourself. Are "you" still "you"? Is that reincarnation?

I can't answer that yet. Little by little though, the pieces will come together. The recipe for Spirit Hurlorn Incarnation – or "incarnation" for short – isn't something you just serve cold. You have to heat it up a bit, add sauce and spices, and then let the idea simmer for a while. Oh, how I miss a real meal cooked to perfection on a potbelly stove! As I said, it will all become clear, soon enough, in the telling.

You are probably wondering why I bothered to ask if there is such a thing as magic. Well, consider this: To take an incarnate form such as mine, you have to first perish... sort of... and then *transmute*. Magic didn't bring me here. It might look like magic and smell like magic, but it isn't magic – unless perhaps you're a troglodyte. Then to you, magic is a good enough explanation. It's all you'll ever get out of me. Trying to explain more to a trog wouldn't be worth my time – precious time – such a primitive mind would never get it. But you're smarter than that, aren't you? Think about it. Magic would be kinder – like the good magic in faerie tales that wakes sleeping princesses and transforms animated china back into the people they once were. Get those thoughts out of your head. It just looks that way.

Don't get me wrong – I'm comfortable in my new form, or rather, "comfortable in my own bark" to butcher a common saying. But I have to say that I'm not exactly sure what I am right now.

"Where does my soul reside?" – I can't answer that either. That's what really gets me.

"Am I still really me?" – yet another mystery to ponder.

"If not, who else could I be?" – well… no one, I suppose, to any observer apart from my former self. It all gets very confusing to my wood-warped brain.

Here comes the rain. I can hear it on the leaves. Wait… false alarm… that was only the angry front of a windy drizzle. Finally, our young storm is building! It's what we've been waiting for all along. Soon, I will have to forsake this grove and seek cover. Pardon any watermarks you might encounter on the coming pages.

CHAPTER XIX

Treasure hunting

Before hitting the woodland trail, Fyorn aimed to deliver each of the boys another one of his famous handshakes. Pockets stuffed full of taffy, Bobbin lined up first. The woodsman hardly squeezed his hand before he squealed like a pig.

Kabor's hands were bloodied, so the two just bumped fists. "Hang in there," Fyorn told him. The Hill Stout had taken a tumble while running near a creek.

Gariff challenged the woodsman by squeezing back with all his might. He gritted his teeth and contorted his body to lever into it, grunting ferociously. Nud couldn't say that Fyorn even noticed. At least, that's how he acted. He even yawned and then excused himself.

"Goodbye, Sir Nud," he said at last. "You and Paplov should come by more often."

"Goodbye, Uncle Fyorn," Nud said – a slip of the tongue.

Fyorn tilted his head slightly and raised his eyebrows. "No need to call me 'uncle' anymore, right?"

Nud sighed. "Old habits are hard to break."

"What?" Holly said. She'd just stepped out of the cabin and into the conversation. The Flipside girl narrowed her eyes and shot Nud a suspicious glance.

Nud shrugged, then sputtered. "I… ahh… well…"

"Humph," she huffed. "Well, Goodbye *Uncle* Fyorn," Holly said, and then gave him a gripping hug. "You can still be *my* uncle." Nud got the impression that the woodsman was not completely comfortable with the idea.

Holly took a step back. "Is this the right one?" she asked, holding up an old spotter's cloak. Fyorn had offered it to her for the trip back. That time of year, evenings on the Mire Trail were either bug-free and cool, or warm and buggy, with little in between. Either way, Holly was ill-prepared.

"That's the one," Fyorn replied. "It was made for someone about your size. Now, listen carefully. It's reversible. When worn one way it's a regular cloak, but wear it inside out and it camouflages – a simple redirecting of light to pass around you. There is also a melding quality… you'll see. It usually takes young spotters a few weeks to get the hang of it."

Smiling, she draped it on. The dark material was light and flowy, yet strong, with an unusual sheen to it.

"How does it look?" Holly spun around.

"Perfect fit," Fyorn said.

To Nud's eyes, the cloak seemed rather long for Holly and on the thin side for warding off flies. He didn't say anything though. She donned the hood.

"Thank you, Uncle Fyorn," she said in her best Flipside hostess voice.

The woodsman waved goodbye and shot Nud a final wink. The Pip felt small for not having dropped in earlier. On his way down the hill and away from the cabin, he felt the urge to look back. Nud thought that maybe he should call out and ask Fyorn why he used to have a giant black spider boxed up in his attic. Nud did look back, but only to wave one last time. Then he turned to the path ahead and just kept on walking, silent. *The visit had gone well*, he decided, and left it at that.

*

The woodland part of the trail was hard-packed and rocky, but once the five broke through the tree line and hit the mud flats, the going was softer. All three Pips meandered off the trail and squished their toes into the soft, cool mud underfoot, while the two Hill Stouts stuck to higher, firmer ground.

Midday had come and gone, and Holly began her chatter as soon as they hit the open territory. Nud wondered if she'd purposely held her tongue until out of Fyorn's woods.

"Hey Leno," she said, skipping past him. She spun around and walked backwards. "Did you see those high cheekbones and lean, chiseled features? I could tell right away he wasn't related to you."

Nud shook his head. "Obviously. I mean, he's Elderkin and I'm not."

"And those eyes… I could almost see the secrets behind them." Holly's own eyes went wide as she spoke. "So much inner strength… and thoughtfulness. He reminds me of Anexxander – oh, you wouldn't know who he is. Anexxander is a woodland hero in one of the Elderkin stories I read." She turned back around to hike in the same direction as everyone else, then slowed her pace until she came to Nud's side.

He had no idea how to respond to any of that, and was glad Gariff interjected.

"Never mind with all that Elderkin fancy now," the Stout called out.

Fyorn's serious words at the cabin still lingered in the back of Nud's mind. *What could be coming? What do the Hurlorns want with me?* Maybe Hopkins knew something…

"Holly," Nud said, "have you seen anything unusual at the Flipside lately?"

She huffed. "Is this another 'Red Room' question?"

"No." Nud put his hands in his pockets and stared at his feet as he walked. "And… sorry about that." He shot her a quick glance.

Holly kept her gaze straight ahead. "All right then. Like what?"

Nud shrugged. "I don't know… any odd people or strange things, weird conversations maybe."

Holly glanced at him and smiled. "Really, Leno? You just described nearly everyone."

"True enough, I suppose." Nud shook off the uneasy feeling. After all, something completely different from what Fyorn was talking about could be on the horizon – like finding the "mother lode." That, in-and-of-itself, would change everything.

Before long, they hit Blackmuk Creek, spilling out of a spruce bog just east of the Mire Trail. The watercourse wound ever southward, fed by crystal-clear headwaters cascading down a broad limestone staircase. The "muk" itself appeared sporadically as they left the trail and followed the water's course towards Akeda, especially in areas where the creek bulged out into sediment rich holes, abundant in plant and insect life. After a short trek, they came to the site of Nud's find. The woodland aroma of sodden leaves filled the Pip's lungs. Gariff led the way to the pit. Nud surveyed the grounds. Something didn't look quite right. He regarded Gariff.

"Are you sure this is the right place?"

The Stout removed his hat and wiped the sweat from his brow. "That's odd, coming from you."

Nud swept his gaze across the scene again. "No. It looks… different."

Gariff shook his head. "Same to me."

Kabor broke in, "This is the same place we looked last time."

Nud scoffed. "You're not even wearing your glasses."

"Well," Gariff said, scratching his head, "the pit's caved in some since last time, that leaning tree fell across it, and the murky water's clear now, but with a green tinge. Other than that, everything looks about the same."

Bobbin pointed to the ground. "Except that leaf over there."

Holly groaned and gave the jokester a gentle push. "You weren't even there." She turned to Nud. "Is this the right spot or not?"

The Stouts were right – the site was *mostly* the same. "It's the trees around it," Nud said. "These aren't the same trees. And the shape of the hole is… different."

Kabor snickered. "Leno, have you been into the barkwood again?"

Everyone laughed except for Nud, who grimaced.

"Just go into recall," Bobbin suggested.

"No thanks," Nud responded. "The whole bog-body experience is not something I care to relive."

"I wonder if Mer made it here?" Gariff said. He put his hat back on.

"Look at the tracks in the mud, nitwits," Holly said. "Someone's been here."

Kabor gave the tracks a sideways look, then reached into his pocket and pulled out his specs. He put them on. "They're not all Mer's tracks, that's for sure," he said. "I don't know if any of them are. I'm no bogger, but by the foot size I'd say old-worlders or Outlanders."

"Well, no one's here now," Bobbin said.

The boys set their gear down near the sinkhole. At Holly's prompting, Nud pulled the stone out of his pocket to let everyone get a glimpse of it before starting the search. He cupped it in his hands so they could see the flicker when it started up.

"Can I hold it?" Holly asked.

Her request caught Nud off guard. He hesitated. The last time he let someone else hold it…

"Can I hold it too?" Kabor said.

Bobbin chimed in. "Me toodly-do."

"I'll give it right back," Holly offered.

The only one who didn't ask was Gariff, and Nud appreciated him for it.

Putting his reservations aside, Nud handed his sparking stone to Holly. Then he swung his gaze to Kabor and Bobbin. "Not you two," he said. "Shoo!" He waved them off. "Kabor, I don't trust you; and Bobbin, your hands are too sticky."

"Aaww," Bobbin said.

Nud closed in on Holly. "Careful," he told her as she rolled the gem in her hands. "I mean… don't drop it."

She cupped the stone in her hands, leaving only a small opening at the top to peer through.

"The light gets brighter whenever you hold it," Nud said.

Holly raised her eyes to meet Nud's. "Thank you," she replied, eyes smiling and filled with adoration. Then Nud realized he'd inadvertently complemented her. What he'd said was true though.

"How does this thing work?" she asked.

Nud shrugged.

"That's weird," Holly said, tilting the stone this way and that way in her hands. "Look… the light's not brighter – it's just gone steady now." She tilted the bog stone again, swaying it slightly left and then right as she did so. "And look, when I move it a little, the spark keeps to the edge, like it wants to go one way, but then it sort of hits the wall from the inside."

She was correct. Moving the stone left to right, the spark hugged the left. Moving the stone right to left, the spark would try to "catch up" to the left side and then stick there.

"Wow… that's odd," Nud said. "I never noticed that. Maybe it's like a compass, except it prefers west to north." He paused. "Sometimes it flashes like crazy too, like it's excited or something." The patterns of light were all a mystery to Nud. Holly passed the stone back to him and he slipped it into his pocket.

In the meantime, Gariff had pulled two shovels from his pack. He kept one for himself and leaned the other against a tree next to Holly. He passed Kabor a pan.

Holly grabbed the shovel and turned her gaze to Gariff. "Where do I dig?"

"That's up to you," Gariff replied. "Before I dig anywhere, I'm visiting these outcrops here." One by one, Gariff pointed out three small, flat rock domes. "If Nud's bog stone is really ancient tree gum like Mer says, then it formed in the *ancient* landscape. Them three hills will tell me something about how it all looked back then, and just maybe yield a clue about where to dig."

"Sounds complicated," Holly said, a little deflated.

Kabor broke in. "I'm sticking to the creek, where the water already did most of the work for me and carved out exposed areas. I'm going to sift through the sand too, like panning for gold."

"That might work," Gariff said.

Holly's eyes brightened. "I like that idea. Nud, what about you?"

Nud thought for a long moment. He peered into the water-filled pit. Wet leaves lined the sloping bottom, along with rotting branches and other forms of detached vegetation. *Nah,* he thought. Then he scanned the pit's edge.

"Tree roots," he said. "I'm going to look for exposed tree roots or ones that are easy to dig under, especially near the sinkhole. That's how I found this one." He patted his pocket.

"The sinkhole with the dead bodies?" she asked.

"I guess…"

Holly turned to Gariff's cousin. "Kabor, mind if I join you?"

"Nope," Kabor replied. "It'll be fun, and maybe we'll find an artifact. I'll show you how to pan for gold too… and old eyeballs."

Holly sent him off-balance with a hip check.

Bobbin's turn came next. He looked around and about, from the treetops to the ground. "I'm going to look under rocks."

Gariff laughed.

Straightaway, Bobbin stooped over and upturned a wide, flat chunk of slate. He pulled something from underneath with a bit of a shine to it.

"What's this?" he said, holding it up for everyone to see.

"Give that to me," Gariff said, reaching, but it was Kabor who snatched the piece out of Bobbin's hand first. He whisked it away towards the creek.

"Hey," Bobbin protested.

"I have an idea," Kabor called back. He waved at them to join him. "C'mon." Everyone followed him to the creekside boulder where he squatted down with Bobbin's find. With the others looking over his shoulders, Kabor gently placed the item in his pan and washed the mud off, replacing the water as soon as it was dirty. After a few refills, when the water finally cleared, it became evident that Bobbin had found a thin strip of curved metal, pitted and twisted out of its original shape. Gariff pincered it between two fingers and picked it up for a closer look. He reached into his shirt pocket for an eyeglass, squinted one eye shut and scrutinized the piece with the other eye, through the glass.

"Old metal," he said, "pitting corrosion for sure. These boggish waters sure did a number on it."

"What is it?" Holly said.

"A bit of plate armor, I'd say," Gariff said. "A band from a… maybe a waist or hip fitting… broken away from the rest of it."

They all took their turns examining the metal item, while Gariff explained what the original gear might have looked like. That got everyone's imagination leaping.

Encouraged by Bobbin's quick find, all went their separate ways in search of more: Gariff and Holly with shovels, Kabor with his pan, and Nud with a flat river stone for scraping and a good-sized stick for poking around in the mud. Bobbin carried his find around with him everywhere he went, overturning stones and pushing aside old logs.

The five of them dug, poked and panned through mud, clay, and sand for hours as the day got hotter. They upturned rocks and dug around boulders and roots, and everyone tried sifting through sand on the banks. Many interesting stones were unearthed, and even some plant and shell fossils locked in shale. Gariff found a few more bits of armor, including a visor, and a pitted blade from an old knife, its handle long corroded away. No one turned up any bog body parts, thankfully, and no one turned up anything like the stone Nud had found either.

All the while Nud searched, he pondered the relevance of their discoveries. It occurred to him that this could be the very site that Harrow was looking for.

Kabor eventually gave up on panning and came to join Nud on the grounds surrounding the sinkhole. The Pip was near his limit of exertion, and ready to call it quits for the day. Gariff, Holly and Bobbin had moved downstream to a fresh location and, according to Gariff, a similar looking formation.

"Be careful near the hole," Nud told Kabor. "The ground is quaky."

"I know," Kabor said. "I can feel it shiver once in a while beneath me." He started digging, using his pan to scrape the mud aside.

"What were you and Holly doing at the market the other day?" Nud asked him.

"Buying books," Kabor said, already in the process of overturning a large rock near the edge of the sinkhole. "Holly likes stories."

"What else did you do?"

"Nothing. Why?"

"No reason."

Kabor pulled up a roundish, fist-sized stone, rinsed it in the pit water, and then tossed it aside. "There's always a reason."

Nud heard a stick snap nearby, a big one. He tilted his head up and scanned the woods around them. "Did you hear that?"

"Trying to change the subject?" Kabor replied.

"What subject?"

"Holly and me."

"No. There is no Holly and you… Is there?"

Kabor passed Nud a sideways glance. "Do you think she likes me?" he said. "I mean, she's always hanging around and getting physical."

Nud didn't answer.

That annoying grin crept across Kabor's face again. "I think she likes me."

Nud scoffed. "What makes you say that?"

Kabor just smiled wider and with overwhelming confidence.

Nud pounded at the ground harder than ever with his slate, grunting and growling with every thrust.

"Ahh!" growled Kabor as he slapped the back of his neck.

Nud looked up at the deer flies buzzing around his head and killed three in a row. "I'm done. It's getting buggy." His arms needed a rest too.

Kabor jerked his head around. "Did you hear that?" He wasn't talking about the buzzing.

Nud waited. Another stick snapped. "Yeah, I heard it too." And another – too loud and detached to be a small animal's skittering.

Nud called into the woods. "Who's there?"

The two of them scanned the forest and the creek banks.

Kabor shrugged. "You're right," he said. "We should go. No more of your stones are here anyway. Even if they were, they could be a mile deep for all we know."

Nud and Kabor soon abandoned the sinkhole and caught up with Gariff downstream, still digging alongside Bobbin.

"Find anything?" Kabor said, on approach.

Gariff responded, "A few odds and ends, is all."

"Where's Holly?" Nud asked.

"Never mind Holly," Gariff complained, "Where's Mer when you need him?"

Nud answered, "When I talked to him last, I told him we'd be here tomorrow or the next day. So, we're early."

"Holly went to try her luck downstream," Bobbin said.

"I was just about to send her away," Gariff grumbled, "…the way she kept going on about Elderkin and all. She nearly talked my ear off. It's hard to concentrate with all that yapping."

"By the way, I found a stake in the ground," Bobbin said, cheeriness in his voice. "Gariff says we're in the clear because of it."

"You're lucky today," Nud told him.

"Yep," Gariff said. "Another claim post. HME staked a property to the south. I already made four claim posts and I have a pretty good idea what territory to cover. It'll have to do 'til Mer gets here. And we'll have to pace it out so's we can mark it on the map for him."

It's really happening. Nud looked over his companions. Despite their slumped postures and being covered in grime, he saw a glint of expectation in their tired eyes, and something else. Something he felt in himself as well – accomplishment.

Bobbin and Nud mostly helped to set the posts, while Gariff paced out where they should go. Kabor sorted out how to draw the boundaries on the map. It would be up to Mer to refine the cousins' handiwork and add more posts if needed. And when the time came, they'd all help cut the claim boundary lines – blazing trees and cutting underbrush between the posts. But Nud knew from Old Remy that only Mer among them, as a recognized prospector, could obtain the special metal tags needed and submit the technical paperwork. They'd all be listed, of course.

Shortly after completing the task, Bobbin and Nud, eager to take advantage of the fair weather, made their way to a choice swimming hole nearby for a quick dip. Gariff and Kabor declined, as expected. Nud stripped down to short pants and dove into the cool, clear water where it was deepest. Kabor managed a seat amidst a cluster of egg-shaped boulders at the creek's edge where he could kick off his boots and dangle his feet in the water. Gariff, on the other hand, had decided to try out Bobbin's search tactic. He meandered along the shoreline overturning stones.

"Miss me?" called a voice. It was Holly. She returned empty-handed.

"Claim's staked," Gariff said.

Her face lit up. "Oh good. I can't wait to talk to Mer about it."

"Watch this, Holly," Bobbin ran to the edge of the pool, spun backwards, and jumped. At the height of his leap, the round Pip froze in a perfect nonchalant pose, as though he'd been resting up there all day in mid-air. At the last possible instant, he curled himself into a ball and barreled into the water with a tremendous splash. Kabor got drenched and even Gariff raised his hands to shield himself from the soaking spray.

Holly flung her cloak down on Kabor's rock, stepped along the creek to a spot where the bottom hadn't been stirred up yet, and then slipped underwater without so much as a splash. She swam over to where Nud was, and popped her head up. Soon, the swimming hole erupted in white water between them, with Bobbin joining in on the fun, whole-heartedly.

Afterwards, laughing and refreshed, the Pips crawled out of the water to sun dry on a few boulders. As resting stones go, they were perfect, warmed by radiance and sheltered from the wind. To the gentle sounds of water trickling over rocks and around twigs, and as the spring breeze slid through new leaves, they soaked up the last strong rays of the evening sun.

"Sorry we didn't find the 'mother lode' today," Nud told Holly. He lay on the river boulder beside her with his hands behind his head.

"It's okay," Bobbin replied, chewing on Uncle Fyorn's taffy. He was right beside Holly. "I still had lots of fun. And now we have a claim!"

Holly rolled her eyes and smirked to herself, lying casually on her own boulder and idly caressing the polished surface of the protected pool at her side. The caress became a sweep when she spread her fingers wide to stretch the thin lines of webbing between them.

Bobbin rose and brought his pack around to everyone, so that each person could grab a snack, then returned to his spot. Gariff had found himself a patch of shade away from everyone, but kept well within earshot. He sat with his hat pulled down over his eyes, ready to doze off. Kabor continued to dangle his feet in the creek. A turtle plopped into the water from its place on a nearby log.

Nud sat up and leaned on one elbow. "Maybe there's only one of these stones in the whole wide world." He felt for the piece in his pocket and brought it out. It shone steady, its point of light still hugging the left side.

"But if this spot is full of them, we'd be rich beyond belief," Holly said.

Kabor eyed the stone with a sideways glance, and then offered his own thoughts on the matter. "Even if there aren't any more bog stones here, there's still lots we could do with this spot. We could sell the whereabouts to a collector."

"Whoa," Nud said. The idea finally hit him. "We could

sell the claim. Harrow is looking for the battleground where they fought the Jhinyari a long, long time ago. This might be it! They've been looking all over the bog lands and staking all kinds of claims."

"Through HME?" Gariff said.

"I guess," Nud replied.

"I can see how their search might've gone wrong," Kabor said. "The way the legend is told, you'd think the battle happened in the middle of the bog. But there are deep pools right around here too, and it's all bog water runoff. Maybe the men from Fortune Bay skirted the edge of Deepweald and met the Jhinyari and the leviathan right here. It sort of makes sense – why try to escape straight through the middle of a bog where it's slow going and open, as opposed to along the tree line where there's hard ground and cover."

Gariff spoke up. "Are claims for stuff like bog iron 'n gems different than claims for stuff like swords and armor?"

"Not that I know of," Nud replied. "Some places do that, but not in Webfoot. You just have to state what you're going to pull out of the ground, and then pay a levy based on assessed value."

"We could be rich six different ways then!" Gariff said. "This is bigger than the mother lode... it's the... it's the—"

"Grandmother lode!" Bobbin broke in.

Holly's enthusiasm was uncontainable. "I'd take my share of the money and run away to Kel Samu. It's hot there all year long, and they are so sophisticated... with such lavish homes."

"Too close to 'the Scar' for me," Kabor said.

"You'd leave?" Bobbin asked Holly.

Holly shrugged. "What would you do, Leno?"

Gariff interjected, "We all know what he'd do."

"Yep," Kabor said. "Leno would be outta here. Where

would you start looking, Nud? North to Dim Lake where your parents were last seen headed? Maybe the Western Tor? No one's looked there. You don't still have your sights set on Harrow proper, do you? Only a fool would try that."

"I don't know where I'd start looking," Nud said, "somewhere like that, I guess. I can't wait to tell Paplov." Nud didn't inform the others, but another plan had entered into his thoughts. *Maybe this is just the sort of leverage Paplov needs to swing a deal and get my parents out, if they really are prisoners.*

Holly tilted her head to one side and regarded Nud. "I thought you liked it in Webfoot. You'll be a town councilor one day…"

"I do like it," Nud replied. "It's just… complicated."

"Great," Bobbin said. "So, everyone would leave?"

"Not me," Kabor said. "I don't need to look for my parents. They're dead."

Bobbin frowned. "You're already in the Bearded Hills though, half the year."

"Well, what would you do Bobbin?" Holly asked.

Bobbin's eyes lit up. "That's easy. First, I'd buy you that dress you were staring at the last time we went to the market. Then I'd show you all the wonders of Webfoot so that you'd stay."

"All the wonders of Webfoot," Kabor repeated. "That shouldn't take long." He looked to his cousin. "Got a few minutes to kill?" The two shared a chuckle.

"Have you ever seen the bottom of Everdeep Pond?" Bobbin retorted. "Well, I have. You'd never believe what's down there."

Gariff scoffed. "No one's been to the bottom. That's why she's *Everdeep.*"

"I have," Bobbin said.

"Bobbin, you're the sweetest," Holly remarked. She reached out and stroked her hand through the young Pip's hair, then leaned over and gave him a big kiss on the cheek.

"Treasure's totally lost on you Pips and yer whimsical fancy." Gariff shook his head. "Us Stouts would put a fortune to more practical uses. That's fer sure."

"I'd use my money to make more money," Kabor said. His scheming smile grew back.

"It's getting late," Nud said, slipping the stone back in his pocket. "We'll catch up with Mer first opportunity and head back here another time with the right equipment, the right paperwork, and daylight to spare."

Gariff nodded, lips pressed together firmly.

Bobbin packed the remnants of their snacks and finished off whatever he could stuff into his mouth. Holly and Nud donned their cloaks; then Nud grabbed his pack. Gariff upturned one last rock before catching up to his cousin.

Nud was the first to cross over to the homeward side of the creek. In the few waiting moments that he stood there, he pulled the bog stone out one last time to gaze at it. Curiously, the spark was still steady, but opposite.

"I guess the spark likes east better now," Nud said to Holly when she drew up beside him. He showed it to her.

Holly gazed into the light. "Some compass that turned out to be. Points every which way."

CHAPTER XX

Stick'n Twine Outpost

Late into evening, the five had hiked as far as the "Stick'n Twine Outpost." Before long, the sun would descend upon the bog and their worries would double, if not triple. The site had already progressed, and now featured a manned gate that restricted access to the Mire Trail. In their absence, a thatched roof had been erected atop the hut, affording the guards refuge from the next rain – if it wasn't too serious a rain. Behind the hut on the east side, stables and a corral were in the works to accommodate more riding lizards and, later in the season, horses. At the rate construction was proceeding, the crew might have something altogether functional by the end of the week.

The young guard that had caught Holly's eye on the way in was working hard, still shirtless and now swinging a sledgehammer. Noting the teens' approach, he wiped his brow with the back of his hand, then blinked from the stinging sweat. He'd been busy erecting a flimsy fence on the compound's west side, a "polite" security barrier to "encourage" travelers not to circumvent the gate.

The second Pip guard – balding, middle-aged and well rounded – still rested on his log outside the hut, soaking in the withering sunshine. He seemed a little slow on the uptake and merely smiled dumbly at them. The third guard hammered away at a doorframe, inside.

Leaning on his sledgehammer, the young Pip doled out a sideways grin to Holly. Then he swung his gaze to her little round companion. He seemed eager to take a break and chat.

"Catch any glowfish lately?" the guard asked.

"Nope," Bobbin said, "we're sparkle free. And—"

"Has anyone left a message for us?" Gariff broke in. He was quick to cut-off Bobbin's revealing double-talk this round.

"Like who?" said the guard.

Bobbin's quick tongue cut in before the Hill Stout could answer. "Mer Andulus – looks and smells like Gariff here, 'cept older and not as sweaty. Mer likes sparkling fish too; wants us to show him where to find them."

Gariff folded his arms across his chest and drew in a slow, deep breath, nostrils flaring. He did well not to whack Bobbin. Nud knew he wanted to.

"That ole rock-hound?" said the guard. "Sorry… not that I heard. Why? Was he supposed to show you the 'mother lode'? That's all he ever talks about."

"He's the one," Nud said. "Can you pass him a message for us, if he comes by?" Nud pulled out the map.

"A map?" said the guard.

Nud nodded.

I don't see why not." He called to the building. "Grof, did you hear that?"

"Yep," said a voice from within the structure. "They can leave it here."

Nud took out the town hall papers as well, which listed all of their names as partners in the claim, folded it in with the map, and then handed the bundle over. The young guard walked it over to his comrade on the log. Next, he looked to the empty corral, then addressed the teens.

"You just missed the handler," he said. "Wyatt set off with a load of merchants from Fort Abandon and he won't be back 'til morning. He's bringing us a fresh new load of sticks and twine."

The words stung Nud's ears like he'd fallen head first on a wasp nest.

"Sounds about right to me," Gariff remarked, the smug look washing over him. Behind the guard's back, the Stout wiggled a nearby gatepost. It was tall and it moved easily, plus the wood was warped. Kabor stood in front of the post and tilted himself sideways to match its lean.

The young guard didn't seem to notice the cousins' mockery. "It's nigh too late to cross on your own," he stated plainly. "As you know, by order of our own Lord Mayor Undle, I must insist that I accompany you back. Jory's the name."

"Pleased to finally make your acquaintance, Jory," Holly said, with a coy smile and a gentle handshake. Her wrist bent up ever so slightly. Jory's gaze met hers, and he held her hand longer than necessary. Holly could pass for an older teen, and she knew how to greet people and make them feel at ease. Not only did she give Jory her name, but Holly told him where she lived, her occupation, and went on to invite him to the Flipside for a free barkwood out back. The rest of the five introduced themselves in turn, with flat words by comparison.

Gariff pressed Jory for more information. "Why all the fuss?" he asked. "Is there a problem on the trail?"

"Nope," he replied. "Not unless you believe in the Boggyman. Truth is, I'm just sore all over and I'd rather sleep on a warm, comfortable hammock in Webfoot than be stuck out here in the mud with these fly-bitten oafs." He waved a hand behind him at his fellow guards.

The guard on the log continued to smile dumbly. The one in the hut leaned out of a window, grunted, and shook his hammer at Jory. He had thick white hair, cropped short, and his eyes were wide and round. He reminded Nud of a great gray owl.

"Did Undle really make that order?" Gariff said.

"Sure did," Jory replied. "The only exception being those who are judged capable of defending themselves… and that ain't yous."

Bobbin puffed out his chest at the remark, and strutted about stiffly. "Sure we are," he said in his deepest voice. Kabor imitated Bobbin. Holly rolled her eyes.

"Is it raiders from Turnsby?" Nud asked, recalling the inn-keep's comments and Mayor Otis' concerns.

"Sounds about right," Jory said. "I haven't seen any signs of them myself though, so I'm sure it's only precautionary. Orders is to escort travelers and be on the lookout for any-thing suspicious."

For the most part, such "town orders" safely can be ignored without consequence, but with Holly keen on Jory they had no choice but to accept the guard's offer. Jory took a minute to gather his travel sack and tie it to his long spear, and then fetch his pot helm, which he hung on the end rather than wear. He also snatched a canteen lying around, which he sipped from often, and a horn that he fastened to his belt.

"You're in charge, Grof," he said to the 'owlish' guard inside.

Grof poked his head out of a window.

"I'm already in charge, Newt!" he spat back. "Don't get lost."

Jory laughed him off and shook his head, smiling.

"You're lucky," Grof added. "I'm letting you off easy today; tomorrow you'll pay double! Be back by dawn or I'll have yer hide."

The five plus one turned their backs on the trailhead and began the trek home.

Along the way, Nud eventually admitted to himself that Jory was pleasant and interesting company. Their private guard displayed practiced manners and had an easygoing way about him. His demeanor made perfect sense once Nud learned that his father was from Everdeep and his mother grew up in Watergarden – a touch of sophistication mixed with down-to-earth friendliness.

The first leg of the journey went quickly on account of all the stories Jory had to tell about strange sightings in the bog, people disappearing, and ghosts that drifted in the mist. On the five's side, they kept the day's events out of the conversation. No one even mentioned the bog bodies, although at one point Nud was about ready to open his mouth and spill the story – it fit in so well with the topic. He never had the chance to.

CHAPTER XXI

The ruse

Halfway to town and just as it was getting dark, Jory closed in on the riveting climax of yet another bog horror story. Gariff – his biggest fan – followed the plot line as wide-eyed as Nud had ever seen him, while Bobbin and Holly hung on his every word. The guard had a way of holding back the telling in such a way that they couldn't stop listening if they tried. Maybe all the attention Jory was getting underlaid the reason Kabor and Nud hung back, both hooded and pretending not to be overly interested. But for the Pip, there was another reason.

"Kabor, I—"

"Shhh."

Nud spoke over him. "I think someone's following us."

Kabor shot the Pip an irritated glance. "It's just the bog stories. You're as bad as Gariff. Now shut up. He's almost done with it and we're missing the ending." The Stout's voice became pleading. "The ending's always the best part."

There was no dismissing instinct though, despite the fact

that all the telltale signs, like the snap of a twig underfoot, or the grassy rustle of footsteps, or wildlife scattering, were absent. It was the little things that made Nud suspect they were being tracked: a soft shuffle in the rushes that didn't quite fit with the wind, a shadow seen out of the corner of one eye, a small splash. And then, above all, there was the gut feeling. The gut feeling summed up all the other little ways the mind opens up to the world that the conscious self doesn't even know exist, the things that can't quite be put to words. Any one of the more subtle signs could be ignored, but together, and with a gut feeling on top, they could not. That would be foolish.

Finally, over Jory's talk, Nud caught the sound of an undeniably peculiar stir in the rushes off the trail. It was not alarming at first, but it was not the natural sort of rustling that a bird or a small animal was apt to make either. The sound was too quick-paced and there was something about it… a soft shaking trying to be loud, perhaps. Nud stopped and pricked his ears. The noise ceased. Kabor, hiking beside him, noticed the sudden change in the Pip's composure. He grimaced and followed Nud's example. The others kept on ahead.

Nud whispered to Kabor. "You must've heard that, right?"

"I think so, that time," he whispered back.

For a brief moment, the two of them stood in the middle of the trail, eyes searching far and near. On the horizon, the pale violet sky warned of a lightless dusk. Jory's voice still floated back to them, but suddenly it seemed half-empty. The mossy silence and stillness of the bog soaked up the other half.

At the end of Jory's story, punctuated by Gariff's loud gasp, Bobbin and Holly groaned and guffawed. Gariff followed with a nervous laugh.

Kabor gave Nud a disappointed look. "Great, we missed it."

"Sorry," Nud whispered back.

In low tones, an unfamiliar sound began to build. It rose from underneath the chatter like a growing moan. It rose and filled the still, boggy air while the laughter of their friends turned uncertain, and teetered off. Then, without warning, the moan shot to the height of a decapitating wail. If pain had a voice, it would sound just that way. Nud's ears hurt to hear it.

The group ahead shot accusing looks back to Nud and Kabor.

Bobbin smirked. "Funny, guys," he said. "You can stop now."

Kabor and Nud shared a glance, then turned to scan the waterscape behind them: between the hummocks and the hollows, the grey standing dead wood, and the hillocks crowded with alders – a great many places to hide.

"It wasn't them," Holly said. Her eyes darted about.

Something slapped the water farther ahead, just off shore. Then another long and dreadful moan sounded from behind. Nud's heart began to pump wildly. His eyes darted this way and that way. *Nothing.* He pricked his ears. *Silence.*

"It's probably just a fish," Kabor said, "or maybe a muskrat."

"A fish?" Nud was astonished. "How could it possibly be a fish? Do fish moan? It's NOT a fish."

"I meant the splash," he said.

From ahead, Jory fixed his eyes on a grassy mound near where the splash came from. "I don't see how it could be a muskrat either," he called back. "Maybe some kind of bird though… or a big frog. I know a story about a giant frog—"

"You go first," Holly cut in, "I don't want to walk right into it, whatever it is."

Jory nodded. He untied his traveling sac from the end of his spear, and put on his pot helm. "Right... I'll scout up ahead a bit." Spear readied, and slightly crouched, Jory moved forward. All eyes were on him. That left Bobbin with Holly and Gariff, Nud with Kabor, and Jory on his own: three groups, divided.

Jory poked his spear into the large, grassy hummocks ahead. As he did so, a crackled old voice called from behind Nud and Kabor, soft and muffled.

"Over here l'il young'ns... ya, ya. <gurgle> I gots som'emm for you... I do, I do." The voice had a motherly quality, but there was something off about it, something wickedly off.

A shiver, cold as winter's chill, shot through Nud. He spun around.

Against the dark blue of a freshly twilit sky, the silhouette of a hunched-over woman rose from behind a large, grassy clump, just beyond the trail's edge. She was not five paces from where Kabor and Nud stood. Her bent frame rose head and shoulders above the tall rushes, in the off-trail dimness. Gariff joined his cousin straightaway, while Nud and Kabor gawked at her.

"Who is it?" Kabor said. He gave the woman a sideways look. "Damn it, I can't see in this light." He reached into his pocket and pulled out his glasses.

The woman waved her long and bony arms to get their attention, as though unsure the teens had seen her. Long dark hair fell in loose tangles past her shoulders. Scant woven rushes were her only discernable clothes, barely concealing a waif body.

The woman beckoned them to approach. Gariff and Nud took a few cautious steps towards her.

"Are you hurt?" Bobbin called, from his place in the middle. He clung to Holly's arm.

"Yesums, yesums," said the woman in the bog, "but I'll be just fine now. I gots som'emm for you… I do, I do."

Gariff and Nud inched closer, Kabor a step behind.

Nud whispered to the cousins. "Can you see what it is?"

Gariff shook his head. Nud glanced back, over his shoulder to Kabor. The Stout mouthed a "No." Nud spotted Jory in the background. He'd planted the butt end of his spear in the mud, and was fumbling for something at his side.

"What's going on over there?" Jory shouted. "Is everything all right?"

"Someone's here," Holly replied. "A woman – starving by the looks of her."

"Be there in a minute. There's something…" Jory's voice trailed off.

Nud turned his attention back to the woman in the rushes.

Bobbin called out to her. "We don't need anything, but thanks anyways." He sounded genuinely concerned, even sympathetic. "You shouldn't be out here on your own at nightfall. And you'll catch a draft if you don't dry off. It'll be pitch black before you know it."

There was no response.

"It isn't safe. Are you hungry?" he added.

Soaking wet, by rights the woman in the bog should have been feeling cold and plenty afraid right about then. Her sunken and shadowed eyes pleaded for compassion.

"Robbers gots to me, hurts me… <gurgle> they did, they did. They stoles everything. They even stoles my clotheses… ya, ya."

The woman in the bog hacked and coughed for a few broken moments, then cleared her throat. Her voice rasped, next she spoke. "Only grasses for me to wear now... ya, ya, and I sneaks around in the water to gets away, I did, I did. Ashamed."

Nud whispered to Gariff. "If everything was stolen, how could she possibly have something for us?"

She heard. "Something special... ya, ya. Something special no one could *ever* steal."

The woman shuffled in the rushes, but the way she moved didn't look right to Nud, and didn't match what the Pip's ears were hearing. Every subtle motion came with an off twist or an unexpected jerk, and the surrounding rushes dithered with a dragging sound underneath, as though snakes lay coiling at her feet.

"Come into town with us," Bobbin pleaded. "You can eat at the Flipside. You can have my cloak. We have a guard." The young Pip still played the gentleman, but just the same, he reminded her that the teens had protection. *Smart.* "You'll be safe with us," he added.

"Safe? Guard? <gurgle> Do you now... hmmm?" Even in the falling darkness, she could not hide her sly smile.

And just like that, as if on cue, Nud heard another giant splash up ahead. They all spun around to look. Then came a thrashing sound from the same direction, a muffled gasp, and the rushes jittered sharply.

Holly's shrill voice cut through the tension. "Jory!"

She shook Bobbin's arms, frantic. "Where's Jory? I don't see him anywhere!"

Something plopped in the shallow water near where the guard was. Nud watched as the rippling disturbance moved alongside the trail, whipping reeds in its wake. Then it stopped at a deep pool.

"It's gone under," Nud said.

Holly's voice rang out over the bog once more. "JORY!"

There was no response.

The woman in the grasses called to Nud and the two Stouts again. She'd approached while their attention was directed elsewhere.

"A little closer this way comes… ya, ya," the woman now begged, "come be safe with me… ya, ya. I'll protects you now, li'l ones."

Up close, Nud could see that the demented old woman was dripping wet and naught but skin and bones, with hair a tangled mess of mud, reeds and half-decayed twigs. But for an instant, Nud saw in her expression something youthful and pure, and there was something steady and unrelenting about her eyes. Nud took another step closer.

The Stouts stood their ground.

"That's right… ya, ya," urged the woman, "closer… closer." She opened her arms, her meek chest scantily clad in her roughly woven half-shirt.

"Protect you… I will, I will." Though the old crone's face was largely hidden in shadow, her eyes gleamed in the twilight. Arms wide, she invited Nud into her embrace. Nud felt compelled…

Gariff lurched forward and grabbed the Pip's arm. "We need to get out of here." When Nud didn't budge, Gariff yanked him back. "*Now.* Something's not right, Leno."

Nud's thoughts in a haze, he tried to walk towards her, without knowing why.

"Stop!" Gariff boomed.

Nud shook his head and came to his senses.

Gariff pleaded with Nud. "That thing… it… she must be a bog queen… just look at her! She'll pull you under!"

Kabor was quick to agree. "Gariff's right, Leno! Don't go any closer!"

Bobbin asked, "What's a... b... b... bog queen?"

"Don't worry <gurgle>," the woman's voice called out again, with a kind intonation. "No worries for brave l'il Pips like you... no, no. No worries for Stoutsies either," the woman assured them. "No worries for the l'il childrens... no, no."

Holly screeched. "Something's on the road ahead!" Two hunched figures had stepped out of the darkness and onto the trail. Holly and Bobbin backed away.

The two newcomers planted themselves in plain view, blocking the trail where they'd last seen Jory. There was still no sign of him. Only the occasional ripple of water told Nud something still lurked in the deep pool.

The two figures ahead were also women, in the manner of the first: old crones, crooked and decrepit.

One of the two misshapen hags – taller and more hunched than her companion – cleared her throat three times before she spat onto the trail. Her shoulders bent in so drastically, they nearly touched. She spoke in a raspy gurgle.

"Give us something. <cough> Yes... give us a present for the Shadow in the Water, and <cough> we'll take it down with us, down, down to the gardens, for safekeeping, yes."

The hunched woman coughed, then spat, then coughed some more and had a coughing fit. When her throat finally cleared, the hag lifted one scrawny arm and pointed a boney finger at Kabor.

"Or maybe we'll take YOU," she hollered to the Stout. Then she swept her arm to Holly. "Or YOU, my l'il princess... you, you... take you where you can be safe, in the gardens."

The first hag, the one in the grasses, whined, shrill and accusing. Her body twisted and contorted as she scolded the others. "No, no... you fools, you FOOLS... you were supposed to wait. WAIT, I said." She sighed heavily and threw her arms down in despair.

Holly and Bobbin continued to back away from the two hags, to join Nud and the Stouts.

The hag who hadn't yet spoken opened her mouth to add her piece. Only a shapeless gargle came out. She coughed and spat and heaved, and gurgled and spat again. She shook her head and, finally, the words took form.

"What have you gots for us, l'il Pipses?"

Nud mouthed the word: "Thieves." He felt strangely relieved. The cousins heard him.

The teens moved into a tight group and looked to one another. Bobbin checked his pockets and shrugged his shoulders at Holly.

"Come'on, give them *something*," Holly said. "Then they'll leave us be and give us back Jory." She started searching through her pockets, trembling. The color had drained out of her face.

"You're right," Kabor said, keeping his calm, "we should give them something, whatever we can."

The two hags ahead whispered to one another, inaudibly.

Gariff took control. He tilted his head up. "Hold on," he called to the whispering hags, "just give us a moment to collect our things." Stout level-headedness prevailed, despite Gariff's earlier fear of the mere *legend* of the bog queens. Strangely enough, he was actually more together when confronted with the real thing. That was his strength.

"You'll have to give Jory back," Gariff added. "Show him to us first, or you're getting nothing but a fight."

The lone hag writhed and twisted and gurgled in the rushes. Nud felt a light spray on his cheeks when she spat their way.

The hunched-in hag up ahead of them responded to Gariff. "Oh… give back?" She chuckled. "Hee hee… no, no, silly l'il ones."

"Silly, silly," said her companion. She wore a ridiculous flower that hung loosely from her hair. It was old and decayed, just like her.

Gariff kept his group on task. "Okay Pips, what'cha got? My pack has two small shovels, a clay jar, a pick-hammer, spare clothes… damn! My compass is in there too."

Bobbin shrugged and bared his palms. "I have nothing," he said. "We ate everything I brought… see." He tore open the pack flap to prove it, and then made a sick face as he glanced down at his ballooning stomach.

Kabor felt his pockets. "I have some change from the market and the stone Nud gave me, and…" Kabor pulled his knife out slightly.

Keep it, Nud thought, afraid to say it outright, for fear of being overheard. Nud just glared at Kabor and mouthed a subtle "Shhh." The Stout closed his fist around the knife and slipped it back into his pocket.

Gariff swung his gaze to the Flipside hostess. "What about you, Holly?"

"Well," she replied, hesitantly. Her shoulders dropped. Holly undid her necklace and passed it to him.

"What else?" Gariff said. "They'll like girl things."

Holly winced and felt at her side pouch. "I have a… I have a…" She searched and searched. "I have a brush, but I doubt they would use it."

"The cloak," Bobbin said.

"Don't be a fool!" Kabor snapped, then lowered his voice to a whisper. "A thief with a cloak like that would be unstoppable. Just turn it insi—"

"Shush!" Nud said. *Too loud.*

Holly nodded, then handed the brush over to Gariff. He fumbled and dropped it.

"Let's put the loose stuff in your hat, Gariff," Kabor offered, "since you'll be handing it over anyway."

"Huh?" Gariff seemed a little taken aback by the suggestion, and Nud could almost see him debating internally. But with the hags waiting, there was no point delaying any longer.

"Come on Gariff, we don't got much else," Kabor urged. "They might like it."

Gariff grit his teeth, took his hat by the rim and gave it one last farewell look before passing it around for the offerings. "I suppose… I guess you're right," he admitted.

Holly picked up her brush, wiped it on Bobbin's shirt, and placed it in the hat. Then she pulled a clip out of her hair and dropped that in as well. Kabor's change jingled as he allowed each coin to slide out of his hand and into his cousin's headgear. He took off his glasses and dropped them in as well.

"No way!" Gariff said, on the loud side. "D'ya know what Pops paid fer those?"

Kabor took them back and squirreled them away. Gariff just shook his head at his cousin.

Bobbin put in a crust of bread after all. He found it at the very bottom of his pack. The hat still looked more empty than full though.

Holly shifted her gaze to Nud. "What about you, Leno, don't you have anything to offer? Stuff is practically spilling out of your pack."

"I have some wood… but what value would that be to them?" Nud said.

No one even suggested that he include it, even as filler. There was also the short bow strapped to his pack. In the dark and unstrung, it was likely to be overlooked. Nud didn't offer the remaining deepwood arrows either, for fear it would tip them off.

Satisfied they'd given their all, Gariff called out to the hags. "We have your present, a REALLY good present… yes, yes… really good indeed, but you can't have it until you give us Jory… no, no."

The two hags blocking the trail exchanged confused looks, and then faced the travelers again. The hunched hag shrugged. Her statement was abrupt.

"Him's gone," was all she said, high-pitched. A sinister grin crept across her face.

Her companion jerked her head to a sideways tilt. "All gone," she repeated, just as abruptly. She sounded the parrot and acted the bubbly clown.

The hunched hag shook her head slowly. Her jaw dislocated oddly from her face when she spoke. "Him's not comin' back… no, no. Not from where him is."

"No, not comin' back, him's not," the other repeated.

All three hags erupted in a chorus of cackles.

Holly scanned the trailside nervously. "What do you mean he's not coming back?"

Gariff narrowed his eyes at the two hags ahead of them. "What did you do with him?"

"Us?" said the hunched hag, raising one hand daintily to her cave-in chest.

"No. Not us," her companion assured, looking innocent.

Holly called out: "JORY!"

The hags found Holly's antics amusing in the most sinister way, and more voluminous cackling echoed through the bog. When the parrot hag finally regained her composure, she lifted a horn – Jory's horn – to her mouth and gave it a little toot. She smiled, and then tossed it aside into the rushes. The pair ahead shared a knowing look and giggled madly to one another, then hysterically. The parrot hag fell sideways and rolled on the ground, bent over, in a bout of cruel laughter. The hag in the grasses joined in.

Gariff turned back to his friends. "Let's just give them what we have and be done with it," he said. "Maybe we can't save Jory, but we can get out of this and send for help."

"They'll do the same to us," Holly said.

Careful to conceal his actions from the hags, Gariff snuck the rock pick out of his pack and stuffed it under his shirt. Then, with slow, cautious steps, the burly Stout made his way towards the two hags on the trail ahead. Holly, Bobbin and Kabor stayed put, and Nud hung back to keep an eye on the other hag amidst the grasses, quiet as she was and eerily watchful.

With an outstretched arm, Gariff made his offering – the hat and its contents. He rested it on the ground in front of them, along with his pack. They watched with eager eyes.

"Here you are," Gariff told them, as he backed away slowly. "That's all we got that's worth anything… and you can keep the hat. Now let us pass."

The hunched-in hag peered into the headgear, and then kicked it aside. "More. Need more… ya, ya, you gots to give us more." Then she spat in the hat.

"More, more" repeated the parrot hag, dead flower swaying with her stringy hair. She sucked back a huge glob of phlegm, then spat it out in Gariff's hat too.

The Stout flushed with anger. "But that's all we got," he said through his teeth.

"Them's won't do… no, no. Won't do at all." The hunched-in hag shook her head and crossed her arms until it looked like they were on backwards. She looked to her partner who began shaking her head in unison.

The hunched over hag pointed to the reeds. "The Shadow in the Water won't let you pass… won't let you pass, he won't."

"More, more," said the parrot hag.

It was the hag in the grasses that spoke next, from behind. "The l'il girlsies," she started, then waved her hand at Holly *and* Kabor. "We want the l'il girlsies – that's all."

Kabor leapt toward her and raised his right fist. "Girl! Who are you calling girl you demented… swamp thing!"

Under different circumstances, the look of disgust on Kabor's face might have been humorous – a contorted blend of terror, disbelief and embarrassment, all rolled into one.

"I'll take *HER*! Take *HER*!" said the hunched hag as she raised her hand to Holly.

"HER, HER," mimicked the parrot.

The hag in the grasses agreed. "She pretty… she is. Take her… ya, ya. Pretty for our garden beneath the moss."

Gariff gasped, "That's it! They are bog queens!"

"I'll take the other girlsie," the hag in the grasses continued, pointing to Kabor, "not so pretty though… a shame… ugly. Fix her up nice I will, ya-ya, really nice. Take time, it will, she'll look pretty like the rest. Pretty pretty."

Kabor drew his knife. "I say we skin 'em all. We can do it – there's five of us and only three of them."

Holly pleaded. "Wait Kabor, STOP! It's what they want you to do."

Gariff drew his pick. "I'm with ya, Cuz!"

"No Kabor," Bobbin said, siding with Holly. "There *were* six of us, plus there's something in the water, that makes at least *four* of them, maybe more."

Gariff scowled. "Then stay out of the damn water."

The hags had finally grown tired of their ruse. Perhaps it was not quite working out the way they'd hoped it would. The time had come to collect. Morbid playfulness at an end, the trio succumbed to their primal urges.

The hag in the grasses commanded the others. "Take 'em all… down, down. Save the li'l children… we will, we will." She jerked her gaze directly to Nud. Her voice wilted. "Let me save you," she told him. "Down, down deep to the safe cool waters. I must save you, my child, my promise."

That was all Nud could endure. The five stood together, back to back, with the Stouts brandishing their weapons defiantly. Holly picked up a stick with a jagged, wicked point. Bobbin brandished a butter knife from his pack.

Nud made a sideways glance at the quivering ball of flesh at his side, then at his utensil.

"Seriously?"

Bobbin shrugged. It still had butter on it.

Nud considered his own options: Assembling his bow would take time – unhooking from the pack, stringing it, fumbling for the arrows amidst the deepwood… *No.* His eyes darted around him. Holly had taken the only good stick.

Fyorn's words echoed in Nud's mind: about the light of the bog stone, the Hurlorns, and the wise Elderkin. And how the Hurlorns had given him the Mark, had chosen *him* above all others, for reasons even Fyorn didn't understand. Was this to be the end the woodsman spoke of, as foreseen by trees? *I think not.* In his mind's eye, Fyorn's words rationalized everything. Nud repeated them aloud. "The Mark does nothing for the path ahead, but at the end is another journey waiting."

"What was that, Leno?" Bobbin asked.

Those Hurlorns must know something we don't.

Nud made his decision. He would let things happen the way they must've been meant to happen. He reached into his pocket and pulled out the bog stone, the gift of the Hurlorns. He held the gem high above his head, in full view of the crooked hag in the grasses. It flared bright in his hand. Sparks flashed and danced beneath its facets. Nud held the sparking stone in a manner so bold that anyone watching might have thought it to be a great weapon – a nexus of energy to be unleashed upon the world, to strike foul creatures down. Nud truly believed the stone would do *something*. He believed in the mysterious power of a glowing hunk of ancient tree gum.

The bog stone flickered, as usual.

Gariff's jaw dropped. He shot Nud a sideways glance, a baffled expression on his face. "Leno, what'er ya think'n? That won't do anything."

"Mine! All mine… MINE! I loses it!" cried the hag in the grasses as she dashed at Nud. Her ropey fingers reached for the stone. "Mine, l'il one."

Knives flashed and Gariff's pick rose to halt her advance. The hag backed away slowly, writhing in the rushes as she did so, eyes fixed to the stone.

"I know what I'm doing," Nud said.

Gariff kept on, "You've got to be kidding. Put that thing away and take out yer knife! Are you daft? You do have a knife, right?"

Nud hadn't packed a knife.

"Throw it!" Holly shouted. "Throw the stone. They'll chase after it!"

Holly tried to grab it from him. Nud kept it out of her reach.

The hag in the grasses erupted in a hoarse shriek: "Gives it to me!" She jerked her gaze to meet Nud's. "Listen, listen l'il pipses. Hear the children's whispers, ya, ya. *All the saved children like to whisper.*"

Nud heard the whispers rise up around him. His heart froze.

The parrot hag repeated the words, stupidly: "All the children's whispers."

"What do they mean, Leno?" Gariff said.

"I don't know," Nud replied. Really, though, he knew. They all knew, but they didn't want to know.

Nud glanced to the other two women. With a crouched stance, the parrot hag and her hunched master hobbled closer. In his peripheral, the rushes betrayed the Shadow in the Water. Surrounded, the five stood ready to fight, in the middle of the trail.

But the fight didn't start the way a fight usually starts.

As the hag in the grasses slithered to and fro, she relaxed her stance and, with those sunken-in eyes, she intensified her gaze on Nud. In a gentler tone, the hag invoked her motherly tongue, forked as it was. "Be a good l'il one… a good l'il one and gives it to me… ya, ya. Save you I will. Save you from the light. Your mother *wants* it. She asked me to tell you."

"Look away," Holly said. "One of the Elderkin stories…"

Nud turned his gaze from the hag in the grasses and concentrated on his wish. He focused on the hags blocking the trail ahead. *Strike them down. Clear the way. We could outrun them if I just…*

Nud felt a surging energy within, dizzying, just like before. Starting with a tingle in his wrist, it coursed throughout his body. Suddenly, the wind blew up around them. Buffeted by the fast-moving air, the two hags ahead of them raised their arms to shield themselves. The wind blew up so strong, it rolled Gariff's hat over, emptying its contents. Then a rogue gust sent the monstrosity airborne over the bog waters. Nud stumbled.

With curious expressions, the two hags slowly pivoted their heads in unison as they watched the hat sail past, tracking its course until it landed in the far-off rushes. Then they swung their gazes back to the five. In a dance full of anguish, the hunched-in hag squirmed and writhed. "Bad l'il ones. Bad children! Bad! BAD!"

The parrot hag beside her opened her mouth to speak, but choked on a glob of phlegm. She wretched it up and expelled it onto the moss.

The world blurred around Nud, everything in a haze. He heard Kabor's voice, hollow sounding. "Leno?"

That's all I get? A breeze? Nud thought, the second before everything went black.

*

Nud didn't know exactly how much time went by, but when he finally came to, all was in chaos. His friends were scattered. He glanced up the trail in time to see a fallen hag push herself to her feet, then pull a long, pointed stick out of her belly. Her and her companion took chase after Gariff, Holly and Bobbin, leaping with sudden and unnatural bursts of speed.

Nud lost track of their battles as he stepped up his own fight. He felt a strong hand pushing on his chest. Kabor had wedged himself between Nud and the hag in the grasses, who had the Pip in her clutches. The Stout cursed as he stabbed at her arms with his knife. Grunting with the effort, he whipped around to pull Nud free. The Pip struggled against the hag's wiry grip, having become the rope in a deadly game of tug-of-war.

Finally, a break — as Kabor yanked, Nud lurched free and stumbled towards him.

But the hag in the grasses was quicker than she looked for one so old and decrepit, and she could lash out at a distance. She snagged Nud and Kabor with vine-like tendrils. Nud rolled into her entangling arms. The hag's rancid breath smelled like the bottom of the bog.

"Down now children, down we go," she whispered, "down to safety, down to rest."

Kabor and Nud kicked and screamed. Nud bit into the

flesh, soft and unnatural. Kabor tried to slash the hag, but she
held his arm firm. He managed to switch hands on the knife and
swiped at the tendrils. But they were slippery, wood-strong, and
tightly wound. When he did cut her, black liquid oozed out of
every slit, and the wounds did little to impede her.

Nothing seemed to work. The hag had overtaken them. She
dragged them knee deep into the bog waters.

Kabor kept the fight up and cut one tendril away, while Nud
squirmed and kicked trying to muscle out. Still, she wouldn't let
go. The tendril roots and grasses that were somehow a part of
her shot out repeatedly to twist around their limbs and trunks.
Kabor cut them away, but there were always more. They twisted
together, tough as rope.

The worst was yet to come. That hag opened her mouth
wide, and even her tongue lashed out. It wrapped around Nud's
neck. The Pip did all he could to keep her leash from choking him.

With Nud and Kabor firmly in her grips, the hag proceeded
to drag them under. They were no match for her wiry strength.
Nud glanced to the others, half-expecting – fully hoping – to
see Gariff charging to their rescue. But all Nud beheld was the
Stout's entangled, sturdy bulk being pulled under, just as him
and Kabor were being pulled under. Holly screamed. Nud had
lost sight of her and Bobbin.

Nud forced a raspy whisper. "Play dead," he told Kabor.
By the terror in the Stout's eyes, Nud had little hope he'd listen.
"Just do it and wait for my signal," Nud added, before he gulped
his last breath.

Down they went under the mosses; down into a cold,
deep pool.

CHAPTER XXII

Queen of the garden under

A deathly chill engulfed Nud as he crossed into a layer of icy water and descended into a hidden drop-off. Nud bit his lip and tried hard not to flinch. The woman in the bog had to believe that he'd drowned.

Don't struggle.

Nud allowed himself to slip, deeper and deeper down the watery path to doom's end. He gave himself wholly to the hag as though accepting the bitterness of defeat.

She has to believe she's won.

The hag's relentless grip and that twisty strength of hers had caught Nud off-guard. Not only did her tendrils hold Nud and Kabor firm, they latched onto roots and debris at the bottom of the drop-off to pull them along.

As far as Nud could tell, Kabor had followed his lead after all, and was holding up well for a Stout. *Just a little longer, Kabor. Don't worry, we'll have our chance.*

In return for giving in, yes – Nud and Kabor would adorn her cursed garden and roll with the bones of children from long ago, the lost innocents of Fortune Bay. But not for long. She was not to spend too many precious moments lingering about in admiration of her ornaments on display. She was to leave them be. That was the secret deal that Nud had made with her. The hag didn't know it, of course.

The woman in the bog kept to her undertaking, creeping along the sloped bottom with Nud and Kabor in tow, oblivious to the Pip's schemes.

Then something unexpected happened.

Nud felt a sharp tug forward, then a pause as the bog queen's ropey tendrils slackened. Soon after came another tug. The Pip bided his time. *She's testing my resolve,* he thought, like testing a fishing line to see if the catch was still there, gauging the creature's will to survive by the fight left in it. Nud yanked back the next time, to imitate that last feeble trace of desperate resistance. He played the hooked fish, except Nud was baiting her instead of the other way around.

After twitching just for show, Nud gave in and allowed himself to simply drift, and be pulled along. He kept his eyes shut. The hag seemed satisfied enough with the performance. She even let loose her grip a little. The depth of water pressed hard against Nud's ears.

I could break free now, he thought. Pips are built for speed and quick dekes in the water. *I could definitely out-swim a blundering old woman, especially in an open stretch.*

But then there was Kabor. Nud couldn't just leave him behind.

Nud fought the urge to breathe – already, at only twenty counts, despite his record being one hundred and ten.

The hag dragged them deeper than Nud had imagined possible anywhere in the bog lands, except perhaps Everdeep Pond. The pressure in his ears mounted. For Kabor, it would be nearly unbearable. The two teens' limp bodies bumped while being towed along. Nud didn't feel Kabor kick or resist at all. Then again, he wasn't supposed to… not yet.

The hag changed course, abruptly, and sped up. She began to skitter sideways. Nud's arm clipped something – a stump at the bottom of the hole. The Pip hazarded a glance and half-opened one eye as he skipped and spun along the bottom, stirring up mud and debris. He'd counted to thirty in the time it took for the hag to bring them all the way down. At most, Kabor would have that much endurance in him again to spare.

Nud spotted the "garden" – not much of a garden at all, really: shallow mounds set within a ring of long, sharp sticks – like pikes. Someone should have told the bog queen that gardens are for living things. In hers, decaying things, long dead, drifted from the ends of sticks. One pike skewered an oddly familiar, dark round mass, wrapped in reeds – a remnant from Nud's buried past. He did a double take. *Could it be?* Paralyzing fear gripped him. His heart raced. *Stay focused,* he told himself, and tried to calm himself down. *Your mind is playing tricks on you.*

Nud held on to his resolve and shifted his gaze to Kabor. Still, the Stout hadn't flinched.

The hag slowed her pace, wrapped her tendrils around the bases of several sticks, and carefully glided through the pike barrier. She coasted to a halt in the center of the garden and set the two of them down on the muddy bottom. The wood in Nud's pack kept him floating back up. The hag kept a tendril latched on him at all times, to keep him down.

The Queen of the Garden Under hadn't thought twice about the act of drowning them. Yet, there seemed to be some hint of affection in the way she went about her gruesome business: the way she so delicately wrapped Nud in braided rushes the way a spider wraps its tender prey in silk. And the way she so gently stroked his hair away from his forehead, like a mother might, to fully appreciate the precious face of her sleeping child. Kabor's death shroud was next.

To the hag, Nud and Kabor were more than mere show-pieces. They were her emotional treasures, to cherish and protect until the end of days. Nearly forty-five counts had passed and the hag had not yet honored her secret deal. She wasn't about to leave them alone any time soon either. Worse, after hoisting Nud up and floating him over the garden ring, she started feeling at his pockets. What a lovely beacon his sparking stone would make, flashing at the bottom of the bog for all eternity, a last sight for future victims.

Nud had just then gained his water lungs and comfortably suppressed the urge to breathe. All the while, the Stout had drifted death-like, just out of Nud's reach, and loosely tethered to a stick. The time had come to make their move.

When the hag's rearranging brought Nud close to Kabor, the Pip thought to grab for an arm or a leg and give it a tug — the signal. Kabor's reflexes bordered on precognition though, and his swift action is what set their escape in motion. Before even laying a hand on Kabor, the Stout sprung to life.

Something else stirred that instant as well, wholly unexpected. The spiked round mass fixed to the end of one of the pikes began to quiver. Tens of legs shot out, fan-like in all directions. Kabor lurched himself upwards as the central mass of the dark ball spun about its axis. Nud had encountered the thing years before — four years, to be exact. Somehow, the hag had acquired Fyorn's spider — the prize attraction in her gruesome collection. And somehow, it was still alive.

A sensation of dread overwhelmed Nud. His heart pumped wildly. Frantic, he propelled himself upwards after

Kabor, kicking the hag square in the face as he did so. His braided bounds quickly became undone. Kabor tore at his own bindings and set them adrift as he wriggled upwards. Hand over one eye, the hag batted at the spoiled ropes sinking in her midst. She let out a muffled screech.

Barely into their escape, Nud felt a wavering tremor. *The Shadow.* Water pushed into him in the wake of its passing. He glimpsed the dark tail of the hulking creature as it disappeared into the dimness.

The Shadow in the Water circled round and came back at them like a blur out of nowhere, crossing above and stifling Nud's and Kabor's ascent. Then it swam out of sight again. The bog queen gained water on them in that instant, and her groping tendrils lashed out. Nud felt her ropey grasp on his ankle. He glanced to Kabor – already snagged.

As they succumbed to the hag's grip once more, the Shadow maneuvered to make a third advance, this time angled from below. Suddenly there was turbulence and mayhem, thrashing and swirling water. Nud could barely see anything. He was thrust aside. The Shadow passed him with something in its jaws. All he spotted was a flailing limb.

"Kabor!" Nud screamed into the depths.

A muted wail of anguish reverberated through the water. Nud flipped head over heels, yanked by his ankle. Then the grip on Nud released.

The Shadow had taken the wrong prey and disappeared into the inky depths. Nud felt for Kabor and grabbed a hand. *There he is.*

But which way was up? Nud had lost track of time and direction. In the confusion, he went still for a moment and just let himself drift. The buoyancy of his backpack pointed the way, and off he went, Kabor in tow.

The two friends barreled straight into a mass of ropey vines. Although not fixed to anything solid, the vines were so entangled with one another that they opposed their every move, wrapping around limbs and pushing at their shoulders. Nud had to let go of Kabor to clear the way with both hands. He powered up with his legs.

Nearly out of breath, the Pip finally broke surface. He gulped for air – foul air and bitter on the tongue, like something dank and decayed. He looked around – only darkness. *This isn't right.* With no time to spare, he felt through the water for an arm, leg, anything. *Where's Kabor?* The Stout should've been right behind him.

Nud's heavy breaths pulsed through the silence. His heart still pounded.

He's not coming up. Nud whipped his pack off and dipped underwater, feeling everywhere with his hands.

Down into the tangles he dove, groping about frantically in complete darkness. He searched the water column around him, end to end and through and through.

Half a minute later, Nud's leg brushed against what felt like a hand in the weeds. He grasped it and pulled, but there was no life pulling back. Kabor's limp body was caught in the tangles. Nud twisted, jolted and finally yanked him out, then dragged him to the surface, and to shore – but not the sort of shore he was expecting.

Exhausted, Nud laid his best friends' cousin on the stony ground. He fumbled in the darkness to find the middle of his chest. No rise, no fall. Nothing. Nud felt for the Stout's face, plugged his nose and gave him two short breaths. He pushed down on Kabor's chest fast, repeatedly, to jumpstart his breathing. *Nothing.* He kept at it. *Nothing.* With every last bit of strength, Nud raised his fist up high and belted it down on Kabor.

He heard the spurt of water first; then coughing and a gasp for air. A long moment passed, and the Stout sucked in a single divine breath.

He's alive.

Kabor rolled over onto his stomach, retching.

CHAPTER XXIII

A hidden passage

The soggy and exhausted Stout lay face down on the dark, rocky shore, coughing and spouting bog water. Short, eager breaths regulated the urge to cough up a lung.

"I feel sick. <cough> Leno? Where am I?"

"A safe place," Nud said, scanning every direction. There wasn't a glint of light anywhere to break the darkness.

Nud collapsed beside him on the cold, wet stone; smiling, breathing, and indulging in the rush of having just cheated death. It was a selfish moment. The air was stale and smelled of all things that crawl into the earth to die. Nud didn't care. A long, black minute of well-deserved tranquility floated by as his body normalized to the new environment. He breathed in the heavy air, saturated with stagnant water. Side by side, they lay still and speechless. Their breaths grew even and steady. Kabor cleared his throat.

"Ahem. I… <cough> was trapped. I couldn't get out." The half-drowned Stout's fist thudded on his chest.

"I pulled you up," Nud said, "then I lost you in the tangles."

There was a long silence. Breathing.

Stones grinded under Kabor as he shifted his position. "Was that some kind of giant eel?"

"Dunno," Nud said. In the long pause that followed, he waited for a milky "Thank you."

"This is all your fault," Kabor spat, instead. The acid water he'd swallowed must have turned his words sour. "You were supposed to fight with us, but you weren't even moving… you let that hag get a hold on you." His voice began to waver. "I tried to help… <cough> and look where it got me." Kabor's hands fumbled in the dark. He grabbed Nud's arm. "What's the matter with you anyway?"

I was… seeing. A tall tower again, black with a dull sheen. But Nud couldn't tell Kabor that. Nud couldn't say that the hag wasn't what made him act that way. He didn't know what to say.

"Let go," was all that came out.

Kabor released his cold and clammy grip. "Where is that damn rock of yours anyway? It'd be nice if we could see down here. Did you *forget* to take it out?"

"No." Nud fumbled through his pockets. "We just got here and I spent most of my time saving your life." One by one, Nud stretched his soaked pockets wide open and felt through them.

"Well?" Kabor said. "<cough> Cough it up."

"I thought it was…" The stone just wasn't anywhere. Nud suddenly felt flush, heated. He patted himself down. "I don't know where it is."

Kabor let out an impatient sigh. "Did the ole crone take it?"

Nud snapped back, "I DON'T KNOW! Let me think."

He stopped what he was doing and thought through everything that had happened during the fight. The last thing he
remembered about the stone was looking into it after it didn't
blast away the hags the way he'd hoped. *I was dizzy.*

An unsettling feeling crept over him. He felt hollow
inside. *Where could I have put it?* He started searching again,
from the very beginning. Right pocket, left pocket, back pockets, shirt pocket…

Kabor egged him on, "I thought Pips were supposed to
have perfect memories."

"Shut up!" Nud's voice reverberated through the cave
system.

Finally, Nud remembered the backpack. "I know…"
When he undid the clasp and pulled back the flap, a pinch of
pale red light filtered out between the soaked pieces of deepwood. Tucked away at the very bottom corner was the stone.

Nud breathed a giant sigh of relief. During the mayhem,
he'd had half a mind to cast off the pack, for speed's sake. "It's
in the pack," he told Kabor.

"Yeah, I saw the flash."

"I don't even know how the bog stone got there," Nud
added. "It started in my pocket, then I took it out, and then…
no matter."

Nud fished the gem out. In the palm of his hand, the
point of light danced and played, trapped in its gummy
prison. There was scarcely a moment of calm between the flur-
ries of red flashes. It seemed… excited, if unliving stones can
be assigned such emotions.

Nud took a few minutes to empty his pack, shake the
remaining water out, wring his cloak and dump the water out
of the boots he'd packed. Kabor did what he could to make
himself less waterlogged as well.

"You know we can't swim back." Nud glanced to a nearby exit tunnel. By *we* Nud really meant *Kabor*, mostly. Nud was actually surprised the Stout could swim at all.

The Pip neatly repacked the wood and the boots, and left the flap open so everything inside would dry over time.

"We have to swim back," Kabor replied.

"I don't even know how I'd backtrack," Nud said. "It was dark and I was disoriented. If we try, we could get turned around and lose our way underwater. And what's to say you won't get stuck again? You could get us both killed, even if we did figure it out. And then there's the Shadow…"

"I think it ate the hag," he said.

"Hope so," Nud replied.

Silence. The Stout shook his head. "What about Cuz?"

The last Nud had seen of Gariff, he was in the process of being pulled under, just like them. He didn't answer.

The light of the stone steadied for a brief moment. The Stout and the Pip locked eyes. Nud didn't want to say *it*, or even to think *it*. The light vanished. When it returned, Kabor was still staring, but sideways-like.

Nud's lack of words spoke volumes.

Kabor let out a defeatist sigh. "You saw something, didn't you?"

In the uneasy silence that followed, Nud backed away and rested against the rock wall. A fist of stone jabbed him in the back.

"Gariff's okay. They're all okay," Nud said, trying to convince himself that such words could be true. He began to rationalize: "They weren't brought to the garden, plus the Shadow and one of the hags were tied up with us. That leaves two old ladies. Gariff is skinning one alive by now, and Bobbin's sipping tea with the other, exchanging turtle soup recipes."

Kabor smirked. "I believe the Gariff part. And either way, Bobbin's practically a floatation device."

Nud couldn't help but chuckle, despite his worries.

As the pair sat deluding one another, and themselves, chains of flickering light scattered off the bumpy stone walls, revealing the natural chamber around them. Fingerlings of tree roots jutted out here and there, while fossil imprints of small, insignificant creatures from an ancient sea embossed the stone. Above the wide pool from where they'd entered was a pitted and well-rounded dome. There were two ways out – the pool itself and an irregular, tube-shaped cave to one side. The chamber walls and the tunnel showed the elongated signs of shaping by water.

Nud scuttled over to the tube-cave and peered in, stone aglow. "A tight fit," he told Kabor. They'd have to stoop mainly, and crawl through some parts. Dense mats of fine roots dangled from the ceiling, nearly blocking passage in some areas, and thicker roots hugged the curvature of the rock wall. The roots played host to a nest of old cobwebs and vermin sheddings. The floor was chunky gravel. Despite all the signs and sheddings of past life cycles, as far as the Pip could see, no living thing dwelled there.

"We could probably dig our way up and out," Nud said, examining where the roots punched through. "The ground must be soft in some places."

"I doubt we can do that," Kabor said. "Roots work their way through small fissures in the rock and then expand into them. Besides, we could be underwater and underground at the same time."

Nud grimaced. "No. How is that even possible? Wouldn't we still be underwater then?"

Kabor sized up the chamber carefully, repeatedly rubbing

his scruffy chin as he closely examined the walls, the roots, and the floor. He put on his glasses, went right up to each feature and stared at it, inches from his face. When prompted, Nud described the overarching dome to him.

Kabor said, "Water *used* to run down through that big conduit, that's for sure."

"I can see that," Nud said.

"And did you notice the side openings?" the Stout added. "They're drains. They relieve pressure when she fills up."

"Why is it dry now?" Nud asked.

Kabor shrugged. "I don't know. The bog's ability to retain water, maybe. These tunnels are flooded regularly... a cycle. And I'd guess we're near the end of that cycle."

That didn't sound good. "How long?" Nud said. "It's as wet as it's ever going to get in the bog right now. And that BIG rain we just had—"

Kabor bit his upper lip and started shaking his head. "Dunno... years, decades. Maybe only during floods, or maybe it takes time to soak through. Or it could be that the ground shifted and there is no cycle to it anymore. Maybe..."

"Everything's dead," Nud said.

"Yeah."

In the minutes that followed, Kabor came up with a half dozen other theories, but none so convincing as the first few.

Nud broke in, "We should start moving."

With a tilt of his head, Kabor gestured to the passage. "You really think that's our best bet?"

Nud nodded. "We can always come back."

Kabor grunted. "Humph." A grim look came over him. He removed his glasses and put them away. "Lead the way then, Leno."

Holding his sparking stone in front of him, Nud peered

ahead into their would-be escape route. "It does seem to slope up a bit, right?"

"Yep. Good sign," Kabor assured him. The Stout seemed quite comfortable underground, having had experience working in one of the mines outside of the Bearded Hills. According to Gariff though, the younger of the two cousins was too easily distracted and never really accomplished anything productive on the job. In part, it was because – according to his cousin – Kabor avoided any and all honest work. That seemed about right to Nud. Gariff even commented once that Kabor used up more energy trying to get out of work than he would've expended just doing the job – always a workaround or a shortcut, never the straightforward and sensible way. At the mine, he'd spent his time roaming the drifts and getting into trouble, not to mention danger, until he was eventually let go.

To Kabor's credit though, he did apparently find a few stray mineral veins while picking away where others hadn't thought to look or had given up the search.

But this place was very different – the network of caves under the bog was nothing like the organized, reinforced tunnels of a Hill Stout mine. Water sculpted them, and water was a Pip's element.

Nud started along the passageway, gripping the bog stone in one hand. Every few yards he stopped, held it up, and waited for the flicker to reveal the way.

Kabor continually and repeatedly asked about what was coming next, how tight the fit was going to be, and whether the tunnel looked safe. "The flashes are fast sometimes" he complained, or "the shadows are confusing."

"Just follow my lead," Nud told him.

The Pip soon discovered that the easiest way through was to crawl and wriggle his way along the gravelly floor, abandoning walking upright altogether. After several long minutes, they came to a divide in the passage. The main course abruptly widened and leveled out. An offshoot tunnel veered off to one side, curved, then ran nearly parallel as far out as Nud could see.

A light breeze refreshed the air at that junction. It was a good sign. Their luck seemed to be turning. They kept on through the larger tunnel.

"Out in no time," Nud said, spirits raised. "Imagine what it'd be like without my stone." As they crawled over the cold gravel on hands and knees, Nud's mind began to drift towards the world above and the fate of their good friends. *What are their chances?* he wondered to himself.

Gradually, the passage gained in height and became high enough to walk along, without stooping. Over time, the bed of gravel disappeared, replaced by larger, rounder river stones. Footing became an issue in the dim and fractured light, and after stubbing a few toes Nud began thinking boots might be a good idea. They reached a zone where dark crevices loomed above, adding even more height. And a new odor filled the air – pungent, a bit like old fish. Nud stopped to rest by a small offshoot tunnel and hauled his boots out of his pack. That's when he noted the first signs of life – the floor was splotted with animal scat.

"Look, Kabor," Nud said, pointing to the droppings.

"I ran into some a while back," Kabor said. "They're all over the place."

"Bats?" Nud asked.

"Maybe." He tilted his gaze to the ceiling. "They might like those fissures in the roof. Did you hear anything?"

Nud shook his head.

The boots were still dripping wet, so Nud tied them

upside-down to a shoulder strap on the pack, for later use. He glanced to Kabor's feet.

"How did you swim with those clunkers on?" Nud asked. *Only a Stout would go swimming with his boots on, and leave them on afterwards.*

Kabor shrugged. "I gave it my all, I guess."

Nud almost replied "At least they're not as bad as Gariff's," but stopped himself. *No one can swim with boots that big on.* The thought sickened him.

Over the next leg of the journey, the scenery more-or-less repeated itself many times over – a dark, winding tube-like passage of smooth limestone with no major offshoots, small cracks and crevices here and there, and a stony path beneath their feet. At times, it was difficult to tell if they were traveling up or down. Certainly, there was no way to determine their bearing – they could've been directly under Webfoot Hall, for all they knew, or on their way to Turnsby. Along the cave roof, fewer and fewer roots showed through until there were none at all.

So, after a long crawl and a doubly long hike, Nud and Kabor came upon a choke point in the passage. Rubble covered the ground and stacked up along the sides – a partial collapse. Nud inhaled the sweet air – high quality. The breeze had become stronger and it carried a pleasant water and mineral scent.

Kabor noted the change in Nud's demeanor. "What is it?"

"Water. Don't you smell it?"

"I hear it."

They stopped to poke at the fallen debris. Nud found a weak point in the pile and punched through to the other side.

"Ahhh!" Nud yelled, as he toppled forward. Arms reaching, he scraped at the wall when he felt himself drop. A rush surged through him as he whipped over the edge of a dark abyss, hanging by two fingers jammed in a crack.

"Leno?" Kabor called.

Teetering in mid-air, his dangling foot felt out a solid rock hold. Kabor reached out. Nud grasped his hand and the Stout pulled him back into the tunnel.

"Whoa, that was close," Kabor said, when they were back on solid ground. "That's a huge drop."

Nud turned around to examine the deep crack in the earth, looking it up and down. "The passage opens straight into it," he said. Across the gap – no more than a few feet – water trickled down from above and sprayed slippery doom on the glistening cliff wall. The mist chilled Nud's cheeks and forehead.

Holding the light over the drop, Nud stretched his neck out and peered into the depths of the dark rift. Below, a proven drop to sudden death beckoned. He shuffled forward, the gravity of the downward plunge drawing him closer to the edge, as though inviting him to join the scattering of bones at the bottom. Staving off dizziness, Nud described everything he saw to Kabor, who stood behind him. The Stout stretched his own neck out to have a look.

"Wow," he said. "Now that's a doozy."

"Death by plummet." Nud waited for the next flurry of flashes, then tilted his gaze up. A second cave opened into the gap, a dozen feet higher on the far wall, and offset to the right another five feet. By its size and shape, it appeared as though it'd once connected with the passage they stood in. A steady stream of water sputtered off the edge of the high opening and fell like red rain, glimmering in the light of the stone.

Kabor pushed Nud aside to get a better view. "I've never seen anything like this before."

After a few minutes, the two friends retreated into the tunnel a safe distance, then collapsed, backs to the cave wall. They pondered their predicament.

*

A knot developed in Nud's stomach as he sat peering through the rubble and surveying the obstacle ahead. *Did we go the wrong way?*

Kabor, as usual, was thinking the opposite. "We can scale it," he said.

"I don't kn—"

"There's only up or back down," Kabor cut in. He said it like it was an obvious, everyday problem that required an equally obvious plan.

"What about that one side tunnel, not too far back?" Nud reminded him. "That might be the way."

"Too tight," Kabor said. "I say we go up. That's the way out. The fissure is narrow enough for us to wedge in as we climb."

"It's slippery," Nud said.

Kabor was either fearless, reckless or completely oblivious to the incredible peril that went along with his recommendation.

"Listen," Nud said. He grabbed a loose stone and tossed it through the break in the rubble. It smacked the far wall and fell into the rift. The stone dropped for a count of two, then ricocheted several times before coming to rest at the bottom. "That's a long way. Why do you think there are bones down there?"

Kabor huffed. "They're probably ancient animal bones." He stood up, shuffled to the edge, and ran his hand along the inside wall of the chasm. "Look at all the holds," he went on.

"No able-bodied Stout – or even a Pip – should have any trouble scaling that wall. Just shimmy up where it pinches in."

"That would be suicide," Nud said.

Kabor snapped back, "Suicide is sitting here doing nothing."

The argument continued, more for the sake of argument than for finding alternatives, but in the end, the choice was clear. Being the lighter and more agile climber, Nud would climb first. The plan was that Kabor would brace himself to catch Nud by a limb or the pack strap if he slipped. Once he made it up to the other cave entrance, Nud would help to pull Kabor in. The plan was a terrible plan, but it was the only real plan they could come up with.

"Strap the pack on tight," Kabor said. "It might be your lifeline."

To start the climb, Nud planted one bare foot firmly at the very edge of the opening on his side. He took a deep breath, gripped the bog stone in his teeth, and then led off with a forward lunge over the divide. He jammed his other foot into a cleft on the other side. Stretching his arm as far as he could, he finger-gripped a small ledge jutting out above him. Water trickled over his hand. Nud held the "splits" position for a second or two, and then shifted his weight to the opposing side of the chasm. One leg dangling, he felt out a second foothold and, slowly, began his ascent up the slimy wall.

"Wha ish som'ens up there?" Nud grumbled, jaw clenched on the bog stone to illuminate the climb. "Wha ish I shlip and fall?"

"I told you I'd catch you," Kabor said. He firmly straddled the two walls just beneath the Pip. Then sarcasm tainted his echoey voice: "But I already changed my mind, so you *should* worry about falling. As for someone up there – not a problem, there's nobody here but you and me… and *her?*"

"Wha?" Nud's foot slipped on the grimy surface. Kabor caught the sole of it. His large hand cupped the Pip's foot as he gave Nud a boost.

Kabor chuckled. "Be careful, Leno."

"Vewy shfunny," Nud said, and scrambled up a little higher.

"That's good," Kabor coached, "you're doing it. Just keep doing what you're doing."

Nud gripped the ledge of the high cave, and muscled up into it. He waited for a flash, and soon saw that the chamber was large and empty. Rubble was everywhere, and the ceiling was high and irregular, but roughly domed. Water poured in from above just two or three steps in, creating the streamlet that spilled and splashed into the drop. A passage cut across the cave. It ran roughly parallel to the rift. That tunnel was tall with smooth, straight walls – very different from anything they'd seen up until then.

Nud waved the Stout up. "All clear," he hollered.

Kabor was already reaching for the ledge. Nud waited until the Stout had a firm hold, then grabbed his other arm and yanked him up.

Kabor scrambled through the opening, then turned to regard Nud. "See – easy. Did you notice the walls on your way up?"

"What about them?"

"The side we were on is limestone. This rock is something else altogether. I can't quite place it." Kabor's eyes darted about the new cave. "Man-made," he said, straightaway, and started feeling the stonework. He almost laughed. Kabor waved Nud over to a spot along the chamber wall, then crouched down in front of it, eyes only inches from its surface. Nud brought the light down close. Every flicker revealed something new.

"You're right, it's man-made," Nud said.

Kabor nodded. "But this isn't mine construction – that's for sure." He pressed his index finger into a groove and ran it along the wall horizontally, then vertically. "There are bricks underneath the dirt and grime, and there's no such thing as a brick mine."

"Where do you think it leads?" Nud said.

"The ceiling height is about right for an old-worlder," Kabor said, then scratched his head. "It must lead out one way or the other." He paused for a long moment, then drew his eyebrows together. "But why is it here in the first place?"

"How did they keep the water out?" Nud said.

The Stout just shrugged and shook his head. "More importantly, why did they leave?"

Kabor judged the left passage to be up-sloping. Nud loosened the straps on his pack and they started along the path. Partially caved-in areas became commonplace along the way, and once they had to dig their way through a heavy choke point. Over time, new openings began to appear on either side. There were brick throughways, wide at the top and narrowing downward in a slow curve to the earthen floor, nearly to a point. To Nud's untrained eye, it looked upside down to what it should be.

They kept to their path with few words. Again, Nud brought to mind the Mire Trail incident. It almost seemed prophetic how Kabor had only recently recited the "Legend of the Bog Queens" and now they were hopelessly entangled in the story's inner workings. He'd told the tale and they'd shared a good laugh at Gariff's expense. *Good Gariff,* Nud thought. *He probably had nightmares. Did the hags hear us that day? Was this some kind of punishment? Poetic justice?* They'd gone from telling the story to living it in a matter of days. A kind of morbid recurrence seemed to be at play in the world.

"What do you think happened to Gariff and Bobbin and Holly?" Nud asked, his tone solemn. Nud knew Kabor was thinking about them too.

The Stout scrunched his shoulders, and then shook his head; his expression uncommonly blank. Nud left the conversation at that.

*

Farther along, the pair came upon a new source of running water. Mist and the noise of random patter filtered into the passageway. Rounding a corner, the tunnel suddenly lost most of its man-made features and opened up into a large, airy chamber with a domed roof again. The original construction was fractured. Piles of rubble lay scattered about, and water poured through a gaping hole in the ceiling. It splashed down into a pool that spanned the room from side to side. Water swirled in the center and drained to unknown depths, and a gentle streamlet spilled out of the chamber on the far side, down through another tunnel.

Nud eyed the water flow. "We're down-sloped, now," he said.

Kabor nodded. "Could be a temporary dip to get around something."

"Like what?"

"Another structure, a pond… the mayor's basement, hard rock… anything you wouldn't want to dig through or run into."

"I wouldn't mind running into the mayor's basement right about now," Nud said.

Kabor laughed. "I bet he has some nice wine down there…
up there, I mean."

Crossing the pool was easy enough, owing to the rubble
that littered the floor. They stepped and hopped from pile-to-
pile as far as they could, towards the rushing column of water.

To complete the crossing, they had no choice but to get
wet. After cupping a drink, Nud removed his pack, placed
the bog stone gently on top, and waded into the cold waters
of the pool. He gently pushed his pack so it would glide to
the other side, and then dove under and swam to the bottom.
Nud floated there for a long minute, hovering, arms and legs
spread wide apart, ears tuned to the pacifying rush of the falling water. The weight of the fluid surrounding Nud kept him
intact physically, the way it gently pushed in from all sides, and
mentally, the way the muted hush released his tension. Not
only was the experience refreshing, and healing, it was almost
spiritual in the way the rest of the world just disappeared.

Eventually, Nud resurfaced and ferried his pack the rest of
the way to the other side. He clambered out of the pool, dripping wet. Kabor had tossed his clothes across and was already
waiting there, tying his boot laces.

Muscles sore and aching, knees and elbows scraped, and
ever-so-tired after a the longest of days, Nud slid his pack
over his shoulders and set out on his way once more. Kabor
slumped along beside him.

The events of the day still haunted Nud's thoughts. Kabor
hadn't seen what he'd seen, just before being pulled under.
Maybe it wasn't right to keep the information from him. But
Nud needed Kabor to stay focused. He needed them both to
stay focused. *You never know,* he told himself, *they might be safe
after all.*

The sinking feeling in Nud's gut told him otherwise

though, and the echo of Holly's scream etched in his memory left the Pip little doubt about their fate, and his role in it.

Nud squeezed his eyes shut. *Kabor's right — this is all my fault. I wish I'd never found that stupid stone.*

CHAPTER XXIV

Flicker

In time, the schedule of flashes became so familiar to Nud that the intervening dead-times – the dark intervals – went by unnoticed. When the Pip relaxed his eyes and let his mind wander, the gaps seemed to fill in all by themselves, phantom-like, smoothly morphing one illuminated scene into the next.

With the mystifying light as their only guide, the heavy feet of the two lost travelers fell into the monotony of a steady march through the underground cave system. The going was good when they kept to the sturdy tunnels, and progress was even-paced for what seemed like hours. Spurious noises became commonplace: scratching, clicking, drips, drops, echoes, and the hollow sounds of wind were all present. That meant life, food, water, and circulating air. Kabor took them as signs that the surface was near. "Cave dwelling animals don't venture far underground," he'd said. Nud wasn't so convinced.

Again, the Pip's senses rose to high alert, having picked up on a repetitive scratching sound, nearly hidden in the clutter of familiar cave noises. It was a rare and subtle thing, but distinctive, and only barely within earshot when it was there at all. If Nud stopped to listen, it would silence, and the Pip would be left to question whether or not the sound was ever really there. But it was. The signature pattern of scratching persisted for long minutes at a time before disappearing for a stint, only to return later.

Chk-chk-fwip… chk-chk-fwip.

Most times it came from behind them, but sometimes from ahead, and once, even from above, after they'd stopped to rest in yet another domed chamber – the fourth of their journey. Nud's gut feeling was acting up again. Kabor, who was better at picking up noises overall, seemed unconcerned when Nud pointed them out. "Just critters," was all he'd said.

The going, although good, was by no means direct. Three times along their course, debris-choked passages blocked passage and forced them to backtrack and take a side tunnel. With all the winding about, eventually they entered a new zone. The air seemed fresher again and there were less structural problems. Despite marginally lifted spirits, the traveler's legs were simply too weary to carry them much farther.

At first, they talked to keep one another awake, mostly about the events that shaped their predicament: the chance meeting with Mer at the Flipside, the visit to Fyorn's, Jory's enthusiasm to accompany them, Nud's decision to brandish the stone… Mer – whatever happened to Mer? Nud wondered aloud if the hags had gotten to the prospector as well. Kabor commented that the Shadow in the Water probably tried to chew him up, but spit him out – too tough.

Kabor continued to stumble along for some time, barely cognizant, having nearly fallen asleep mid-step on several occasions – he'd start to mumble incoherently just before tripping over his own feet. The Pip caught him each time, before he ever hit the ground.

"We need a break," Nud said, finally. "It's late. And you can't keep my eyes open…" Nud tried to shake the tiredness off.

"I mean, I can't keep your eyes open." Nud shook himself again.

Kabor spoke for him. "Whatever the specifics, our two pairs of eyes cannot remain open much longer." He let out a soft chuckle, followed by a sleepy nod of agreement.

The pair took half a moment to settle into adequate, if not comfortable, resting places on one side of the passage they were in. The floor was earthen with a few scattered stones and pieces of brick protruding. Nud shrugged the backpack off his shoulders and slumped against a dry and plain looking section of wall. His body ached everywhere and his were shoulders raw where the straps rubbed against his skin. The simple act of taking the load off his legs felt like absolute luxury. He tucked the stone away and decided that he wouldn't be getting up again for a long, long time.

As sleep began to wash over Nud, he pondered the prospects of endless days persisting on bugs for food – if it came to that – and imagined all of the corners and cracks they might be hiding in.

Kabor was already snoring by the time Nud's dragging fatigue pulled him under the liquid gloom. He quickly succumbed to the cloak of unconsciousness and plummeted into a deep sleep. In the netherworld of dreams, Nud envisioned the vast wetlands outside of Webfoot, with fields of green reeds swaying in a light breeze on a drizzly day. Only a faint patch of light shone through the grey sky where the sun crouched over the horizon.

It began to flicker.

Nud jolted awake, startled, with the scent of bog water heavy in his nostrils and the sound of the whirring wind still in his ears. Except the scent wasn't bog water – it was the dampness of the cave. And the whirring sound was not wind – it was Kabor's raspy, early morning voice. Nud didn't know the words. Nor did he care.

"Go away," Nud said. *How long was I asleep? A minute?* The Stout's choppy speech suggested he hadn't slept much either.

"I heard something," Kabor whispered. He shook Nud's shoulders.

"You heard nothing," Nud countered, and promptly fell back asleep.

Kabor shook Nud again. "Leno, we're almost there. The way out is just ahead – we should go."

The Stout was beginning to sound like a recurring night-mare: "just around the corner" or "maybe up that way" or "I can smell a Stout mine on the breeze" – Nud'd heard them all. And he wasn't the only one fool enough to proclaim they'd be out in no time. Wishful thinking – dangerous thinking – all of it.

Nud didn't open his eyes or say a word. He just shook his head.

"What if the hags are following us?" Kabor pleaded. "We have to keep moving – we don't have much food – just a few berries I picked and some maple candy from your uncle that I didn't tell Bobbin about."

"He's just Fyorn now," Nud said.

"Huh?"

"Those hags… just let me… think for a bit," Nud said. "If we run out of food, we can… well… if we have to… I hear all kinds of scurrying sounds in the walls."

"Yeah, bugs and moles," Kabor said. "Fine fair for a Pip maybe, but not for me."

Chk-chk-fwip... Chk-chk-fwip.

Nud's body tensed. He forced himself awake, unnerved by the sound. The Pip sat up and retrieved his bog stone. In the first flash of light, something moved along the far wall. Nud pointed.

"There!"

A shadowy thing about a quarter their size scurried into the darkness.

The spider?

Nud scrambled to his feet and stared down the passage, holding the stone above his head. With dead eyes and a sideways look, Kabor stared too.

"Do you see anything?" said the Stout.

Nud waited for the next burst. "Nope... wait... nope."

"Is it a hag, do you think?"

"Nope... it might be a giant spider."

"Shit," Kabor said. "That's just great."

They both held their breath and listened intently. The air was dead and the passage deathly quiet... the regular noises that cave things make in the dark had subsided. Only the sound of water dripping into a shallow puddle persisted.

"I don't like this," Nud said. "You're right. What I'd do for a simple torch."

"What about your bow?"

"A shot in the dark?"

"Better than no shot."

Nud passed the bog stone to the Stout and unhooked his bow from the side of the pack. It took half a minute just to untangle the bowstring. In the meantime, Kabor picked up a rock and whipped it into the darkness.

The Stout watched and waited while Nud strung the bow, gathered the arrows, and notched one. The Pip swept his gaze over the chamber. *Nothing.* Slow and quiet, they gathered their things and, shoulder-checking as they went, footpadded deeper into the cave system.

Kabor had grabbed the pack this time. He offered to carry the stone as well, so Nud could shoot unhindered – Nud let him. The Pip kept an arrow notched and his bow slightly bent for a good long time as they continued on their way. Not surprisingly, the way out wasn't "just up ahead" as Kabor had thought. The air did shift again though. Nud couldn't quite place the difference. Kabor said it was a mine smell.

After that encounter, they spent a daylight's worth of hours exploring the network of tunnels.

Legs weary, they gave in to the notion that they'd be stuck underground at least one more "night," and so once again settled to rest. This time, they chose a section of passage that they'd passed twice already and taken special note of. The area was home to a protected cubbyhole for sleeping.

Nud cleared a space to rest and used his pack for a pillow, then felt the need to put his boots on, finally, before cocooning into his cloak. They agreed to take watches, Kabor's being the first. The moment Nud's head hit the pack was the moment he found himself somewhere in Deepweald again, at least in spirit. A normal sleep just wouldn't do though, and so Nud slipped into recall. Having seen the spider-thing in the hag's garden had stirred up old memories. Memories he needed to explore more thoroughly.

CHAPTER XXV

Heart of Darkness

Hatchet in one hand, box in the other, Nud made off towards a part of the woods that he knew would be clear of Fyorn and Paplov. The woodsman never brought them that way. "Best keep out of those thickets," he'd once said. "There's no good wood that way, and the bugs'll eat you alive." But it was some hidden place that Nud sought, away from prying eyes, and the bugs shouldn't be out yet, so early in spring.

Nud trampled over the last remnants of melting snow, twigs crunching underfoot. His heart quickened with anticipation. The buzz of old growth forest urged him on, alive with its earthy scents. Nature had just been jarred awake by a late rush of spring air and was making up for lost time. Nud sped up, faster. Small birds flitted from branch to branch as he passed, and foraging chipmunks scooted up tree trunks. Excitement seemed to loom beneath every strip of bark, behind every bush, and below every winter-trodden leaf. Nud didn't think much about where he was going.

He'd never been alone in *those* woods before. Countless times, Fyorn had led Nud and his grandfather along forest paths looking for wood salvage: branches or even entire trees felled by windstorms or lightning. He'd dragged the good pieces all the way back to his workshop, no matter how big they were, or how small. Nud thought he'd been following one of the woodsman's paths, but when he glanced back over his shoulder, the path behind him simply wasn't there – like it'd disappeared. In fact, the forest around him looked the same in every direction.

And that is how Nud came upon a clearing he'd never seen before.

A rocky outcrop formed the foundation of the spot, surrounded by tall pines. It opened to a small cliff that overlooked grassy lowlands, still snow-packed in the hollows. Chilled air billowed up the precipice and into the grove, carrying with it the dank scent of wet earth. In the middle of the clearing, a crooked old oak tree stood sentry over a thick bed of fallen leaves. The tree's low, outstretched branches cupped a family of warblers, puffed up and warmly nestled in.

Finally, the time had come. Nud set the axe down on the rock dome and weighed the box in his hands. After a long, examining look, he wedged his fingernails beneath the lid and pulled up firmly. Tap… tap… tap… came a sound from inside.

A cloud blocked out the sun, the temperature dropped sharply, and the warblers scattered in a whirling flurry.

Try as Nud might, the box wouldn't open. It had no latch and no hinges, so he tried using the axe, gently forcing the blade into the slim gap beneath the lid. Working the keen edge inwards and twisting, the nails gave some and he pried the lid up, just a bit. He jammed the tips of his fingers into the box to keep the lid from tensing back down.

From within, cold goo oozed out of the box. And something nudged his fingertips.

Nud jerked his hand out, but the lid didn't snap shut. Instead it bowed. Nails screeched. A slithering, fleshy mass pushed up on the lid. A black tendril whipped out, with the uncanny speed of a coiled serpent.

"Ahhh!"

Nud flung the abomination into the air and dashed to the trees. The box smashed against a branch with a splintering crack. Before Nud could get anywhere, he tripped over a root, let go the axe and smacked the ground. Something landed on the side of his face.

The Pip let out a muffled scream. It was the thing, sticky and oozing, its tendrils writhing over Nud's face like a dozen snakes. Two slimy appendages drilled into his ears, and another pair twisted up his nostrils. Others pressed at his eye sockets and tried to get in his mouth.

Frantic, Nud ripped the black mass off his face and tossed it aside. He leapt to his feet, then grabbed the axe. A blur shot across the ground in front of him, between sharp rocks and beneath patchy underbrush. Brandishing his weapon, Nud pursued.

The creature scurried up a mossy boulder at the edge of the clearing, and perched there. It bore likeness to a giant spider, crouching in the way that jumping spiders crouch, as though poised for a spring attack.

The body of this thing was black and insect-like, but meaty in the middle. Its weight was borne on long, spindly legs – tens of them. The thing dripped black oil and the centre throbbed like a beating heart.

With a slight tilt and roll of its eyeless central ball, the thing measured Nud's presence. The two stood facing one another, the spider-thing and Nud, at an impasse it seemed. They stayed that way until a tremendous buzzing sound roared up from the earth. A cloud of flying insects swarmed all around – insects that shouldn't have been there in the first place. Nud waved frantically to keep them away. They landed on his arms. They got into his hair. Some crawled up his sleeves. In a frenzy, he swooshed the axe at them, which of course didn't help. More crawled down the back of his neck and into his shirt. They bit and stung, repeatedly.

Running in circles and flailing about, cursing and squishing the bugs in his hair, Nud found no practical way to defend himself against the swarm. And when he came to the edge of the drop, he froze. For a foolish moment, he considered making the treacherous leap off the rocky outcrop and down to the fractured ground below. He backed away instead.

Then something unexpected happened, as if enough of the unexpected hadn't happened already. That old oak tree in the middle of the clearing began to *move*. Not just by swaying in the breeze. It moved over the ground, from one place to another. The tree closed in on Nud, frozen in place. And this tree wasn't alone. Slender conifers joined in from the perimeter, forcing Nud back towards the precipice. And the insects persisted. The Pip's next step would meet open air instead of solid earth or rock, and there was nowhere left to go but down. Nud reconsidered his odds of surviving the plummet to the rocky bed below.

No… Instead, the Pip planted his feet as firmly as he could and adopted a wide stance. Precariously perched on the cliff's edge, he gritted his teeth and readied the axe with both hands. Bugs crawled over his face, but he ignored them. Sweat stung his eyes.

The crooked old oak tree led the advance. With a deafening

crack, it bent down in front of Nud. He swung Fyorn's axe with all his might, but missed his mark. The momentum of his swing nearly sent him spinning off the edge. He teetered for a long moment, but held his own.

The tree paused and made a deep, windy sound. A large hollow in its trunk opened wide like a gaping jaw, twisted and contorted. Black, pointed thorns made for jagged teeth.

Nud's body tensed. He swallowed his breath. With a deep inhale and sudden burst of energy, Nud feigned to the left and lunged right, intent on making a run for the "real" tree line. But he was a beat too late, for in that very same instant a branch lashed out and struck Nud hard in the chest. It lifted the Pip right off the ground and sent him flying backwards, out of the clearing and over the drop.

Up and then down Nud flew, in a rush of backwards acceleration, farther and faster. He cringed, anticipating the coming smash to the back of his head against a tree, or a stray boulder, or hard ground.

Nud's recall suddenly warped. *Something's wrong.*

The sky flickered, and then went dark.

When it flashed back on, Nud was in freefall, and a thousand disembodied eyes filled the space around him. They watched him as he fell, floating and swirling everywhere; they studied him and they studied everything. The world went dark again, and in the flurry of red sparks that followed, the eyes were gone.

Nud should've hit the ground in a pair of heartbeats after being thrown off the cliff, yet his plummet continued. A stinging branch whipped him on his way down, and then another. Soon he was crashing through a canopy of whipping branches. All at once, the foliage became so thick that it broke his fall. A branch caught Nud and he hung there, suspended, facing down the trunk of a colossal tree.

A young woman with beautiful auburn hair stood on the ground below. It was Holly, staring up at Nud from some fifty feet beneath him. Except it wasn't Holly for long. The young woman looked to her feet before the next dark interval, and in the light of the next flash, she tilted her gaze to Nud and he saw she was a hag. Soothing olive eyes begged for affection in a soft, motherly way. Her hair had turned stringy and dripping wet, and she was covered from head to toe in muck, moss and grasses. The hag-Holly started to regurgitate something, shuddering in the midst of her effort. On her second try, the young woman heaved and spouted bile. And while greyish fluid oozed down her chin and neck, gargled words rolled out from deep within her gut.

"Down… down… down," she chanted in a drowning voice. "Down… down… down…"

With a rising roar, a strong gust shook the branches and flung Nud off. Arms flailing, he grabbed at anything, and landed solid on a spread of thick branches. He locked eyes with a gnarled face set in the tree trunk. Panicked, he let go. The face glared after him as he began his third descent – it had Fyorn's visage. Again, the branches whipped past Nud, until he landed in a giant web. The black spider-thing scurried out of its spider hole and rushed the Pip. Nud jerked and slashed at the strands, until he broke free. But there was nothing left to cushion his final descent.

The inevitable happened; his back struck the ground with a tremendous CLUNK! He heard his own spine snap. His body crumpled. There could be no denial.

Then all went black, and in the instant that followed, Nud beheld a grim figure of death. The figure stood at Nud's feet as he lay, looming tall and dark as a long shadow. He wore a thick, hooded cloak. The grim figure grasped a long scythe taller than he was. The tip of the wicked blade was a hook for the unwilling. His face – if indeed he had one – lay shrouded in the black cloud of his cowled hood. Death stood there, judging. And… flat, as though lacking depth. Nud's heart seized, his chest tightened.

Shroud's Well. I'm dead and the Grim Reaper has come to claim my soul.

In the flurry of that realization, the budding of that free and rational thought, the dark apparition began to dissolve. First, he flickered, and then he faded into tiny specks of patchy, utter blackness. One by one, the dots disappeared until there was nothing left to see of the Reaper. Nothing but empty space.

*

Nud opened his eyes. Slowly the pale glow and familiar flicker of the gem melted into view. His head was spinning, his mind charged. It'd only been a recall, but the transition to reality had not been without doubt. And some of it, at least, had been false.

Nud lay frozen in a cold sweat, afraid to stir. His neck felt stiff and sore. He found himself wishing that he'd flattened out the lengths of deepwood in his pack before resting his head on them.

The Pip reminded himself that what he'd just relived was not an accurate portrayal of how the events really unfolded. He reminded himself that the gaping maw in the oak tree had opened a second time and swallowed the spider-thing, and that Nud, when thrown, had landed far afield on a bed of thick moss with only slight injuries and a nasty cut from the axe. He reminded himself that he'd fled back to the cabin afterwards, with no word to Paplov or Fyorn about what'd happened.

CHAPTER XXVI

Interlude - Reckoning

Recall can be a strange and finicky thing for some; especially those who cross the thin veil of reality into something else; something beyond. Is what they experience still real?

Surely, that world of shadow they enter is formed of real things, twisted and contorted as they may be. But so difficult to tell what is real and what is not, while spiraling up and away from imagination's abyss – climbing countless layers of cryptic illusion – and then crashing through the paper wall of consciousness.

Many years would pass before knowledge of the strange creature unleashed in the forest ever came my way. It was not a mere spider. The thing, the *Heart of Darkness*, was a danger to us all, returned to the hands of its maker for destruction. Just possessing it violated the Treaty of Nature. My uncle would have to answer for that, eventually.

Oh, how easy it can be to twist a selfish desire into something justified by good intentions –the means by the ends, and such. Everyone does it...

CHAPTER XXVII

He who holds the light is king

Kabor lay beside Nud, breathing shallow and steady. *Fast asleep – so much for guard duty.*

The bog stone rested between them. The Pip stared into the shadowy red void for a long minute, pondering his dream and the notion of death. He hadn't really thought much about death before. Sure, in recent memory he'd known Pips and Stouts with relatives who'd passed on. He just never really thought much of it. Nud was a young child when he'd lost his own parents and when his grandfather, Paplov, had taken on their roles. Apart from a few scraps of distant, but fond, imprints from the earliest times, all that really stuck with him about his parents was a feeling... kindness. Nud could still picture the blur of light behind his father's head as the man stood tall above him, looking down kindly. "Little Newt," he'd say as he patted the young Pip's head. But in his mind's eye, Nud could never see the face. And his mother...

Nud shook off the sensation. Morning or night, they'd have to measure time by the number of "sleeps," which got Nud wondering just how many sleeps they could last. *And what if the light goes out…*

His scalp prickled with the implications. *No one will ever find us here.*

Nud reached over to the Stout and shook him until he pushed back. Kabor moaned and rubbed his eyes.

"Where… What is it?"

"Wake up," Nud said, giving the Stout a strong nudge. "Get your stuff together; we have to go back… we have to go back and swim out. This was a mistake."

Kabor responded by closing his eyes. Nud shook him again until he was fully awake.

"We might not last if we continue this way."

"Go back?" Kabor said. "That's crazy. No, you were right. You said we can't swim back – you can't just flip sides like that, not now. We've come too far."

"We tried, okay. We gave it our all. We tried, but now it's taking too long and we're just getting deeper and deeper into this system. Who knows where it ends, or if it ever ends."

"But the animals… we can't be too far from the surface. We could live off them, like you said."

"What if the light goes out Kabor? What if it just stops? Then what?"

"It won't go out."

"How do you know that?"

"I just know. Have you forgotten about the bog queens?"

"I don't forget."

"That doesn't mean you know what you're talking about, Leno." Kabor turned away and rolled onto his side. "And this tunnel leads out. I can feel it in my bones. Go back to sleep."

Nud paused. "We don't know where it goes or what's waiting for us. Worse things than bog queens could be skulking about in these forsaken caves. Besides, in broad daylight with people looking for us all over the bog, the hags will make themselves scarce."

"Who's looking?" Kabor said.

"Well… Paplov knows we're overdue, and Gariff's father, and the Numbits. The guards at the trailhead would be wondering what happened to Jory. They must *all* be looking for us."

Nud stood up, determined to get moving. He hooked in his bow and slung his backpack over his shoulders.

"If we leave right now," he urged, "we can get there for daylight – I think. I can make it to the surface; I know I can. Once I'm back on the trail, I'll fetch help to bring you up… and maybe a long rope would be all we need to guide you. You could follow it and—"

Kabor huffed, then rose to his feet and brushed the dirt off. "No. I'm going with you from start to finish."

"You'll drown. I don't know the way, and I don't want to have to babysit you trying to find it."

"You want to leave me alone down here? I'll need the stone to see."

"You're half blind anyway, just sit in the dark and wait."

"I'm not half blind. If it's daylight like you say, you won't need it. Just swim towards the light."

"I'll need it to see through the dark water, and to get back to you."

"You have a perfect memory, just use it."

"What's to remember about the dark?"

"At least if I have the bog stone, you can just swim to the light again to find me."

"If I have the light with me, I can probably remember my way."

"Probably? Weeds are weeds, Leno. And if you don't find your way back, what then? I'm left here to die, alone and in the dark."

Neither of them said a word for a long moment. When the light flickered on, Kabor turned his head sideways to fix his gaze directly on the stone. Nud sensed a scheme forming behind those dull eyes, lurking. Kabor broke the silence.

"Maybe we can bust it into two pieces," he said, "and each take one."

"That's the surest way to snuff it out," Nud retorted, "and way too risky. You'll just have to wait in the dark for a little while. Like I said, I'm sure someone's already looking for us. All I need is some rope and…"

"No. I'd rather take my chances moving forward than backtracking. Up is up, it's not that complicated."

"We're lost down here. There's only one way out! We have to go back."

"I'll make it on my own then," Kabor retorted.

Stubborn Stout.

"If we stick together, we stand a better chance," Nud said.

"Something's following us," Kabor countered. "You saw it last night. No way. I'd rather take my chances with whatever's up ahead than be left in the dark wondering who will find my bones."

"I'm done arguing." Nud turned to go back the way they'd come. He glanced over his shoulder. "We're going back and that's final," he said, and went to take a step.

Kabor grabbed for the bog stone with a sleight of hand so fast, Nud didn't know what hit him. The Stout swiped it and danced away, deftly.

"What are you doing? Give it back!"

"No."

"It's mine! Give it back!"

"You stu—"

Nud cuffed him in the head. Kabor lurched backwards.

"Filcher! Liar!" Nud grabbed for the stone. Kabor pushed back, holding it out of reach behind him. Nud muscled in closer, swiping to regain his prized possession.

"You… would just leave me here?" Kabor said.

"Temporarily."

Kabor executed a swift maneuver and wriggled free. Then he backed away. "You need my help to get—"

"You're the only one that needs help," Nud cut in.

"We'll see about that," Kabor replied.

The chamber went dark, and stayed dark. Nud took advantage of the moment and charged at Kabor before the stone lit up again. But the Stout wasn't where Nud thought he'd be. Kabor had sidestepped. Nud tumbled to the floor of the cave.

Kabor asked, "So, what will it be?"

Scraped and bruised, Nud regained his footing. The light shone again. But it had grown dull and barely flickered for long at all. Kabor stood in front of an undiscovered section of passage. He was panting.

"I'm getting out of here," Kabor said. "If you don't like it… TOUGH!" A kind of venom began to seep into his words. "And if you try to take the stone, I'll cover it up and bolt. I'll smash it in two before I give it up. You might never find your way out, unless you follow me."

Heat flushed over Nud's temples. The fire welled up and burned from the inside. *I never should've turned my back on the filcher. How dare he, after all I did for him.* Nud hadn't ratted out Kabor when he'd stolen from the town, Nud was the one who'd introduced him to an Elderkin, Nud cut him in on the claim, and Nud had saved his skin when he was drowning. *I was stupid to think he was selfless back at the Mire Trail,* he thought. *Kabor just wanted the sparking stone for himself, all along – my stone.*

"Last chance," the Stout taunted, poised for a sprint.

Nud played out the situation in his mind: Kabor knew the Pip could easily outrun him. But with his blind sense, he could cover the light and disappear in the dark tunnels. He could even hide in plain sight, or double back while Nud fumbled for him in the dark.

"The light is getting dimmer," Nud said. "It doesn't like you."

Kabor hesitated.

"It's just a *thing*," he replied. "It doesn't like or dislike anyone. And I'm not kidding about what I said. You'll get your stone back when we reach the surface. Until then, it's mine."

"It doesn't belong to you, Kabor. Give it back. You're making it go out. Then we're dead meat."

"Oh ya?"

All went black again. Long, lightless seconds passed. A shuffling noise sounded away in the tunnel, away in the dark.

Chk-chk-fwip… chk-chk-fwip.

Nud screamed at him. "STOP!" He had the eeriest sensation that this wasn't going to end well.

Kabor didn't respond at all. The shuffling sounded again.

Chk-chk-fwip… chk-chk-fwip.

Then silence.

Nud spun around, eyes searching for a glimmer of light.

"Open your hand! It's coming closer!"

Kabor made Nud wait for it. He made sure Nud understood what it meant to be alone in the dark with the lurking presence of danger nearby. He made sure Nud understood who was in control. Finally, after a long minute, Kabor opened his palm. The light erupted into view.

"This place is full of strange noises in the dark," Kabor said. "Do you want to be one of them?"

Nud said nothing. The anger still burned inside.

"Well, do you?"

"No," Nud said, clenching his teeth. He felt a hardening in his stomach as he gave in. "Okay then. We'll do it your way. Give me back my stone and we'll see what's up the passage."

"I'll give it back when we reach the surface," Kabor responded.

Nud grimaced. "Fine," he said, but his compliance was a thin veil. In bitter silence, the Pip vowed to retrieve his gift from the Hurlorns at any cost, the first chance he got. He also vowed to never trust Kabor again.

"One more thing," Kabor added.

"What now?" Nud said.

"Promise you won't try to take the stone back before we get to the surface."

"But it's mine."

"Just promise," he repeated firmly.

He knows.

Nud crossed his fingers behind his back. "Fine, I PROMISE," he said, drawing out the syllables to the point of mispronunciation. "We'll do it your way, BUT… it's my stone and don't you EVER forget it."

The matter was settled. Nud gathered his gear that'd been scattered during the scuffle, and then adjusted his backpack and belt. Kabor didn't have much of anything to collect, but the one thing he did have was everything.

In utter darkness, he who holds the light is king.

CHAPTER XXVIII

Interlude - Dark daemons

Does it matter if you break a vow that you were forced into? I didn't really know the answer, at the time. Had I not surrendered to Kabor's demands and had the Stout followed through with his threat, I might have been left to flounder in the dark, cursed to die in those tunnels. I wasn't sure if he was capable of doing that to me, but I wasn't about to test the waters one way or the other either. So, I forced myself to follow the footsteps of my new master, faithfully. Naught but a faint, flickering glow led the way. And with each desperate step, my mind raced and my rage multiplied. There had to be at least fifty ways to take someone down.

With that sentiment, the steps forward became easier. An uneasy calm came over me as I plotted. In an odd way, I reveled in the notion that I would get back at Kabor. I began to imagine all sorts of machinations about exactly how his demise might come about by my hand, or by fate. But one thing nagged at me. I'd once taken something that wasn't mine to take, something of great importance. I was very young when I did it, but that was no excuse, and the reasons were not as grand.

After some speechless wandering and ample time to cool off, I concluded that the best way to inflict revenge on Kabor was to bide my time and let Paplov know about what happened once I got home. He would bring in the town guard and Kabor would be in a mess of trouble when it came time to answer for his actions. Of course, there was one flaw in that plan – it would mean that he would have been right all along and that his plan led us out, making him impossible to criticize. He would be a hero for standing firm and hanging tough. Webfoot folk admired that sort of perseverance and Stouts idolized it.

Kabor held my bog stone tight in his thick fingers the whole way, as though it were a gold nugget. His mason-like hands were typical of Stouts from the Hills – like his uncle's. Honest hands built for honest work, not for thieving.

And yes, in the perpetual night of the underground world, he who held the light was king. But even a king must sleep, eventually…

CHAPTER XXIX

Forsaken

The passage leading to a way out was brick-lined, just like all of the other subterranean halls in the area. And in the tinted glow cast by the stone, the walls flickered as red and pale as any they'd stumbled upon. Nevertheless, a brief excursion inside was enough to confirm that they'd entered into yet another new zone, and that something was very different about it.

For starters, the air seemed vaguely familiar. It had an earthy scent to it, more like that of the original point of entry than of the intervening cave system, but pleasant – without the underlying stench of decay. There was even a hint of freshness. On the wall, signs and markings began to appear in an unfamiliar script. Directions of some kind, it seemed, combined with arrows pointing to side tunnels or down. The down arrows were a mystery, drawing attention to unremarkable sections of the debris-laden floor. The two lost teens cleared the area beneath the first few, searching for covered openings, more signs or hidden trapdoors, but found nothing of the sort. It wasn't much of a concern, really – they were on the lookout for ways up, not down.

It wasn't until they came upon another dead-end that their prospects heightened. Cave fill from a ceiling collapse fully blocked passage from top to bottom. On the face of it, the dead-end seemed like just another disappointment. The automatic thing to do was to backtrack and find a suitable side passage to try instead. And that is exactly what happened, or began to happen. But as Nud gazed back into the dim, empty tunnel, something compelled him not to abandon the spot just yet. Call it a gut feeling. Whatever it was, something about that spot gently tugged at his instincts.

"Wait," Nud called out to Kabor, already well on his way back. "The ceiling."

Kabor's shoulders slumped. Annoyed, he turned about and dragged his heavy feet back to where the Pip was standing. After so much effort that had yielded so little, Nud didn't fault him for his lack of enthusiasm.

"All right," Kabor said. "What is it?"

"Just a minute," Nud told him, and clambered to the top of the pile.

Water trickled down from a cavity in the ceiling, just above the blockage. It wept onto the jumble of shale and clay and ran down the side of the pile, settling in a shallow puddle at the bottom.

While on top, Nud cleared enough debris from beneath the break in the ceiling to stick his head up into it. The cavity was too dark to see anything. Nud stretched his hand out. "Give me the stone."

"Nice try," Kabor responded.

"Then have a look yourself," Nud said, and slid down the rubble.

The Stout sniffed at the drafty air. "Do you smell that?"

"I know," Nud replied. "That's *real* bog air, I'd recognize it anywhere… I know the place… it's… it's…" Nud trailed off. Unfortunately for Pips, smell is the sense least linked to memory. He couldn't quite place it.

Kabor climbed the pile and stuck his head right up into the cavity. Light in one hand and eyes an inch from the inner surface, he examined it closely. He said nothing for an excruciating minute.

"Well… what do you see?" Nud said.

"Ahh!" he screeched, jerking back. He scrubbed at his face, now covered with grime. "Damn it! Right in my eyes." Muck had slopped onto him. He wiped around his eyes until he could see again. A sly grin crept across his lips.

"What?" Nud asked.

"Come'ere. Look for yourself." The Stout moved aside and held the light up to the cavity so Nud could see in.

Nud peered into the opening, round and tubular in shape, with a glistening surface of wet clay. It was more than just a gap in the ceiling; it was a natural shaft extending nearly straight up into the darkness. Nud felt a pulse of air waft his face – definitely boggy.

The wave of realization hit him. Nud laughed and cried out. "We found it!"

"Hold on." Kabor nudged the Pip aside and began to inspect the shaft acutely. He took on that engineering look that Gariff sometimes gets when sizing up a job.

"I don't know… might be a blind shaft," he said, still peering into it. "Plus, those walls are slippery and unstable. If we fall—"

"We're dead and buried if the wall gives," Nud said.

"But on the upside," Kabor offered, "the sides are soft

enough to dig your hands and feet into. On the downside, even you barely fit."

The two friends stood pondering for a long minute.

"Sometimes you have to follow a blind passage to know that it's blind," Nud said.

Kabor nodded in agreement.

"I can chimney up," he said at last. "I've done this sort of thing before in some of the old workings. There were some really narrow shafts in there – downright dangerous if you didn't know what you were doing." Kabor glanced at Nud.

"We have to go up one at a time though," he continued. "There's no sense in you having your head stuck up my rear. I'll go first and find solid holds and footings. I'll dig them in a bit so you can use them on your turn."

"I bet I can squeeze through the tight spots easier," Nud said.

"Maybe so, but I'm going first anyway. If I can get through, you'll be sure to and we'll both make it out."

"It's a good thing Bobbin isn't with us," Nud said, not thinking. Even during the utterance, the words didn't sound right to his ears. A sick feeling formed in his stomach.

Kabor turned his head sideways to look Nud in the eye. "That's the plan, right? That we *both* get out."

Nud nodded, feeling somewhat selfish about his earlier notion to abandon Kabor in the dark and return later. But there was more: their current predicament brought the flag incident to mind. Truth is, Nud wanted to be the one to climb that time as well, but fear had gotten the better of him. Fear of climbing to the top of the flagpole and fear of being caught in broad daylight. It wasn't even the flag Nud wanted, it was the adventure. Once again, the Pip would let Kabor take the risk.

"How am I supposed to see the walls when it's my turn?" Nud asked.

"Follow the light. Don't worry, I won't leave you behind. 'Never leave a hand behind.' That's as much a sacred code of honor as you'll ever find in the Bearded Hills. And that's not just for Stouts either. It applies to anyone, even boggy-smelling Pips."

"What if the shaft isn't straight, or what if it's too long and I can't see the light?"

The pile shifted and Kabor braced himself as debris slid beneath his feet. He shuffled against the flow until it stopped, then stroked the wispy whiskers on his chin where his beard rightly should be, at least by Stout standards. As he stood there, a blob of runny muck splatted onto his head. He shook it out of his hair.

"I'll drop the stone down to you," he said.

"What?"

"We're in this together, right?"

"It might hit something hard or get stuck along the way," Nud said. "I'm not sure about this."

"Do you have a better idea?"

Nud hesitated. "Not really."

"Look, I'll call before I drop it down. It'll be up to you to catch it. You can't miss it – it's the only thing lit up around here. Have a little faith. Look for the glow."

Kabor was convincing enough, not just in his words but also in the conviction of his voice and the confidence that emanated from every pore. There would be no stopping him.

"Okay," Nud conceded. "Good luck."

"I could use a little luck today. This would be a lot easier with rope. If we had—"

"We don't. Get going. I don't want to be down here any longer than needed."

"I was just saying… ah, forget it." Kabor brushed a few mud-soaked strands of hair away from his face.

"Stay clear of the shaft at first or you might be sorry for it," Kabor added.

With those words, the Stout clenched the bog stone in his teeth as Nud had earlier. He began his ascent, leveraging the walls to pull, push and twist his way up. Nud slid down the rubble and backed away as mud splattered down on to the pile.

"Don't swallow the spark!" Nud called after him. Not long ago, the Pip would've wished he'd choke on it so Nud could rip it out of his throat. But that moment, he watched with hope as the wiry Stout slowly scaled the shaft, up and away, until the red glimmer of the stone grew dim in the distance.

Nud removed his pack – it would be too cumbersome for such a narrow climb. He was reluctant to leave his bow and the deepwood arrows behind, but bows and arrows are replaceable. Pips aren't.

Kabor grunted and groaned about the climb, but made fair progress nonetheless. Judging roughly, he must've chimneyed a good twenty feet before disappearing around a slow bend, out of direct sight.

"Can you see daylight yet?" Nud yelled up the shaft.

"I'm not sure," he hollered back. "It's hard to see anything up here. There are roots and—"

That was the last of their conversation, those final words lost to echoes in the dark.

A tremendous WHUMPF! followed. Nud scrambled back from the pile. Suddenly, a pulse of water shot out of the hole. The Pip backed away farther. The next instant, a loud sloshing sound funneled through from above, and the opening sighed with a strong rush of air.

Oh no! Something big is coming. Nud dashed down the tunnel, but stumbled and fell. A muddy mess crashed down behind him.

A long moment passed in the dark before Nud processed what had just happened. All was quiet. Dark.

Nud tried to feel his way back to the pile under the cavity, but cave fill blocked the passage. He couldn't get through. Kabor was nowhere to be found.

"KABOR!" Nud yelled.

The Pip threw himself at the debris. Desperate, he clawed and dug his way in with his bare hands. Nud groped for a rock that could help and found a suitable piece of shale.

"KABOR, ARE YOU THERE? CAN YOU HEAR ME?"

Silence.

"KABOR!"

Scraping at the cave fill with his rock, Nud managed to gouge out a tight space. He tried digging upwards, where he thought the hole might've been, but his efforts were repeatedly undone as runny sludge seeped down. *I can't see. I need to see.* Nud called out again.

"KABOR, ARE YOU THERE?"

There was no answer.

Nud plunged his fists deep into the soft regions of muck, reaching and grasping for a limb, hair, clothes… anything.

It was no use.

The sludge was overwhelming. The frantic Pip dug and clawed and scratched at the earth, grunting with the effort until his arms went weak and his hands began to shake.

Soaked in sweat, fingers raw and stinging, Nud finally slumped down and crumpled against the wall of the passage, exhausted. Warm blood trickled down along his battered knees as he gasped for air.

A minute went by way too fast. Nud forced himself to his feet and returned to the pile. He tried tapping rocks on the ceiling, hoping the sound would carry through – that Kabor might be trapped nearby, in the cavity.

There was nothing in response.

Then a horrible thought occurred to Nud. He had to stop.

He had to stop and shake his head.

Then, he had to move.

Nud began to walk in circles. "No," he muttered. The thought wouldn't go away.

"NO!" he screamed, to stifle that unfeeling, inner voice.

"no…" he said quietly, to himself.

I will not think or ever say that he had it coming.

That was for everyone else to say. And they would, if only they knew.

CHAPTER XXX

Cloaked

No respectable Stout would leave someone behind to perish underground. But what's a Pip to do about a Stout that might already be dead, was *likely* dead? *Did they all perish… all of my friends? Am I the last?*

Back and forth… back and forth… the monotony was strangely reassuring, a diversion from all the mulling over things Nud couldn't control. Pacing, even if it produced nothing, was better than pure inaction. Pure inaction would have been unbearable. Somehow, the motion kept a part of Nud's mind busy; a part that just wanted to curl up and die, or scream, or do something drastic… something *extreme*.

Such was the doom and gloom that consumed the Pip as he paced in the dark hallway of the collapse, tugging at his fingers. It seemed to Nud that as long as he continued to pace, some grand idea lurking in the back of his mind might take shape, propelled into being by the sheer momentum of his stride and the sharpness of his turns. But nothing brilliant came of those dark minutes, and the gray matter of Nud's intellect left him holding little more than a black list of sad alternatives to choose from.

"A hard choice," Paplov would've said. He'd warned Nud about hard choices, having to face situations where there were no clear paths or easy answers. "There's value in waiting," he'd said on one occasion. That meant do nothing until you know what to do. Years later, on another occasion, he'd told Nud to "just choose *something*, follow through with it, and hope for the best." He never gave his reasons.

Nud halted, bowed his head for several long minutes, and prayed to the nameless gods of his father. It was more of a complaint, really. He promised to be good. Praying was not something he did very often.

All the same, the exchange left the young Pip feeling refreshed. He revisited the blocked shaft with renewed energy and dug some more. He dug with fervor, numb to the pain of his raw, bleeding fingers and broken-back nails. He dug with his elbows when he had to. He kicked when he had to. For all Nud knew, the Stout could be stuck in an air pocket, on his last breaths. Nud quickly settled into a routine: dig – tap – listen; dig – tap – listen; and so on. Every so often, he took a break to resume the pacing, in case something new came to mind. Something that could help. A connection, maybe. Through it all, Nud pondered the situation at hand.

Kabor should've come out with the initial rush of water. He must've either dug in his heels – a typical stubborn Stout thing to do – or gotten stuck on his way down. Either way, if the collapse started higher in the shaft, he should've come down with the cave fill, otherwise there'd be a lot less of it because the space was too cramped to let that much material pass around him. Since Nud didn't find him in the pile, odds seemed not terrible that the collapse started *beneath* Kabor, perhaps in a spot he'd disturbed that took some time to react, or maybe he'd started an avalanche with his foot…

Beneath… it had to have started beneath him…

With Kabor's chances of survival stabilizing in Nud's mind, he began to consider his own prospects. In utter darkness, it would take every bit of razor-sharp memory and every pinprick of heightened awareness to make it back to the entry cave. There were enough turns, dead ends, pits, climbs, and circling paths to make the darkened course deathly treacherous. The hard choice was clear though.

I can't stay here. At some point, I'll have to leave and take my chances.

How long? – One day? Two days?

But suppose Kabor did make it to the surface, got help, dug his way back down through the shaft and didn't find Nud waiting. Then what? He'd still know the general layout of the caves, and he would've brought with him lanterns and loud horns and experienced miners.

No one is coming, warned a small voice inside. *Hopeless.*

So deep underground and so far away from everything that matters, Nud contemplated his Mark and the idea of transmuting skin to bark: free from pain and weary limbs and pangs of hunger, free from infections or maladies of the flesh, plus no need for sleep…

But if the inevitable were to occur while still trapped underground, the re-becoming's leaves would have no choice but to unfurl in utter darkness. *Would they sustain the new being? I think not. Trees need light, but do Hurlorns?* Nud didn't have the answers.

Defeated, Nud began to dig slower. Much slower. Limbs dragging through the motions, he finished up one last round of dig – tap – listen. Finally, he got a reply.

But it wasn't the reply he was hoping for.

Chk-chk-fwip… chk-chk-fwip.

Nud's heart skipped a beat. *The spider-thing.* He froze and didn't dare breathe. The scraping sound was close – *really* close. Emboldened by the dark, the creature scuffled overhead and then down the opposite wall. Then silence. Only the plunks of dripping water echoed through the cave.

With a slow, steady creep, Nud felt through the sloppy rubble until he gripped a sharp, fist-sized rock. He lifted it high above his head, and waited in the dark, ears pricked, breaths thin.

The silence and waiting amplified Nud's heartbeat, resonating in his ears so loud he feared the creature would hear the wild thumping. *Can the thing somehow see me?*

The noise started up again, but softer.

Shsh-shsh-fwiph… shsh-shsh-fwiph.

And the pattern had slowed – suggesting a disciplined and willful motion, like the careful, muted footfalls of a cat stalking its prey… just before the pounce.

Nud's muscles tensed, ready to strike. Then it came. It came like a whoosh of air. A moist, sticky mass smacked Nud in the face and stuck there, with gripping suction. The Pip gasped, but his breath was stolen from him.

Nud lurched back. He dropped the rock and grabbed at his face. The thing was thin and flat, but solid like pure muscle – it wouldn't come off. He couldn't breathe. He yanked and pulled, but its back was slippery and coated with slime. It wriggled on for a tighter seal. With all his might, Nud tried to rip the creature free. His ripped so hard his own skin tore, but the creature remained clamped.

Can't breathe!

Frantic, Nud dropped to the ground and rolled, pulling

and clawing at the thing on his face. Under the slimy coating lay hard flesh, impervious to his few remaining nails. The beast wrapped a long, winding appendage around Nud's neck. It felt like a tail. It squeezed.

Grunting and struggling, the Pip rolled onto his face and scraped the creature against the floor to get it off. The thing only squeezed tighter.

Near his cheek, Nud felt the smothering creature's mouth open. A ring of razor-sharp teeth scraped against his skin, and something rough – a tongue to lick his flesh down to the bone. Desperate, Nud planted his face on the stone floor. He head-butted the creature again and again. The teeth retracted.

Reeling and rolling, Nud pried at the creature again, to peel it off his face. It let loose slightly, and Nud gained a sense of its weak spot. Feeling dizzy, he tried another head butt, this time targeted. The thing reeled back and emitted a shrill screech. Nud tore the thing off his face and gasped for air, then flung the slimy mass away.

Free at last, the Pip scrambled to the pile. He swept his hands through the muddy debris, searching for another rock. All at once, the darkness lifted. The mud suddenly lit up, and then went dark again.

The stone!

Nud's wayward gem had found its way back to him. When it flashed again, Nud grabbed the bog stone and wiped the grime off. He held it like a burning torch and waited for the next flash.

When it lit up, the passage appeared empty: the walls were blank and fill covered the floor. During the next flurry of sparks, a thick glob dropped next to him. Nud tilted his gaze up. The creature was above him, perfectly blended into the stone. The light went out. Nud scrambled away.

On the next flash, he noticed a flap of black skin that seemed out of place on the thing, loose and hanging with fluid dripping down. *I must've cut it.*

The stone went dark for a long moment.

Chk-chk-fwip… Chk-chk-fwip.

"YAAW!" Nud yelled, waving his arms wildly in the dark. He picked up a rock and threw it. "GET OUT! BE OFF!"

He picked up another as the light flashed on. The creature was an easy target, wide and flat, and far too confident in its disguise. Nud dinged it, square on the back. The creature jerked and fell. And as it fell, the thing twisted and contorted in mid-air. Like a falling cloak caught by a gust of air, it floated for an instant, then spread itself out in an arc and *flew* away down the tunnel. The thing flew with the pulsed grace of a bat – long, smooth glides punctuated with abrupt shifts in height and bearing, barbed tail swaying behind it.

That's no spider.

Nud groped for another rock and tried his luck once more. The shot sailed through the air and missed by a wide margin, smashing against the cave wall. The flying thing accelerated around the corner and out of sight.

Nud collapsed. He cursed at the creature. He cursed again and then started laughing. Blood streamed down his face; flesh torn. His fingers bled, jammed and smashed. His arms and his legs bled. Even his toes were jammed and bruised. He was covered in grime.

The Pip sat for many long minutes, tens of minutes, before yanking his half-buried pack out of the cave fill. Hands quivering from their brutal treatment, he readied his bow. Then he crouched with his back to the pile, one arrow notched and the others stuck in the ground beside him. He trained the bow on the corner, and waited. Nud crouched for a very long time, watching and listening for the creature's return. The veins in his head pulsed; his heartbeat steadied.

Once Nud realized that the creature was truly gone, he relaxed. He started to peel the sticky residue from his face. Then he stood up, legs shaking.

Before turning to leave, Nud made one last feeble attempt to find Kabor. In a small way, he was glad not to find him. Not finding him meant he could still be alive… although without any ancient tree gum to light his way.

The bog stone will light my way instead, he thought, *as it should. As it was meant to be.* After all, it wasn't Nud who did the choosing, it was the Hurlorns.

The Pip put away his arrows, hauled on his pack, slung the bow over one shoulder, and then turned to the open passage. He started along it.

As he strode away from the heap, Nud called to mind something Kabor had said.

The Stout was right, Nud thought. *It isn't beyond me to abandon him, alone in the dark.*

And that is exactly what Nud did.

CHAPTER XXXI

That stupid hag

Now I set out to tell you the tale of how I became the gnarly beast that I am, and ere I have brought you to the very time and place when and where I felt less deciduous than ever before or ever after… at least in that life. A world away from sunshine, rain and the free wind that carries it. Deep within the element of earth, so deep even roots chance not to go, I sat skulking in the dark, my only company retched vermin and once animated fossils locked in shale, long ago having met inevitability. I contemplated the notion that I would never see the true blue sky again; and that my bones might one day be found amongst those fossils, encased in a silt sarcophagus, with evidence of being gnawed upon.

The storm has finally arrived and Amot is off making preparations. He has more Fyorn in him than he cares to admit. I have taken shelter in a west-facing grotto. It is cramped, but dry and the good ranger set me up with enough light to see by and enough ink to mark the pages. May these words find the right reader when the need is greatest.

Back to what's important. Never lose sight of what's important.

I have somewhat spoiled my own tale, the story of my great adventure, in the way I have dished it out. Dishes… Ha! My dish is the massive granite formation that cups the overburden. I eat dirt now.

You must have reasoned that *somehow* I escaped the recesses of the dark zone in order to be here, writing this. The only real mystery is how and when I met my fate. For the time being, I continue to reserve the telling of that part of the adventure, while you continue to wonder – if you are the type to wonder about such things.

I will no longer hold back that which is rightfully yours for having read this far – the tale of Holly, Bobbin, Gariff, and Jory on the Mire Trail, in the sights of the dreadful bog queens. For this compilation, I borrow the collective accounts of all those able to speak of the incident afterwards, together with those who later joined the Hurlorn consciousness, whose memories now flow unimpeded through my mind. This part of the tale is not an adventure, sadly, so much as a tragedy, and the sap runs free whenever I must think it through and through. If you abhor sad tales, skip this part. You have been warned.

*

The mangled mass that was once easy-going Jory lay half-sunken in the bog water, wrapped in decaying grasses and moss.

The search crew was quick to find the first of the missing teens – their guardian. But with such a distressing discovery, optimism for finding the others in good health withered. Mer Andulus was among the volunteers.

"What could have done such a thing?" Mer said, shaking his head as he reached out with his walking stick to comb through some brush.

An air of impatience still lingered in Holly's voice, and worry kept the skin tight around her eyes. "I told you all a thousand times already," she said, "we were ambushed… bog queens… remember?"

"There is no such thing as bog queens, child." The old prospector sighed, eyes fixed on the horizon, the grey in them reflecting the morning sky. Mer took in the wideness of the scene for a long minute. He always thought the bog was beautiful. He also thought he'd seen it all.

Mer reached over to lay a hand on Holly's shoulder, to comfort her. But Holly would not be comforted. She spurned him, turned aside and left him hanging.

"I believe you experienced something treacherous," Mer said. "Of that there's no doubt. Thieves out of Turnsby, or so I hear." His voice trailed off into stoutish mumblings and inaudible curses.

Holly did her best to tone down her whimpering. She'd heard the rumors. There were many, many rumors, ranging from the mundane to the extreme. Indeed, "thieves out of Turnsby" was one of the more sensible speculations.

"Ya know," she'd overheard an old-timer say, "sometimes them bog lights is swamp gas and sometimes they's wicked spirits." For all Holly knew, there might've been some truth to that one too. There were others.

"The Numbit boy went mad and ran away. He's always been a little off. The rest got lost trying to find him." That one, at least, was quickly set straight by Mrs. Numbit, proud owner of the Flipside rumor mill, along with her husband. No one dared to say "He got so hungry he ates them" to her face. Mrs. Numbit was always great that way. She pushes her nose right into people's business and gets the better of them. Holly received more support from the Numbit family than she ever got at home. And when hurtful whispers arose out of Turnsby about Holly's upbringing, Mrs. Numbit was there to stomp them out.

Holly tried not to think of poor Jory. Jory was young, and good, and charming and handsome and brave. *Was.* She never got a good look at the body that was found. She was glad for that. Though the corpse was mangled beyond recognition, the crew had been able to surmise it was that of the young guard. Shredded remnants of a once dapper uniform, found scattered in the near vicinity, made the identification certain.

It had been two days since the disappearance of her friends. Determined to do whatever she could to find them, Holly had insisted on joining the search crew during the day. It was tiresome recanting the events to official, after official, after official as volunteers rotated on and off the job. None of them fully believed her. And she didn't like the looks they gave her. Some offered pitiful stares; some looked at her as though she'd gone mad. Others, she thought, glanced and pointed as they conspired with one another, whispering that she was holding something back and that her version of events had been falsified, or that she was purposely leading them astray. *Let them think what they want. They're just stupid.* All these things Holly imagined as she meandered about the site.

Even Fyorn had heard the news and showed up to help. He was a marvel to behold in his tall helm and leather armor, with an impressive sword strapped over one shoulder as if he expected to do battle. As out of place as he appeared, Fyorn at least had believed her. Holly was sure of it. He'd gone out with the boggers in their small watercrafts and even down under with the divers where Bobbin was last seen.

The woodsman was up the trail a ways at the moment, pointing across the bog waters as he conversed with volunteers in his mild Elderkin accent. He insisted there was a trail in the grasses they could follow, if they looked hard enough. The boggers were skeptical.

"There are two distinct trails," he told them, pointing into the bog, "but they break off out that way… there and there." Fyorn's hand chopped at the air in one direction and then the other. The outdoorsmen continued on about that topic for some time.

Rumor had it that Nud's grandfather had immediately set out to join the search when he heard the news. "Not again," he was heard saying, as he gathered his hat and cane.

Mayor Undle delivered the ill tidings personally, and had assured the aging Pip that every possible measure was being taken to find the missing teens. "Then why are you here?" he'd said to the mayor, "You should be out there too."

Despite Undle's insistence that he stay in bed, while still in his night robe Paplov shushed the mayor and stormed out of his hut. He collapsed before even reaching the gate, far too ill to exert himself.

Such information had come to Holly through eavesdropping – an activity she never would've even considered were it not for the spotter's cloak and the prevailing circumstances. In the course of her information gathering, Holly learned many other useful and interesting things about Webfooters, some of which were exceedingly private and unsettling.

One of the councilors had a mistress while another, Mrello, accepted bribes; a group of Stouts from the Hills – not Gariff's clan – were charging double the fair price to straighten out a sinking building that they built purposely deficient years earlier and, to make matters worse, they were cutting corners.

As a hostess at the Flipside, Holly was used to overhearing such talk and, for the most part, looked the other way or, on occasion, might drop just the right hint to a patron she sympathized with. But with the power of wild elderkin camouflage, she found darker secrets too, either too disturbing or too damaging to repeat.

Holly Hopkins paused by the tree where she had donned her cloak, searching for signs of the bog queen's passing. There was nothing. Up ahead she could see Gariff and his father talking with Pip divers near the last known location of Nud and Kabor.

The events of that dreadful day consumed Holly. *It was dark and we were divided. The witches planned it. Where are my friends? What am I missing?* She closed her eyes and slipped into recall.

*

Holly's pulse quickened, her heart palpitations surged as she watched the hag pull Kabor and Nud underwater. Frantic, she couldn't believe what she saw, what she thought she saw. Her dear friends just gave up without a struggle. *The hag has them by a spell,* she convinced herself. *They won't take me that way.*

Gariff fought on relentlessly. Hopeless or not, he would never give in – stubborn and Stout to the bone he was. Pushed under repeatedly, arms swinging, he kept bobbing back up for air. He desperately tried to land a punch on the hunched-in hag, grabbing and pulling at anything he could get his hands on. Even when underwater, Holly could hear his muffled grunts of determination – overtaken, but not yet beaten.

It was the parrot hag who chased Holly down. She tackled the hostess and pulled her into the bog water. The Pip's webbed feet were all that kept her from sinking into the moss.

"Let me go, you stupid witch!" Holly cried, struggling against her. Scratching and kicking and pulling at her hair.

Holly's nails dug deep; she gouged the wretch's face. But the hag didn't seem to notice, or care, and squealed in delight as she forced Holly's head down with ease, like a mother dunking a stubborn child in the bathtub – except the hag held her there.

On the brink of suffocation, and without known cause or warning, the parrot hag relaxed her grip. Holly pushed and wriggled her way above the waterline. She gulped for air too soon and took in a mouthful of the quaggy water, and heard a voice over the sounds of her own sputtering – a singing voice, and the source of the hag's hesitation. It was not a change of heart or feeling of pity that saved Holly, it was Bobbin. At the Flipside, the baker boy sang all the while when preparing food. Apparently, he did the same when seeking a hag's attention.

The still air echoed with his taunting. Bobbin stood at the trailside on a patch of moss, waving his arms and mocking the hags. He explained by melody exactly how they became so ugly, and why they had to steal children – "because no man would ever have them." Abruptly, he stopped, and pulled something out of his pocket.

"Na-na-na-na-na… I-have-your-sparkle-stone." The immature Pip wiggled his mid-section foolishly and pointed at the hag that held Holly in her wiry grasp.

He plugged his nose. "You-oo-oo sti-ink… bog breath!" Then Bobbin lifted one hand high above his head, with the palm opened just enough to reveal that he held a stone there, obscured by the dim light and completely unrecognizable at a distance. It wasn't even flashing.

"Want a kiss?" said the parrot hag.

"Come and get it, you dirty old bag of weeds… I-know-you-want-it."

The dim-witted parrot hag shook her head twice, blinked, then stopped what she was doing. Her eyes rolled up to the whites and she shivered violently, then they rolled down again. She looked about her, as though confused, like she didn't know where she was.

Then the hag homed in on her mark and glared at Bobbin. Her eyes fixated on the stone he held. A sudden crazed look came over her. The blank, stupid expression, ever present on her face, was ripped away by maniacal rage. The hunched-in hag saw the change and scolded her for it.

"No, no! <gurgle> Stay! Stay!" she spat. "Lose them both, you will. Stuu—pid."

Bobbin sensed the shift in character as well, and the way he stumbled back hinted of lost nerve. He carefully shuffled farther out onto the floating moss, to the very edge of the water.

But the hag who was no longer a mere parrot had set her sights on Bobbin. She must've taken his subtle retreat as a sign of weakness. Immediately, she let go of Holly and bounded towards the uncertain Bobbin, like a wolf on a scared rabbit. A scared, pudgy rabbit. And a really ugly wolf.

In the time taken to snap at her disobedient accomplice, the hunched-in hag had turned her attention away from the struggling Stout. That was a big mistake. Gariff had been pushed around, dragged underwater and was short on breath, but he was determined like no other.

Taking full advantage of the distraction orchestrated by Bobbin, the burly Stout ducked under the hunched-in hag and lifted her above the water. She gurgled and writhed and squirmed in protest, and it wasn't long before she twisted her way back down. But Gariff had gained a few steps towards the trail, tethered as he was to her. It was all he needed to gain solid footing.

Holly, free at last, gasped, coughed and spat out bog water as eloquently as her nemesis. With one hand pounding her chest, she cleared her throat and hollered out.

"No Bobbin! <cough, cough> What are you doing?"

But her words came too late to change the sequence of events that he'd initiated. The parrot hag ignored her master, took the bait and closed in on the gentle Pip with alarming vigor.

"Catch me if you can!" Bobbin squealed, just before hitting the water in a ripping dive. The adept swimmer propelled himself under with the grace of a bullfrog. In the blink of an eye, only the slowly rising depression in the moss and wide ripples in the water betrayed that he was ever there. Holly staggered to shore, hunched over and gagging.

The parrot hag screeched and plunged in after Bobbin, a tangled mess of flowing grass and thrashing limbs.

Holly glanced about her. As far as she could tell, no one was looking when she removed the cloak Fyorn had given her. She turned it inside out and put it back on. Just before closing the hood, she glared at the hideous leader, still battling Gariff.

The unmovable Stout had his heels dug in, braced for a wrestle. And when the hunched-in hag turned back to him, with firm quickness Gariff diverted her grapple, and when she fell, with solid leverage he lifted her right up out of the water again.

"Uggh!" she screeched, unable to contain her frustration. Gariff used the hag's own tether on him to keep her twisting, writhing body in check. But before he could take full advantage of the situation, more tendrils wrapped around his face and neck, even creeping inside his mouth, his ears, and his nose. She would have him suffocate, above or below the boggy water. The hag was determined to have her way.

Holly slipped into the water and the mayhem. A new demeanor washed over her, cold and placid. Moments later, the Stout looked down in terror at the strangely swirling water and the subtle splashes around him, unnerving and phantom-like. A ghastly whiteness spread across his face.

The hag eyes darted about her, uncertain.

From behind the hag, Holly raised a waterlogged stick, long and jagged. It was especially solid, and the jagged edge especially sharp. She took careful aim and plunged it through the wretch's back. The stick punched through the waif body to the other side, beneath the hag's ribs. She arched backwards, wailing in pain.

Gariff stumbled away as the hag released the tendrils around his face and neck. She fell into the shallow bog water. The old woman's eyes went wide in disbelief. She stared, gaping, at the ooze-coated point of Holly's stick protruding from her belly. The hag spun her head around to face her attacker. It was the only time she ever appeared fearful, for all that she beheld was the serving girl's disembodied face set atop a blurred, dripping form. Holly wrenched the stick free and stabbed the hag again, and then many more times for good measure. The water went inky-black around her. Holly couldn't have stopped herself if she tried. Each strike, the wretch jerked and writhed. After a flurry of piercings, exhausted, the Flipside girl ended it all with one final thrust to the neck.

She let go of the stick, hands shaking. Her arms dropped.

Gariff took over from there. The Stout grabbed the beaten creature with his strong, determined hands. She still had tendrils on him, but they weren't moving. He carried her to shore as she writhed and moaned. She tried to pull the stick out of her neck, but it was held fast by a knot in the wood that had passed straight through the wound. The stick would not draw free. Eyes glazed, and in senseless desperation, the dying hag rolled the stick in small circles, inscribing an invisible cone in the open air. Stretching the hole only served to open the wound. Thick, dark liquid pulsed out.

"She's not done fer yet," Gariff called to Holly. A level of sternness that only Stouts possess infused him. He laid her down and tore at the hag's twisted tendrils, severing the last remnants of her hold on him. Then he lifted her above his head and firmly carried her to a half-submerged log, spiked with a rat's mouth of jagged old branches. Gariff thrust her down upon the broken tips, impaling the wretch. The despicable bog thing didn't so much as twitch after the impact.

Full of battle rage and with one opponent down, the Stout turned his aggression to the remaining hag, the parrot, and charged after her. But that hag was still within the pool where Bobbin had disappeared, continuing her dives to find him. When she caught sight of the berserking Hill Stout, and after she beheld the dismal fate of her sister, the parrot-no-more hag slipped under the mosses and disappeared. Gariff stopped at the edge of the bog pool, glaring into the moss-filled depths. He knew better than to enter. The ripples in the water dampened as he stood there watching, waiting. He glanced back to where he'd last seen Holly; she was gone too. Gariff jumped a nervous jump when he heard a girl's voice so near.

"Come here," said the voice.

Gariff spun left, then right, then all the way around. It sounded like someone was standing right next to him, but where?

"Holly?" he said to the wind.

Gariff spotted the eyes first. On meeting her floating gaze, he realized it could only be Holly in her elderkin cloak.

The hostess had already gained a full appreciation of the

benefits of invisibility. As long as she kept the hood closed, everything about her was hidden. But if she wanted to see the outside world, she had to reveal at least her eyes. And the cloak worked in water as well as air, apart from the displacement of fluid around her physical being, which could not be helped.

Holly Hopkins opened her cloak to Gariff and revealed herself fully, beckoning him to join her in the safety of its confines. She was shivering.

"Wow, that really works," Gariff said, dumbly.

Holly nodded. "We have to hide. Hurry, come in."

Gariff obliged. They crouched down and hid together for a time, and fixed their eyes upon the scene where Bobbin had dived in. Together, they peeked through the hood of the cloak. There was plenty of room for two in there. He kept her warm. She kept him hidden.

The impaled hag remained motionless, and the other never returned. Bobbin never came up for air. Kabor, Nud and Jory were long gone. The Shadow in the Water was nowhere to be seen either. It was almost *too* calm, eerily calm, with only the gentle drone of insects breaking the twilit silence. The two waited together a bit longer.

After a time, they convinced themselves that there were no more dangers lurking anywhere near. Holly and Gariff abandoned their hiding place. Gariff emerged from the cloak, and both scanned the bog from the trail's edge to the horizon, for signs of those gone missing. They saw little evidence that their friends had even been there.

There were many tufts of grass, mounds and stumps to provide hiding places, so they called out for their companions as well, mindful of the possible consequences of drawing attention to themselves. Their voices bellowed out into the quaggy expanse and were lost on the absorbing mosses. There was no response.

Defeated, Holly bowed her head and walked along the trailside to where Bobbin was last seen. She stepped out onto the moss and gazed into the night-shimmering pool.

"We have to go back to town for help now," Gariff told her. "We've done all we can. I can't cross the water or search underneath it."

"I can," Holly said. Gariff took her hand.

"No," was all he said.

Holly swung her gaze to the skewered hag, then up at Gariff, sobbing. "We as good as killed her, didn't we?"

Gariff sighed. "We did what needed to be done… besides, she looked half dead already, right? I mean, she wasn't really alive to begin with… a bog queen from down under is unnatural. She couldn't have been a *regular* living thing." Gariff paused to glance at the hag. "And I'm the one that finished her off. Remember?"

Holly nodded and wiped her eyes. "That stupid hag," she said, then painted her face with a forced smile.

"We have to mark the spot," Gariff said.

Under the darkness of a new moon, the two survivors set out for Webfoot together. They reported the incident to the first guard they met at the Wet Wall. A search party was quickly organized in the night and many hands deployed to the bog, even before the rising sun burned off the mists of the new morning.

9 781988 363172